FRESHMAN CLUB

GAY EROTIC TALES ANTHOLOGY

EDITED BY
DAVID MACMILLAN

companion press

laguna hills, california
http://www.companionpress.com

MW01141894

Student Union © 2000 by Barry Alexander
Teacher's Pet © 2000 by Sam Archer
Straight—As a Board © 2000 by Jordan Baker
Randy Roommates © 2000 by Richard Bellingham
Rally 'Round the Flagpole © 2000 by Robbie Cramer
Dirty Laundry Boys © 2000 by Bill Crimmin
Jock Itch © 2000 by Grant Foster
Farm Boys © 2000 by J.L. Gorden
Phi Beta Sucka © 2000 by Dak Hunter
The Boys Club © 2000 by David MacMillan
Frisky Frat Boys © 2000 by Howie Marshall
Cherry Boy in the Big Apple © 2000 by Roddy Martin
The Coming Out Party—Spent Youth © 2000 by Alan W. Mills
Summer Blow Job © 2000 by Bryan Nakai
Confessions of a Camp Counselor © 2000 by J.D. Ryan
My Sex Education © 2000 by Simon Sheppard
Camp Out Orgy—The Initiation © 2000 by Jay Starre
High School Reunion © 2000 by Chad Stevens

COMPANION PRESS, PO Box 2575, Laguna Hills, California 92654

Printed in the United States of America
First Printing 2000

ISBN: 1-889138-27-4

Cover photo of porn star Steve O'Donnell, courtesy Per Lui, Copyright © 2000

CONTENTS

INTRODUCTION

Remember your first time? We all do. And that's what the **FRESHMEN CLUB** is all about. It's a collection of 18 gay erotic stories by and about that endangered species known as the 18 to 21-year-old "All-American Virgin" —who's doing his best to become an ex-virgin. Fortunately, there's no shortage of fellow virgins, born-again virgins and former virgins willing to help him out.

From dorm room encounters to frat house orgies, from randy roommates to raunchy rites of passage, the **FRESHMEN CLUB** takes you inside the University of Youthful Sex. And your tour guides are the hunky young twinks who don't mind cramming for finals, are happy to hold after-school hand jobs and are eager to display their school spirit by running for prick tease President. Not all the guys are in school, but they're all college-age.

Though written as fictional tales, the authors claim that the stories are based on true events. Most are based on their own lives or were told to the authors by the college students who lived out these stories. Featured are some of the best gay erotic authors writing today, such as Barry Alexander, Sam Archer, Jordan Baker, Dak Hunter, Howie Marshall, Roddy Martin, Alan W. Mills, Bryan Nakai, J.D. Ryan, Simon Sheppard and Chad Stevens. Some are old pros—others are virgins: these are their first published stories. As they say, you never forget your first time. Well, I guarantee you're going to have a hard time forgetting some of these stories as well.

David Macmillan
Atlanta, Georgia

STUDENT UNION

Barry Alexander

I STEPPED OFF THE BUS INTO THE EARLY MORNING DRIZZLE AND WALKED across the deserted campus. Classes wouldn't start for another hour, but public transportation kept its own schedule. The rain on my glasses made everything look blurred. The tall pines were charcoal smudges against the gray sky. The few maples that still held their leaves glowed like Van Gogh suns. I scuffed through the fallen leaves littering the sidewalk towards the Student Union.

In high school, I'd seemed to be the only guy more interested in good grades than sports and getting laid. I also liked swimming and biking, so I kept in pretty good shape. Usually, I'd bike out into the country, find a quiet spot, and write my stories.

College had come as a shock. I'd been used to being the brain in class. Suddenly I was just like everyone else. Well, not quite—the guys at college could argue about Nietzsche one minute then brag about scoring on the football field and in the backseat the next. I didn't have anything to brag about.

Commuting, working my part-time job, and studying didn't leave time for a social life. All the fun stuff seemed to happen in the evenings when I was working. Maybe if I lived in the dorms …

I stumbled down the concrete steps into the Student Union. It wasn't officially open yet, but no one said anything when I slipped through the door left unlocked for staff. I thought about doing a little last minute studying, but I was exhausted. I'd stayed up until 3:00 AM studying for my humanities test.

I cleaned my glasses on my shirt and walked past the dining tables bristling with upturned chairs. I dropped my books beside one of the purple couches on the upper circle of the lounge. The lower level had a

5

concert grand piano in the center and was ringed with sturdy chairs in golden maple and purple cushions—school colors.

I figured I could catch a nap before my first class. I stretched out on the cushions, bending my knees so my long legs fit onto the couch, and I closed my eyes and listened to the rain tapping on the skylight.

I opened my eyes, unsure where I was for a moment. The most exquisite music I had ever heard vibrated through the air around me. I heard the sound of a book hitting the floor and realized where I was.

The music didn't stop. It flowed around me. I had never heard anything like it—delicate, precise—like water rippling, or voices laughing, it sounded like sunshine.

Someone giggled. I sat up and looked around. Across from me, a guy and a girl slouched at opposite ends of a couch. Books and papers were scattered on the floor beside them, forgotten, as the girl burrowed her foot under the guy's shirt. She giggled again. Her voice was discordant, a jarring, too human voice, interrupting the angelic sounds filling the room.

The couple chattered away, totally oblivious to the music washing over me. I gathered up my books and walked down to the circular pit of the lower level. I wanted to be closer to that wondrous sound. I seemed to be the only one. An empty ring of chairs surrounded the concert grand. I set my books down quietly as I settled into the chair closest to the piano.

I could only see the back of the guy playing the piano. Drops of water sparkled in his dark curly hair, and rain spots dappled the shoulders of his navy blue sweatshirt. His long torso swayed back and forth as he stretched to reach distant keys. He should have looked out of place in his jeans and sweatshirt, sitting at an instrument I associated with tuxedos and candelabras. He didn't. His body looked slim and elegant and totally at home as he filled the room with music.

His fingers stilled. He sat silently for a moment while the last notes echoed in my head. I started clapping, hitting my hands so hard it hurt. He looked around, startled, as if he hadn't been aware he had an audience. I heard someone laugh and I blushed when I realized I was the only one clapping and saw that what-a-geek expression I'd seen all through high school on the face of passing students.

Then the pianist smiled at me, and I didn't mind at all. His eyes were the blue-gray of a lake at twilight—quiet, but with the first stars sparkling in its depth. His nose was aristocratic, but his mouth was too large for conventional good looks—there was something about him that was compelling. Maybe it was the impression of good humor and intelligence, maybe it was the memory of the music surrounding him like an aura.

I realized I was sitting there like an idiot. "That was wonderful!"

His smile deepened. "Thank you."

I stood up and held out my hand. "I'm Brian."

He looked a little surprised. When I realized how old fashioned I was being, I felt stupid for a moment. His warm fingers curled around mine in a firm grip and put me at ease. "Good to meet you, Brian. I'm David."

"That was so beautiful. I've never heard music like that before. It made me ache inside," I said, then felt dumb for saying it. "Did you write it?" I asked quickly to cover up.

"I wish. That was Mozart's Piano Concerto in D minor."

"Mozart? Is that what he sounds like? I always figured he wrote that high brow music that rich people pretend they like to prove they have good taste. But what you played—it sounded like angels must sound."

"You've never heard Mozart?"

He sounded astonished. I wondered why for a second, then realized he probably thought I was older. "I'm just a freshman. I don't take Music Appreciation until next semester. I've heard it's tough."

He threw back his head and laughed, though I didn't see what he thought was funny. "Don't worry. Somehow, I think you're going to love it."

"I hope I get to hear you play again," I said, figuring we'd both run out of things to say. "I'd better take off for my comp class."

"I'm here almost everyday at this time. I like the acoustics in here better than in the practice rooms in the music department."

I stared at him. "But I'm here everyday at this time. I've never heard you before."

"Wait, did you say Freshman Comp? Professor Wheeler?"

"Yeah, why?"

"You're a bit late. He always has that one at 9 o'clock, semester after semester. It's 9:20."

I looked at my watch. "Oh shit! I better run." I grabbed my books, but David put his hand on my arm.

"Wait. Wheeler's been known to eat freshmen for being late. Why not skip it and come have coffee with me?"

I was tempted to skip class the next day, just so I could hear David play again. But I needed a good grade in comp to take more writing classes. I took out my wallet to reassure myself that the ticket was still there. David was playing at the October Concert in two weeks and had given me a ticket. I wasn't sure how I was going to work out the transportation but I had no intention of missing it.

David and I had talked a long time over coffee. Funny, but it seemed we'd known each other forever. He told me about his plans to be a concert pianist and his hopes to study at the Conservatory of Music in Vienna. And for the first time, I told someone about my hopes of being a writer. My family would have laughed at the idea; business management was a lot more practical. David didn't think it was silly. He said if you wanted something badly enough you had to try. Even if you failed, at least you wouldn't live with the regret of never trying.

Over the next couple weeks, we met several times for coffee or lunch or just to talk. Classes were starting to go better. I was starting to feel less like an outsider. I would have skipped another class just so I could hear him play again, but David told me he wouldn't play a note if I did. He said if I wanted to be a writer, I had to take it seriously and work at it. He even offered to look at some of my writing, but I was afraid he'd look at it and think I had no talent. I was getting A's in comp class, but writing stories was different.

I sat in the crowded auditorium, listening to the buzz of conversation. I couldn't wait. The lights went down and I settled back in my chair with a sigh. The people around me settled into silence. The notes of a single flute rose slow and sweet, almost hesitant, then the curtains opened and the orchestra joined in a glorious swell of music.

David sat center stage. He looked incredible in his tuxedo. Slim, and elegant, and very much in command of this performance. He was so handsome. Every woman in the audience was probably drooling over him. Did classical music buffs act like groupies after a rock concert? Throwing themselves at him as they ripped the clothes from his luscious body? Kissing him in all the most right places?

My God! What was I thinking! I squirmed in my seat, my dick uncomfortably hard. I was missing the concert with these ridiculous thoughts. That's enough, I told myself. Concentrate on the music.

I closed my eyes, letting the music take me where it would. It was dark. I walked through a night wood, following the song of water as it led me along shadowed paths. Then I caught a glimpse of light and hurried towards it. Ahead of me stretched the sea. David stepped out of the waves, proud and naked like one of the Greek gods. Water glistened as it ran down his torso. I took a step towards him, mesmerized by the beads of water coursing down his body. The music stopped. Then there was a great clap of thunder.

I opened my eyes and realized that everyone was clapping. I joined the clapping. I blushed, thankful that no one could see my red face in the dark. Then the lights came up and I realized I had more than blushes to hide. I sat in my seat, pretending to study the program strategically placed over my lap as people squeezed past me and headed for the aisles.

I waited until everyone was gone, then put on my jacket and headed for the door. I sat on one of the stone benches beside the water sculpture and waited for David. He wanted to change first, he'd said, then we could go have pizza at a little place that stayed open late. He smiled when he spotted me. I tried to say all the right things as we chatted about the concert. I hoped he didn't notice how distracted I was. My cock was still half hard, but my jacket was long enough to conceal it.

We cut across the campus, following the paths worn in the grass instead of the brightly lit sidewalks where couples giggled and walked with their arms around each other. Trees shadowed us as we walked side by side. Leaves crunched underfoot. The music still sang in my ears. We didn't talk. There didn't seem a need.

I couldn't stop thinking about his body. I was a bit surprised when his hand caught mine and squeezed. I squeezed back. Blood pounded in my veins and the music soared through my head. It was a moonless autumn night, dark and chilly, but in my head it was suddenly summer and fireflies danced in the silver glow of moonlight on water.

I don't know how long we walked. Time had stopped. I was only aware of the warmth of his fingers around mine and the occasional brush of his hip or shoulder against mine.

"Do you mind very much if we skip that pizza?"

I shook my head. Food was the last thing on my mind. When he turned towards me, I was ready for him. I had thought of nothing else all evening. His lips touched mine and, suddenly, I knew what every-one got so excited about. His kiss was nothing like a girl's—it was fierce and demanding and gentle all at the same time. His arms wrapped around me, holding me close. The warmth of his body penetrated the layers of clothing separating us.

I reached under his jacket and tugged his shirt tail out then slipped my hand underneath. I'd caught tantalizing glimpses of his chest hair before, but I'd never seen him bare-chested. He was a lot furrier than I'd expected. I splayed my fingers and ruffled the abundant hair cov-ering his torso, delighting in the warm silkiness of it as I explored the planes of his chest. My finger tips bumped against the tiny nubbin of his nipple.

I couldn't help being a bit scared. This was so different than it was with a girl. His skin was smooth and soft, but stretched over hard muscle. The arms that held me were strong. Our bodies matched. I knew where everything was, but I was afraid I'd do the wrong thing. What did guys do? I knew how it was supposed to go with girls.

I didn't have to guess. David showed me the rest. I could feel how much he wanted me. The hard length of his cock pressed against me. My dick fought to escape. I wanted us both naked, nothing blocking the touch of skin to skin. I wanted him so much my hands shook when I tried to undress us.

David took over. He pushed my jacket off my shoulders as he explored my mouth. He unfastened the buttons on my shirt and I shuddered while his tongue traced the inside of my lower lip. After the first couple of buttons were undone, he slid his hands inside my shirt and gently pinched my nipples. I moaned in protest when he pulled his mouth away from mine, but I was soon glad he did. His warm lips nuzzled against my pec. I gasped at the first flick of his hot tongue. His mouth closed over my nipple, sucking it to hardness. I loved the way he rubbed his tongue over the sensitive peak. I was too lost in the sensations to notice when he slid my shirt off.

He dropped to his knees and licked at my belly button while his hands tugged at my belt. He tugged my slacks down to my ankles. I kicked off my shoes and stepped out of my pants. He combed his fingers through my bush and looked up at me. My cock quivered, dripping pre-cum all over the grass. I could barely hold still when I felt his breath on my cock.

His tongue flicked over the head of my cock. The moisture quickly cooled in the evening air, but I barely had time to notice that sensation before he took my cock in his mouth. My knees trembled. I had never imagined such an exquisite pleasure. I knew I wouldn't be able to take much; David was just too good with his mouth. He seemed to know exactly the right pressure, the right pace, the right places. He must have sensed my urgency. After a couple of minutes, when my shaft was slick with his saliva, he stood up and stripped quickly.

He looked like the David from my symphony dream, standing proudly naked before me. I could hear the music just as I had then. It was dark between the trees, but for a moment he stood in a pool of diffused light from the security lamps that lined the sidewalks. He looked like some woodland god standing before me, his body half in shadow. He took a step towards me, and the shadows fell away. Not a god, a satyr. His cock would have shamed all those statues of naked gods.

He spread our jackets over the grass. Leaves crunched as he pulled me down beside him. I planned to spend hours exploring his body—another time. I wanted his cock—now. I'd never touched any cock but my own, and I couldn't wait to touch it and taste it and feel it inside me. David lay back and let me. His pre-cum tasted a lot like my own, but muskier, more exciting. I loved the way his cock felt in my mouth, hard and soft at the same time, and so thick it stretched my lips wide. I tried to copy the things he had done to me, but I kept gagging myself in my greed to take all of him. I loved the way his pubic hairs tickled my nose and I eagerly licked all around his crotch, wetting down the silky hairs on his balls and rolling them around on my tongue. I could tell I was exciting him. He started squirming and his cock kept leaking a steady stream of pre-cum.

He pulled me back up into his arms and kissed me.

"I want you. Will you let me?"

For answer, I rolled over onto my back and held out my arms. He reached into his pants and pulled out something I couldn't see before he leaned down and kissed me again. I felt him tremble. I knew he wanted to take me as badly as I wanted to be taken. But he went slowly.

He rolled on top of me, his mouth locked to mine. His arms and knees took most of his weight, but his body was pressed firmly against mine, covering me and pinning me in place. His cock throbbed against mine. I slid my hands down his back and over his smooth buttocks. At first they were hard and cool, like marble, but they warmed beneath my palms as I cupped them and pulled him even closer to me.

His fingers played as delicately over my body as they did over the keyboard. He touched me gently, caressing my body and slowly exciting me, and showing me the places that sent fire through my body, places that no one had ever touched before. He squirted a glob of goo onto his fingers and warmed it in his hands before he worked it inside me. I blushed at the intimacy of his touch, but I loved it. It was a little tight at first, but he slowly stretched me until two of his fingers slid easily inside me. My cock jumped every time his fingers bumped my prostate.

I tried to roll the condom on him, but I had it backwards and it wouldn't roll. I felt stupid, but David just laughed and pulled another one out of his jacket pocket. I lay back and locked my knees in the crook of my arms, exposing the most intimate part of myself to him

David moved into position. His cock brushed the bottom of my ball-sac, then centered on my quivering hole. I held my breath.

"Relax," David said. "There's no rush."

I took a deep breath and let it out. I really wanted him inside me, but I suspected pain. His cock was so damned big. It had to hurt, didn't it?

I hadn't counted on how patient and gentle David could be. There was pressure, and a slow stretching as my body opened for him. His cock was so hot. Just when I thought I couldn't stretch anymore, the head of his dick popped inside. It felt—strange. Part of another human being was inside me. I could feel his pulse, beating just inside me.

Experimentally, I moved my hips. His cock pushed at a different angle, exciting a whole new area. It was starting to feel good, really good. I sighed with pleasure as he slid another inch inside me, then another. I wiggled my butt to take more of him. He gave a last push and his balls smacked against me. He held for a moment, looking into his eyes as he smiled up at me.

He began a series of slow, deep thrusts that made me aware of every fat inch of his cock as it filled me over and over again. God, he felt so good, so warm and alive inside me. I wanted him deeper inside me. To get so close, nothing could separate us. He moved my legs to his shoulders, leaning over me so we could kiss. My dick rubbed against his stomach with every thrust. I was leaking so much pre-cum it felt like I was fucking him, too. Our mouths locked together, forming one more connection as we rode towards the peak.

He pumped faster, changing the angle of his thrusts. The blunt head of his cock kept bumping my prostate. I couldn't hold still. I squirmed beneath him, shifting my body to meet the force of his drives and wrapping my legs around his ass. I slipped a hand between us and grabbed my cock. I pumped my fist as David pumped me.

I thrust upwards, locking my heels against his buttocks. We made music together. An ancient, primitive music of love and lust: the wet slick sound of his cock reaming me, the smack of his balls against me, a duet of mingled sighs, and grunts, and gasps. My body arched as crescendos of pleasure sang through my body. Hot semen gushed over my fist and belly.

David slammed against me in renewed frenzy, as if trying to drive every inch of his body into mine. He gasped against my neck, his hips riveting me as his cock spurted inside me. His arms gave out and he fell heavily against me. His heart hammered against my chest.

I pulled him down into a kiss neither of us had the breath for. I could feel the slow, steady beat of his heart against me. We lay twined together in the dark for a long time, until we started to get cold.

The next months were the best of my life. I still had to work and study and go to class so I didn't get to see David as much as I wanted, but every second we could find we were together. Sometimes we managed to have quick fucks in out of the way spots. I loved the thrill of having sex in almost-public places. But most I loved the rare times when we could spend hours making love, then fall asleep in each others arms.

I'd finally dared to show David one of my stories. He encouraged me to send it to a magazine. They turned it down, but I had a real rejection slip just like real writers get. So I sent the story to another magazine and started a new story.

One snowy afternoon before winter break, we met for coffee in the Union. God, he was gorgeous. Melting snow spangled his dark hair. Every time I saw him I got half hard. I forced my attention back to my good news—I'd gotten an A on my last paper in comp and the professor had written "you may have possibilities" on it.

David had news of his own. I let him go first. I could see something was really bothering him.

"There's something I've been meaning to tell you. My application came through. I'm going to be transferring to the Conservatory of Music in Vienna in two weeks. Hey, don't look like that. I told you about it. It's what I wanted. But now—" He bit his lip and looked like he was ready to cry. "I have to go."

Of course he did. This was his chance. It didn't make it any easier. I forced myself to stay calm.

"Of course, you do." I pulled him into my arms and kissed him. "Congratulations, David." I hoped I sounded a lot more sincere than I felt.

The two weeks went by in a blur of music and sex, joy and sorrow. We made love for hours the last night, but it was flavored with goodbye. After, I lay in the dark, unable to sleep.

He gave me his address, but we didn't promise each other we'd wait or that we'd write everyday. I think we both knew that some romances don't survive distance. It doesn't make them any less real, just more fragile.

I couldn't say goodbye. I didn't trust myself. I slipped out of his bed before dawn and dressed quietly in the darkness. He was sprawled across the bed, the comforter half over him, his chest pale against sapphire blue sheets. The scent of our lovemaking still hung in the air. I leaned down and brushed my lips against his for the last time. His breath caught for a second then resumed its steady rhythm. I'm pretty sure he was awake, but his eyes didn't open.

I said, "I love you, David," picked up my backpack, and opened the door. I didn't expect an answer.

I wanted to give him something. Something he would remember as much as I remembered his music. Something that captured what he meant to me. If I were an artist, I would immortalize his face for eternity. But he deserved music. I didn't have the notes to give him, but maybe I had the words. I had to try. I took out my notebook and wrote down the title for a story—"Sonata for David."

I hoped he would hear the music behind the words.

TEACHERS'S PET

Sam Archer

AS USUAL, JAMES DRAGGED HIMSELF INTO CLASS EXACTLY SEVEN MINUTES late and slouched into a seat in the back row. I wondered how he had arrived at seven minutes as his personal definition of fashionably late.

Not that it really mattered. James was a good student, bright and reasonably talented. His grades were quite good despite his affected disdain for the system. It would probably kill his soul if I let his GPA slip to that of the other students.

Instead, I glared at him over the half-rims of my bifocals and asked if he'd bothered to pick up the required books for the course.

James snapped his fingers and put his palm across his forehead in mock embarrassment.

"Fortunately," I intoned, "I have a copy of *The Virginian* that you may borrow for today's class, but I'll expect you to have your own by Wednesday's session."

Immediately, he brightened up.

"I won't need a copy," he said. "I've seen every single episode of *The Virginian* at least four times. Trampus was my hero."

"I'm afraid the novel is slightly different from the TV series, James."

"In what way, sir?"

"For starters, your hero Trampus dies in the end."

For a moment, I almost thought the 20 year old's stunned expression was genuine.

"But the Virginian gets the guy who killed him, right? He evens up the score?"

I caught scent of the trap even as I put my foot into it, but James had a talent for tricking people into over-extending themselves.

"The Virginian is the one who kills Trampus."

"Why?"

Losing patience with the game, I answered a bit more brusquely than I should have—which, of course, was exactly what James wanted me to do.

"In the novel, Trampus was a bit of an ass."

This time, the shock on James' face truly did seem to be genuine. His hands were actually shaking as he stood and gathered his things.

"What are you doing, James?"

"You've just told me that my hero—the role model I've patterned my life after—was an ass and that he was killed by another of my childhood heroes," James said. "I'm going to need a moment with this."

By the time he finished speaking, James had reached the door of the classroom.

"I need a drink," he said, then disappeared into the hall.

I caught up with him 25 minutes later at the Sundown West, a rundown little bar just over the railroad tracks from the main campus. All the James Dean wanna-bes hung out there. I knew I wouldn't find James drinking in the frat hangouts.

This time, the surprise on his face was genuine.

"What're you doing here?" he asked.

"I dismissed class early," I told him. "There was no way I could follow that little stunt of yours."

Circling his finger in a water ring on the table, James had the decency to feign embarrassment.

"Trampus really was my hero."

"Yet you've never read the book?"

"I didn't think it would be that interesting. It's just a Western."

"It has significant cultural weight," I pointed out. "For instance, did you know the novel is the first place the phrase 'If you want to call me that, *smile*' was used?"

James stared at me with the blank look of a modern youth who'd never seen a John Wayne movie.

"How can you be a Western fan and not know that cliche?" I asked.

James was slowly tearing his napkin into small strips of paper.

"I'm not a Western fan," he said, fixing my eyes with a cold blue gaze. "I only liked the Virginian because I had a crush on Doug McClure."

The admission lay there on the table before us like a dissected animal. There was an urge to prod it and poke around its insides for meaning, but no one wanted to make the first move.

Finally, I broke the silence.

"I was always more partial to Robert Conrad—he played Jim West."

"Yeah, the guy who dared people to knock batteries off his shoulder," James interrupted. "I've seen the commercials on TV Land."

The silence grew uncomfortable again.

"Well, I've got to run," I said. "Look, why don't you plan on coming out to my farm this weekend? I'm having some of my better students out to workshop a class I'd like to offer next year. I think you'd enjoy it."

"You think I'd enjoy giving up my Saturday to study English?"

The infectious grin was back on James' face as he waited for my answer.

"The class contrasts novels to the movies made from them. We'll look at the way Hollywood bloodsuckers ruin great works of art so moviegoers can have happy endings and plots that won't tax their brains. You'll have an opportunity to learn all kinds of observations that will make you seem cooler than everyone else the next time you get together with your buddies at the coffeehouse."

James was still laughing as I left the bar, but he had accepted the directions I'd scrawled on one of the few napkins he had left untorn.

The rest of the week passed uneventfully. James arrived at his normal time Wednesday and Friday. He wasn't particularly boisterous, but, then, he didn't seem subdued either.

Apparently, our shared confessions weren't going to be an issue for him. Unfortunately, I couldn't say the same for myself.

Don't get me wrong, there was no love interest here. I wasn't falling for one of my students or thinking about carrying on a long-term relationship with a man half my age.

It was purely physical. I'd wanted to fuck James from the first day he entered my class. Learning he was gay just made him more accessible.

By Friday's class, it'd gotten so bad, I found myself daydreaming about the bastard. As the students took their weekly quiz on Theodore Dreiser, I sat at my desk daydreaming about screwing James in the hayloft at my barn.

It was a true zipless fuck. We'd just come together, coupling like rabid weasels in the darkness of the loft. Flames seemed to engulf my cock as James slid his mouth up and down its shaft in steady, measured strokes. His tongue deftly buffed the underside of my eight-inch erection as the stubble of his beard grazed my inner thighs.

James' mouth tightened as he tugged at my cock, trapping the head between his tongue and the roof of his mouth while pulling away. Just as I thought I was about to slip free, he loosened his grip, swallowing me quickly and taking my full length deep.

At the peak of this movement, when I was thrusting my hips upward with all my might, the warning came.

James deepthroated me with bullheaded determination. At least three inches of my cock were down his throat now. His face pressed hard against my pelvis as he refused to withdraw. Instead, he whipped his head from one side to the other like a hound shaking its prey.

"Fuck," I growled, crumbling straw from the loft in my fists as the muscles in my belly convulsed. "Fuck, fuck, fuck."

Out of control, I stabbed my hips at James as I came, mainlining my jism straight into James' throat. His throat muscles worked as he swallowed, their rippling grip working to arouse me even more as he continued milking my cock.

After an eternity, my orgasm ended and I collapsed back in the straw to catch my breath. In the darkness, James coughed and gasped for breath.

He coughed again, a bit more insistently. This time, it seemed to be coming from a different angle, though. Turning to see what he wanted, I realized I was back in the classroom again.

Blushing, I took James' quiz and slipped it into the stack with the others.

At the end of class, he was slower to leave than the others, pointedly hanging around until the room emptied.

"May I help you with something?" I asked when we were alone.

"I wanted to get something straight about the other day," he said, not quite making eye contact.

"Go ahead."

I deliberately kept my voice calm, but inside I was trembling. All I needed was for James to decide I'd been hitting on him and file a complaint. I was relatively certain nothing would come of it, but the scandal involved would be unpleasant nonetheless.

His next statement, though, surprised me.

"I just want to make sure you don't have the wrong idea," he said. "I'm not gay."

"Of course not," I said coolly. "Neither am I. We were speaking hypothetically."

His face clouded.

"Seriously, when I said I had a crush on Doug McClure, I didn't mean I wanted to sleep with him. I meant I wanted to be him."

He seemed so earnest about making himself understood that my resolve faded again.

"I really wanted to sleep with Robert Conrad," I laughed. "But I understand what you're saying. It's not a problem. A lot of kids get confused during that hero-worship phase."

James seemed relieved. I suppose I was, too.

"If the invitation still holds, I can make your workshop this weekend," he said.

"Excellent," I said. "There really was no ulterior motive in my invitation. You're just an excellent student and I thought the class might appeal to you. I'm trying to get a broad range of input before sticking my neck out with the department head." It sounded good and James actually bought into it. I almost did, too.

Saturday's workshop was uneventful. The brightest of my English literature students attended. Naturally, they acted about like I'd expected.

Drieser's *An American Tragedy* was universally despised by students as a long, dull bit of work. They seemed to enjoy the way Montgomery Clift brought the role to life in the film *A Place in the Sun*."

Jim Harrison's *Legends of the Fall* was better received. Students roundly snickered at the pseudo-pornographic translation of his novel *Farmer* into film.

Gore Vidal's *Myra Breckinridge* confused the hell out of hip students who'd grown up watching 250-pound, post-op transexuals having shouting matches on the *Jerry Springer Show*.

By the end of the afternoon, it was obvious the class would sustain student interest. Whether or not they'd learn anything of value was still up in the air, but I was only in the preliminary planning stages.

We'd moved outside to enjoy the autumn weather during the last round of discussion. I thought it was a good sign that my students were still arguing the merits of books over films as they drifted out to their cars. We'd just finished watching *The Witches of Eastwick*—which the two students who'd read Updike's book swore must have been based on some other novel.

As the day drew to a close and the last student drove back to town, James uncoiled himself from my porch swing and stretched.

"Are you going to be able to stay awake long enough to drive back?" I asked.

"I'll make it," he said, stretching again. "I was just up later than I planned on last night."

I couldn't help admiring the way his muscles tightened beneath his shirt as the stretched. The outline of his pecs showed clearly against the taut fabric of his workshirt.

"Feel free to stay over if you like," I said. "There's plenty of room. If nothing else, take advantage of my couch for a couple of hours. Spend the night if you need to. I won't bother you til morning."

James looked tempted.

"Lay down and take a nap," I told him. "I've got work to do in my study. I won't even know you're here."

That was all it took to polish off the rest of his resolve. Sighing gratefully, he followed me into the house and stretched out on my oversized leather sofa.

I was soon busy with coursework and chores and completely forgot he was there. I didn't remember James until I heard the strains of '70s porn music coming from my living room.

Easing the door open a bit, I spotted him. He was still stretched out on the couch, but he'd undone his jeans and was actually stroking off to gay porn. The movie was *Barbarfella*, the horribly dated tale of one man's search for his sexual identity in the future world of the 1980s.

As a rule, porn parodies of B-movies are a bit more dismal than the originals. This one was a complete bore. Its main reason for surviving in my video library was that, back in my younger days when I needed money for college, I'd played the lead in the film.

In fact, the scene James was watching featured me wearing a silver harness while buggering a limp-wristed queen wearing strap-on angel wings. My costar was bent over a styrofoam rock as I pumped my cock in and out of his ass.

I would have been mortified if James had not seemed to be enjoying it so much.

He was so intent on the scene, I think I could have driven the proverbial Mack truck through the living room without drawing his attention. I was just as riveted on James.

His hand slowly pumped up and down the length of his massive cock. Pre-cum glistened along the length of it.

James wasn't even trying to cum. I'm not even sure he was aware that he'd begun to jack off. I couldn't tear myself away from the show. James had a beautiful cock—cut, about nine inches in length, and as thick as my wrist—and the lazy way he worked his fist along its length was utterly charming.

Finally, I couldn't take it anymore. Carefully closing the door so as not to make any noise, I slipped into the kitchen and fixed a pair of Irish coffees. The drinks would offer a good excuse for interrupting James.

Cracking the door again, I peered through to find James still idly stroking himself as the scene played out. I timed my entrance to coincide with the money shot.

I knocked loudly, then shouldered the door open and backed into the room.

"I heard you moving around, and thought you might want some coffee—"

James jumped about three feet in the air. Panic left him unable to act. Hesitating between switching off the video tape and hiding his erection, he found himself unable to do either.

"Oh," I said, feigning surprise. "I didn't realize—"

Zipping his jeans, James stumbled over his phrases as he tried to explain.

"I didn't mean to pry," he began. "I was looking for just any tape— you know, something to watch while I woke up. I didn't realize what this was until—" His voice trailed off.

"It's not one of my better films," I said.

"You looked good in it." James tried to grin.

"You looked good watching it," I smiled. "I'm no Doug McClure, but I hope it had its intended purpose."

I was impressed that James was able to blush even more deeply.

"I don't know why that turned me on," he said.

"Neither do I," I grinned. "The acting was atrocious and that nelly little queen I was humping never really did anything for me."

A wan smile rewarded me.

"You've got a nice cock, though," James said, blushing again.

I let my hand fall on his thigh, stroking his cock through his jeans.

"So do you," I said, steeling myself for possible hysterics. "I'd like to take a closer look."

He hesitated, then turned to look into my eyes. After several long moments of soul searching, our lips met in a deep kiss.

Soon, the kiss became more insistent. Our tongues delighted in dancing, swirling and chasing one another as we ground our bodies together. Our hard-ons also rubbed each other as we embraced. Through the thin fabric of my slacks, I felt James' arousal grow.

I traced the outline of his cock through the denim of his jeans and began stroking it. Even through the cotton, he felt hot. His breathing grew strained as I pumped my hand faster.

"Stop," he pleaded. "I'm on the edge already."

Smiling, I unzipped his fly and began fishing around until finally I felt the hot flesh of his cock fill my hand. Hauling it into the open air, I worked it furiously, until his climax approached. Dropping to my knees, I engulfed James' cock, swallowing each pulse of his orgasm.

As he collapsed on the couch, I began gently massaging his chest.

James reached down and began stroking my cock. It took a moment of fumbling with my fly, but he finally got it open and began to stroke.

"I want you to fuck me," he said simply.

Stripping away his jeans, he bent over the arm of the couch and presented his ass. My hand was still slick with pre-cum from our handjob. I used that and my own spit to lubricate his asshole.

I fished a condom from my wallet. Smoothing the cold latex over my cock, I prepared to take James' cherry. I used my thumb to open him, gently easing it into his hole. He moaned slightly and pressed back against me.

That was my signal to proceed, and I pressed the head of my cock against his asshole. He gasped as the glans began to enter him. Slowly, I pressed onward, careful not to hurt him. James responded by arching his back and squeezing his anal muscles harder around me.

With one last push, I broke through. The last bit of resistance eased and I was inside him. My cock sank to its hilt in James' ass and he cried out. Whether it was in pain or ecstasy, I couldn't tell. Frankly, at that point, I didn't care.

We continued rocking against each other, becoming more and more frenzied as our passion built until finally I couldn't take it anymore. Reaching around his waist, I fisted his cock and began pumping it furiously. He came moments after I did, shooting his seed across my hand and onto the couch.

An eternity later, James was apologizing for the mess on the sofa as my head slowly stopped swimming. So much for any worries that he might be scared.

"I thought you weren't gay," I joked.

"I didn't think I was," he said, grinning. "I blame your VCR. That movie corrupted me."

"Keep it," I said. "I never particularly liked it anyway."

"Maybe you could base a course on it—porn parodies of movies based on books."

For a moment, I actually considered it. The course would definitely be fun to workshop.

STRAIGHT—AS A BOARD

Jordan Baker

THE FOYER WAS TOO PRECIOUS FOR WORDS. WHITE WALLS TRIMMED with a subtle floral pattern. Neat cross-stitch samples and preschool crayon sketches in identical brass frames filled the blank space.

No children lived in this house, though. Anal-retentive orderliness vibrated through the rooms like a high, fine noise only a dog could hear. The hair stood up on the back of my neck as I surveyed the scene in front of me.

"So this is the inner sanctum," I whistled as rain dripped from my denim jacket onto the parquet floor.

"Yep," Mac said. "This is where the queen holds court."

"I shouldn't be here."

"Nonsense," he grinned. "I told Dr. Wells I'd housesit for her this weekend—not that I'd go into seclusion."

Dr. Wells probably picked Mac to housesit because she thought any guest he slipped into her home would be a nice, well-mannered young homosexual. She imagined someone who would appreciate the window treatments and ceramic angels.

Instead, I showed up—a rough, shambling libertine with a penchant for debauchery and destruction. At least that's what the good doctor had called me when she found me making out with a freshman beauty in her office. I wasn't sure if she'd meant it as an insult.

Mac jerked his head toward the living room and padded barefoot to the couch. I dropped my jacket on the bare floor and followed, the fifth of tequila loose in my hand.

"Thanks for coming over," Mac said. "I was going stir crazy. It's like being in prison."

Only Mac would take housesitting literally to mean sitting in a house for two days without a break. But then, that's what I'd always liked about Mac. He was beautifully eccentric. Even now, he was dressed entirely in shades of gray with only a couple of blacks and whites and his own flaming red hair to break up the haze.

His apartment was the same way. Everything was all black and white and gray. No color was allowed. Mac claimed bright colors were the reason society was so screwed up.

"Look at the television we watch," he argued. "It's not the violence or the sex. It's the color. In the 1950s they had violence and sex but it was all in black and white and everybody was happy. No one ever had a problem they couldn't solve in 30 minutes—with time out for commercials."

I could never quite muster a convincing argument. Maybe he was right. Neither of us belonged in this house tonight, swaddled among the cotton candy pastels of Dr. Wells' ceramic menagerie. Shooting tequila with a faggot on a Friday night wasn't my idea of the perfect evening.

Or maybe it was.

Mac and I always seemed to end up together on stormy evenings. I lived a couple of blocks from his favorite bar and when the summer storms blew in, he'd usually wait them out in my living room. And when hurricane warnings closed the university, we were usually the ones who showed up at the student newspaper to get the issue out.

I knew we made an odd couple—a hardcore redneck and a fag—but we were both journalism majors. If you cut us, we would both bleed red ink. Was that enough to build a friendship on? Apparently so.

Besides, I couldn't help but like Mac. His logic was as transparent as my own. He hung out with me because he wanted to fuck me. I went along because it fed my vanity and, at 18, that itself was a primal urge.

The more time we spent fighting deadlines and bitching about editors, the easier it was to forget he was gay.

I shook my head and eased down onto the couch, cringing as fabric crinkled around me. In this overly precious dollhouse, I was marking everything I touched.

"Relax," Mac laughed. "I'll straighten up before Dr. Wells gets home."

Snorting, I broke the seal on the bottle of Torada, deftly tossing the miniature sombrero onto the coffee table. Mac snagged it and settled it atop his tightly curled hair. He looked ridiculous.

"That's a good look for you," I smirked as the first hit of tequila did away with the chill of the rain.

"What are you supposed to do with these things?" Mac asked as he studied the tiny straw hat.

"Somebody thought they looked cute," I shrugged. "Probably a Mexican distiller who thinks all Americans are hopelessly trivial.

"So, Mac, why am I here?"

"I was lonely," he smiled.

For a moment, I studied Mac in silence. Twenty minutes ago he'd called in a panic. He was housesitting for the head of our department and he had an emergency that required my immediate presence— along with a bit of alcohol.

Fair enough. I already had the tequila and no plans for the night. Mac and I had spent our entire freshman year at Louisiana State University working as a team of sorts. Sticking together seemed the right thing to do. I assumed he was having man-trouble again. Mac always seemed on the verge of suicide from being mistreated or ignored by the current love of his life. The objects of his affection changed almost weekly, but the urgency of his despondence was palpable each time.

"You got me out in the rain to come drink with you in a house I'm afraid to move in because you're lonely?" I asked.

"Of course not," Mac said. "I'm also bored. The storm knocked the cable out—and the lights. That's why I've got all these candles lit. I was hoping you could find the fuse box or something."

"Nope," I said. "The whole block's out."

"Cool," Mac giggled, holding a cone of incense in the flame of the nearest candle. "This is more romantic anyway."

"Candlelight and incense?" I asked. "Am I going to have to beat you senseless when you do something stupid?"

"Calm down, redneck," he sighed, producing a cigarette. "I'm not trying to seduce you. I just don't want Dr. Wells to know I was smoking in her living room. She said to go outside."

"Right," I drawled. "Now she'll think you were smoking dope."

Mac stuck his tongue out and settled cross-legged at the other end of the couch. After a long draw on the cigarette, he leaned toward me and we traded even—the bottle for the smoke.

"Not bad," I said, allowing the smoke to relax me. It tasted sugary, almost like candy. Trust Mac to have clove cigarettes. If nothing else, he knew my weaknesses.

"This is horrible," he grimaced, handing the tequila back.

"It may be cheap, but it's still smoother than the stuff our fore-fathers had to swill down at the Alamo," I noted. "Be thankful you didn't have to fight Indians and bears to get a drink."

And that was pretty representative of the conversation that followed. We talked for hours about men, women, history, literature, whiskey and sex. The power came back on. Gradually the tequila and the strains of classical guitar music coming from speakers hidden somewhere in the house lulled us into that comfort zone that only a truly good drunk with a close friend can offer.

Eventually, we reached the plateau where speech itself was no longer necessary. Our bodies just crumpled onto the couch and we enjoyed not being alone on a dark and stormy night in Southern Louisiana.

Eyes closed, I mentally chased the melody of one of the pieces on the stereo. It was baroque and sinuous and, in my fogged state of mind, following it was like riding an enormous roller coaster in slow motion. I could have ridden for an eternity, feeling each rise and plunge like a lover's caress.

Instead, I opened my eyes and found Mac staring at me, his own eyes focused, but with a dreamy, lost-in-the-smoke look to them as the last embers of the strawberry rose incense coughed up a billowing cloud between us.

"What?" I asked.

"I want to kiss you so badly," he sighed.

There was a hint of sadness in his voice and I studied him for a moment. He was actually quite lovely, I realized. Small-boned and delicate, almost elfin. The tightly curled red hair and bright green eyes leaped out above his pallor. He hadn't shaved and miniscule stubble darkened his jaw line slightly.

Oddly, his feet made up my mind. I don't know why. Maybe it was just that they appeared soft, feminine. They weren't the huge Flintstones parodies most men are weighted down with.

Or maybe it was the tequila.

"Why don't you?" I asked.

"You mean it?" he said. "This isn't a trick?"

"You're not unattractive," I sighed. "And we are friends."

Mac rolled forward, half-falling onto his hands and knees as he climbed over me on the couch. Finally, our lips were inches apart. We hesitate a moment, on the verge of something.

Then we kissed.

His mouth felt hard, firmer somehow than I'd expected. I lifted my hand to his cheek and felt it bristle against my fingers. Mac pulled away, his eyes questioning, and I smiled. His face brightened and we returned to the kiss.

My head began to swim as the kiss deepened and our bodies crushed against one another. Mac ground his hard-on against my thigh with firm, slow thrusts. I relaxed and enjoyed his hunger as he humped my leg.

Soon, however, my own cock craved attention and I pulled Mac to the side until our crotches aligned. It was the first time I'd felt another guy's cock sliding against my own. Even through our jeans, the feeling was intense. As Mac sucked my tongue, I circled my arms around him and squeezed him tighter, trying to pull him through my body.

"Fuck!" Mac swore, burying his face in my neck as his body went rigid. I tangled my fingers in his hair and stroked his curls as his breathing slowed.

"Jesus," he gasped. "I'm sorry."

Stretching, I laughed out loud.

"Right," I said. "Like we're only going to do this once tonight. I'm expecting something really outstanding the next time around, though."

Mac snapped his fingers and leaped off the couch. A moment later, he was rustling around in a backpack and humming to himself.

"I knew these would come in handy one day," he crowed, straightening up to display a pair of handcuffs. "You want on top or on bottom?"

I had to smile. Mac looked so incredibly earnest in his excitement. Taking another deep drag on the bottle, I grinned and held out my wrists.

"I'm all yours, Mac."

"Really?"

"I've never done this before," I grinned. "I'll need you to show me the ropes."

Mac was still laughing as he led me to Dr. Wells' bedroom.

"You're sure she's not coming home until Monday?" I asked.

"Almost certain," Mac grinned maliciously. "Take off your shirt before I cuff you."

At this point, there didn't seem any point in arguing. The idea of our adviser walking in and catching the two of us making out in her bed actually kind of turned me on. I almost lost it, though, when Mac insisted we fold the doctor's down comforter and carefully store it in a chair before continuing.

"Somehow, I'm seeing my chances of hot, nasty sex fade away," I kidded Mac.

"Lay down, bitch," he replied, flattening his hand against my chest and pushing me onto the bed.

"Now, let's get you chained down."

The cool metal sliding over my wrists sent shivers down my spine. Mac closed it with a ratcheting noise until the hoops almost touched my skin after looping the chain around the headboard.

"That's not too tight, is it?" he asked, a little too solicitously.

"You really suck at this," I giggled. "I think you're supposed to be meaner."

"I could cuss you and stuff," he suggested.

"Just suck my cock," I suggested.

Instead, Mac tugged off my cowboy boots.

I relaxed and watched as Mac peeled off my jeans and shorts and then stripped off his own clothes. Naked, his body was better than I had suspected. He was athletic in the way swimmers often are. I admired his flat stomach and long, slender limbs as he moved forward. His cock still glistened from his earlier orgasm.

"I've got a better idea," he said, straddling me on the bed, his cock just inches from my face.

It was a unique position for me. I'd presented my dick to be sucked by girls on more than a few occasions. Somehow, from the other side, it looked somewhat confrontational.

"Shouldn't you wash that thing first" I suggested.

Mac shrugged.

"You're in no position to make demands," he intoned, falling just a little short of the menace I'm sure he was trying for.

I laughed out loud and he humped his pelvis forward, slamming his cock into my mouth before I realized he was really doing it. Mac was bigger than he looked, or at least it felt that way as I tried to press his cock out of the way with my tongue. For a moment, I had trouble breathing as he began pumping my face.

There was no time to get angry, or reconsider. I was too busy dealing with the cock wrestling its way to the back of my throat. Gradually, I became aware of the fine coating of pre-cum that washed over my tongue in waves. The word "aqueous" popped into my mind. Salty and damp around a hard core, and all life flows back into the sea.

Turning my head from side to side, I worked Mac's cock like a dog with a bone, always seeking a new burst of flavor as I massaged it with my tongue. I began pumping it with my mouth in long, even strokes to get as much flavor out of the thing as I could.

Frankly, I became so caught up in the game, I completely forgot Mac was attached to the cock until he began moaning and twitching on top of me. For a moment, I thought he was having a seizure. Then his cock began to spasm and I realized he was cumming.

When he pulled it from my mouth a moment later, I began laughing.

"I'm glad I amuse you," he sulked.

"It's not like that," I tried to explain. "I just forgot you were there for a moment."

"Well, then that makes it okay," he snorted. "Jerk."

"You'll have to try harder to get my attention," I suggested. It was, in retrospect, a dumb thing to say to a guy who had you chained to his bed.

This time it worked out.

Mac's idea of getting my attention was a long, lazy tongue bath. Still mildly drunk, I lay there with my hands chained above me as he kissed his way over my chest. He took forever playing with my nipples and I shivered in anticipation as Mac began working his way over my abs and into the pit of my stomach. His tongue in my navel startled me and then he was kissing my pelvis and hips, licking my inner thighs, running his hands over my legs.

He was paying attention to every inch of my body except the one spot that was screaming for him. Eventually, Mac got there as well, flicking his tongue over the head of my cock. I gasped at the first kiss and he pressed my hard-on flat against my belly as he began kissing his way up and down its length.

Closing my eyes, I let my conscious thoughts fall away as I enjoyed every stroke of his tongue as he worshiped my cock.

The orgasm, when it came, was intense. It was almost deadly in its force and a trifle frightening when I realized it had come from a guy's efforts.

Mac lost some of his delicacy at that point, turning me roughly onto my belly, twisting my wrists above my head as he did.

"Ouch," I protested half jokingly.

"I'm sorry," he apologized. "Should I take the cuffs off?"

"Remind me never to play Dungeons and Dragons with you," I sighed. "You've got no talent for role-playing."

The jibe must have gotten to Mac because he suddenly became more aggressive. He rolled off me and leaned over the side of the bed. A moment later, he was straddling my legs and tearing open a condom packet. I stared at him over my shoulder as he spread it over the head of his cock and rolled it down his shaft. My mind was blank. I certainly didn't think he was actually planning on shoving his dick up my ass.

Seizing my hips with a strength I'd never imagined him having,

Mac began thrusting his cock against the opening of my asshole.

"Jesus," I protested.

"Shut up, bitch," he laughed. "You asked for it."

The pain was amazing. For a moment, I expected to pass out as he thrust his cock into me. I felt as if I were being torn apart. Then, suddenly, the pain was gone, replaced by a kind of warmth as the friction changed. His cock seemed to be rubbing against my insides somehow and for a crazy moment I imagined one of those cut-away anatomy charts as I tried to visualize what he might be stimulating.

Soon, however, I gave in completely. Relaxing, I enjoyed the tremendously satisfying feeling of being filled and desired. As best as I could with my hands tied, I began thrusting back to meet Mac.

I remember noticing my cock was hard again and hearing Mac gasp as he reached orgasm. I came again myself as my cock rubbed against Dr. Well's precisely laundered sheets. Then Mac collapsed on top of me, his chest pressing into my shoulder blades.

"Are you going to be okay with this?" he asked, his voice soft and warm in my ear. I remember thinking the answer I gave him would be very important for some reason.

"Yeah."

I was alone in the bed when I woke up and Mac was nowhere to be found. The television was playing in the other room and the alarm clock was balefully blinking noon at me.

Stretching, I found the handcuffs had been removed during the night. As I pulled on my clothes, I heard Mac moving around in the kitchen.

That, too, was like him.

We sat at the kitchen table and ate in silence. He'd made chicory coffee, French toast, eggs and bacon.

"Wow!" I finally said. "You give great head and you can cook. I may have to marry you."

With a grim finality, Mac settled his fork on the plate and left the room. I should have known it wouldn't be easy. Nothing ever was.

Munching a strip of bacon, I wished plaintively for the simple joys of preschool when I could just offer someone the use of my colors and they'd come back from their sulks. Sky blue could cure any ill and I always felt sorry for burnt umber. It was the longest crayon in everyone's box.

Crossing into the living room, I found Mac watching *Bewitched*. It was one of the original episodes, with the first Darren, in black and white. He was upset about being turned into something he didn't want to be, but he looked perfectly human during his rant.

"He's being too hard on her," I said. "He's the same guy he's always been. Now he just has a new perspective on things."

"She should have asked him first," Mac said. "You don't go around changing people without their permission."

"He said it was okay," I pointed out.

"But he didn't know what he was agreeing to," Mac argued.

We sat there in silence and I realized we weren't talking about the television show anymore.

Maybe Mac was right. Maybe things do work better in black and white. I couldn't help thinking that even in the world of classic sitcoms there were an awful lot of shades of gray. Surrounded by pastel angels and cross-stitched samplers of what America was supposed to be, I studied Mac's profile and decided he was still beautiful.

That much, at least, hadn't been the tequila.

Turning his face gently in my hands, I kissed him and he gave himself softly, passively accepting it at first. Then, as I held him more tightly I felt his own grip growing fierce with need.

"Sometimes," I whispered in his ear, "you just have to let art flow."

RANDY ROOMMATES

Richard Bellingham

MY FIRST FEW DAYS IN ATLANTA WERE PRETTY CONFUSING, WHAT WITH millions of people and bumper to bumper traffic and everything.

I'd been down to Macon once and even over to Athens, but they didn't have even a half a million people together—and Atlanta had over four, according to the counter on Peachtree just as you entered Buckhead.

I was from South Georgia, near Alabama—out in the boonies. The sheer hectic craziness and noise of Atlanta almost drove me crazy. The reality of the place was downright overwhelming.

The folks had driven me to the Tech campus and watched proudly as I became the first member of our family ever to enroll in a college. They treated me to lunch at The Varsity and Mama couldn't get over us having to pay five dollars each for such tiny hamburgers and a drink; Daddy just fumed. Afterwards, we kissed and hugged and shook hands in the parking lot and they sat there watching their boy as he lugged his two suitcases into the dorm.

My roommate arrived that evening and turned out to be a good-looking guy named Scott, an Atlanta boy. My name's Sam, but it didn't take Scott two minutes after hearing my country drawl before he was calling me Hayseed. It seemed good-natured, though, so I didn't pay too much mind to it.

Scott had a swimmer's body. He was around my height and I could see the definition of his muscles when he stripped his shirt off, but he was just a little less muscular than I was. He looked kinda like me, too, although his hair was black and his face a little sharper and narrower than mine. I had kind of a square jaw, where his was more angled. Still, we looked enough alike for people to call us the Hick Twins.

I first saw Scott naked when he stripped for a shower that first night. I just blushed and kinda turned my head, though Scott seemed determined to flaunt what he had right at me. "What's up, Hayseed? Never seen a grown man's wiener?"

He stepped up in front of me and wiggled his prick right at me, and I couldn't help but look. His was different from mine, and it took me a moment to work out he'd been clipped.

Scott's was the first cut dick I'd seen up close. Although I knew about circumcision, it was kinda interesting to see the result and compare it to mine. My first thought was that jacking off must be kind of painful without any skin to roll back and forth over the head.

"Well, have you?"

I realized that I'd been staring at Scott's prick. I just looked down at my feet, blushing fit to bust, and mumbled something about him being very funny, and told him to get into the shower and stop pestering me.

Scott just grinned and tousled my hair, padding off to the shower and leaving me feeling really confused. I'd felt myself getting turned on by looking at Scott's dick, seeing him jiggling it up and down. As I heard the shower run I reached down to adjust my groin because my pole was pushing painfully against the front of my jeans. I wondered what the hell was going on, because men weren't supposed to get turned on by other men.

Were they?

Over the next week or so I got settled into college, and the nickname Scott gave me stuck. Everywhere I went people called me Hayseed. Scott and I got to be pretty good buddies as well as being roomies, and we hung out together all the time. He was pretty smart, and he was soon helping me out with homework. And he still showed his body to me whenever he could.

I was beginning to get really confused about how I felt about Scott. Every time he stripped, or even went shirtless, I blushed and started to get hard and horny. If that wasn't bad enough, he seemed to know it. Everything he did seemed calculated to turn me on as much as possible.

He'd leave the bathroom door open a crack so I could see hints of what he was doing in the shower—the occasional flash of butt or the odd glimpse of his half-hard prick. He once left the door open and jerked off in the shower; I heard every one of his groans and moans.

It was getting so that he only had to smile at me and I'd pop wood. I was jerking off every night, as he slept in the next bed, thinking about him. I really didn't know what the hell was happening to me. Was I turning queer?

My feelings for Scott crystallized the end of the third week of college. I was doing okay in class but getting more and more worried by the weird way Scott kept turning me on. I found it harder and harder to concentrate on homework when all I could think of was Scott and his thick meat. It was a Friday night and I was trying to work on some higher algebra while Scott took a shower. I might as well have been trying to fly to the moon; it would have been just as impossible.

"What you need, Hayseed," he said, toweling himself off to the accompanying jiggle of his balls that I'd come to know well, "is a night out on the town. What d'ya say? It's about time you tried out Hotlanta's nightlife."

It took a little bit of persuading, but not that much. I was getting so confused about my feelings, so frustrated by trying to understand them and deal with homework that getting blasted sounded like a cool idea.

It was about nine when we arrived at the Armory. As we were getting out of the car, Scott winked at me. "This one's a gay bar, Hayseed."

My eyes bulged and I quickly shut the car door and started to buckle back up. Scott sighed. "Do you want a beer or not, boy?"

"Yeah—"

"Well, it ain't gonna happen at most bars, Hayseed."

"So, what makes a queer bar different?"

"This place allows eighteen to twenty year olds inside for one thing. Then, there are usually enough guys old enough who'll buy your drinks for you—if you go up to the deck with them."

"They're going to think—"

"So, slip them the money to buy your beer." Scott shrugged. "They get to cop a feel and maybe get a kiss off you. They get the minimum and you get booze. Come on." He pushed his door open and slid from under the wheel.

"Scott!"

I followed him inside, my ears flaming. It was pretty dead that early, but we did find a single guy staring morosely at an exercise program on the television over the bar and nursing his beer. Scott sidled over to him. I followed.

The man looked up and saw Scott. He smiled tentatively. Then he saw me and frowned. "Let me guess, you're both underaged and you'd like a beer." Scott grinned. "You two lovers?"

"Not yet," Scott told him. "But I'm working on it. The boy just won't let go of his cherry, though." I choked and felt my face flame crimson.

The man laughed and said: "Give me a ten and go upstairs. I'll meet you on the deck in a couple of minutes."

The man was actually sorta nice. We drank our beers and found out what was happening in gay Hotlanta. I didn't jump too high when he pawed my crotch. Scott just grinned when the man groped him.

I spent the ride out to Decatur wondering why my heart fluttered every time I remembered the man's hand on my basket. I didn't much like the logical conclusions that I was tending towards.

Scott pulled into a convenience store and bought us two sodas. Back at the car, he poured half of his out on the ground. "You want a real drink?" he asked.

"I guess—sure."

"Get rid of half that can then, Hayseed—down it or dump it. I've got a pint of Jack Daniels under the seat." Behind a church we filled our soda cans and started seriously to work on our buzz. That I might be turning queer was somewhat less disturbing after I finished my Jack and Coke.

The bar in Decatur really brought my feelings into focus. It was this place called BI-Zantium; if I hadn't been a little buzzed I suppose I could have made an educated guess as to what the place would be like.

The bouncer gave us kinda weird look as we went in, but he didn't ask either me or Scott for ID. I giggled at him and he just shook his head, smiling and rolling his eyes. Scott yanked impatiently on my arm, almost jerking me off my feet. I followed him inside.

The club was noisy and smoky, with bright disco lights that seemed to float around on the billows of acrid smoke and pulsate with the throbbing beat of the music. It wasn't like the other club we'd visited that evening. Instead of being several rooms like the Armory, this was pretty much one barn-sized room split in two. There were two bars, one on either side of the room with a little stage in the middle of each one.

What really knocked me out, though, was the fact that on the stage to the left of the entrance there was a cute guy wearing just a G-string and lots of oily sweat. He was dancing and shimmying, playing to the audience in front of him with pouts and lewd gestures. His audience had both girls and boys in it, both shouting for him to take it off.

I glanced over to the right and found myself looking at a topless lady, playing to an audience equally as large and equally as mixed as the boy's.

It was about then that I began to understand the name of the club.

I gave Scott a weird look, but he just grinned at me and dragged me over to the lady's crowd. I couldn't help taking a look back to the boy who was dancing, and I felt somehow disappointed that Scott and I weren't going to hang around his side.

"See something you liked?"

Scott had thrown his arm around my shoulder and was hugging me friendly-like, and I jerked my head around from the male dancer to look at him. I felt a blush spreading across my cheeks.

"Uh—yeah. She's pretty," I stammered, not really seeing anything through this haze of embarrassment.

"She's pretty? I didn't notice you looking at her."

"Whatever—"

"Awwww—Hayseed, you're so cute when you blush."

Saying that, he grabbed me by the hand and dragged me over to the small dance floor, leaving me reeling with confusion and pent-up sexual tension.

We danced the rest of the evening, jostled together by the press of hot bodies all around us, and by the end of the night my confusion had been replaced by the dawning realization that not only was I queer, but

I was in love. With Scott.

What the hell was supposed to happen next?

I didn't have a clue, but I was sure ready to find out.

I knew I was becoming utterly obsessed with Scott and his dick as we drove back to midtown Atlanta and the Tech campus. I was quiet, trying to accept the idea of wanting another boy. Scott was quiet, too, giving me enough room to work it out.

In the room, he stripped for a shower. I just peeled off my clothes until I was just wearing my boxer shorts. They were comfortable, but they did diddly-squat for hiding a boner. So I was lying down on my stomach to keep him from seeing my hard-on, and watching him flex his buttcheeks as he sauntered to the bathroom.

At the door, he turned back to me and I saw that his dick was standing to attention. He idly reached down to run a clenched fist along the length of his erection and raised an eyebrow at me. "Did you say something, Hayseed?"

I was having a hard time keeping my eyes away from the winking slit in the tip of Scott's prick. It looked moist and inviting, and I suddenly wondered how it would taste. "I didn't say anything."

"I could have sworn you groaned."

I was just shaking my head and stammering that I'd said nothing, and he was walking over towards me with his dick swaying. It was so hard now that it was standing straight out above his low-hanging balls.

"Wrong answer," he said as he reached me.

With that, he practically leapt on me, letting his full body weight come down on mine. His chest was real smooth against my back, and I could feel the little nubs of his nipples pressing into my skin. The thing that really got my attention, though, was the hard cylinder that was nestling between my buttcheeks.

"Hey!" I protested, trying to buck him off. That caused his dick to rub against me, and the feel of that hard, hot meat sliding through my buttcrack felt real good through my boxers. All the fight suddenly went out of me. I moaned.

Scott's arms wrapped around my chest and I could feel his hot breath against my ear. He started to hump my butt and groan in my ear, his fingers massaging my sides.

"I knew you were ready, Hayseed."

A small voice somewhere in the back of my mind told me that I oughtn't to be doing this. The feeling of his hardness down there between my cheeks was so good, though, that I ignored it.

My own prick was fit to bust it was so hard, and I started to hump the bed. He gave a quiet, sexy laugh and rolled off of me. The sudden feel of cold air on my skin made me shiver, and I looked up at him reproachfully.

"Hey! Why'd you stop?"

I could hear the indignation in my own voice and knew that I wanted to do more with Scott. I felt pre-cum slither down my shaft and pool on my balls, felt my butt aching to enjoy the friction of Scott's dick again.

"Because I know something you'll like a whole lot more."

He started to pull at my boxers so I lifted myself off the bed, figuring he wanted to hump my bare butt rather than my underwear. He tugged the shorts down and off, but instead of getting back up on top of me, he knelt down behind me. I flinched nervously as his smooth fingers touched my ass cheeks, but it felt good as he spread them apart and blew warm air against my tight pucker.

I moaned and wriggled against the bed as he kissed me down there, his lips pressing against my ass-ring and his tongue trying to ease into it. Nothing had ever been inside that ring, but his tongue felt really good as it slowly pierced me and slipped inside. Any thought about what was right or wrong simply melted from my brain as that tongue flickered in my chute. I felt an itch deep inside, but I didn't know how to scratch it.

Fortunately, Scott did.

I heard foil tearing as Scott breathed on my butt and kept on reaming me with that warm, slippery tongue. In a couple of minutes, his tongue gave a final lick along my hole before slipping out, leaving me feeling empty.

Scott slapped my butt lightly. "Get up on your hands and knees, Hayseed."

I had some idea of what was coming but I obeyed anyway, kneeling there with my shaft swaying beneath me in time to my heartbeat as he crawled up behind me. I gave an impatient groan of anticipation as I felt his hands parting my butt-cheeks, my dick drooling a torrent of pre-cum to the bedspread beneath.

I groaned and arched my back as I felt the heated rubber of the condom's tip pressing between my buttocks, right on the spit-slicked button of my anus. His hands rubbed gently up and down my hips as he slowly sank the first inch or so of his pole into me.

Intense pain burned through me. My prick lost some of its hardness as it washed over me, making me groan and clench my eyes shut as tears trickled down my cheeks. Even as I hurt, I wanted him to continue, wanted him inside me.

"It'll feel better in a moment, Hayseed," he comforted, the pleasure he was feeling evident in the breathlessness of his voice.

He reached around to grasp my shaft as he sank the next inch into me. I felt the pain blossom into pleasure as he fully stretched me open and nudged my prostate. Pre-cum flowed like sap from my slit and coated his fingers. My dick throbbed with the latent energy of a full erection. He drew my foreskin back and then forward, the pressure of his fingers through the silky skin making skyrockets of pleasure blast through my head. It was only when I felt his balls nudging against mine that I realized he was entirely inside of me. Feeling his balls rubbing against my own and his dick buried to the hilt in my guts turned me on like nothing else ever had. It made me feel that he was a part of me. I started grinding back against him, moaning about how good it felt and how I never wanted him to pull out.

Pull out he did though, and I whined as I felt just the tip against me again. He chuckled and then stroked along the length of my shaft and slipped back inside me at the same time.

The comforting feeling of being full of him came back as he rested for a moment, languidly slipping his fingers up and down my shaft. I felt my orgasm welling up from the root of my dick, and I contracted all the muscles down there as hard as I could to stop myself from cumming right then.

Scott began to fuck me, gently stroking my erection at the same time. I could feel sweat trickling down my flanks and the heat in my rear caused by the friction of his thrusts. I started to buck into his hand, timing my thrusts to be opposite to his. I'd thrust forward and him back, then I'd thrust back as he slammed forward to make his groin slap against my buttocks. Distantly, I heard the sounds of our fucking, slaps and squelches and moans.

I could feel him trembling against me as he tried hard not to empty his load, to keep fucking me forever. I could feel myself going over the edge though, and I yelped out loud at the intense feeling of my orgasm.

The fullness in my rear made the jolt of pleasure a thousand times more intense than in any jerk-off session I'd ever enjoyed, and I shot thick jets of cum on to the bed and over his hand. I could feel my ring clenching involuntarily as I came, and I think it was that spasm that sent him over the edge. He gasped and shuddered against me, and I felt his hot jizz rippling the condom as it filled it.

He collapsed on top of me with his shaft buried deep inside of me, both of us panting breathlessly. Eventually he managed to untangle his limbs from mine and slip his rod from my chute. He stripped the condom from his shaft and tossed it to the floor, then looked at the creamy cum on his fingers and grinned. He brought the hand up to his lips and licked my jizz from his palm and fingers, watching me as he swallowed every drop.

I studied him curiously and reached out to dip a finger in the cum coating the tip of his shaft, tasting it tentatively.

"Salty," I noted, licking my lips. "But not bad. What did mine taste like?"

He quirked his lips in a grin and tousled my hair with his sticky hand. "Like Hayseed's seed, of course."

With that, he made a dash for the shower.

I readjusted my still hard prick, feeling the sticky, slippery residue of cum. I didn't know exactly what was going on between Scott and me, but I had hopes and wanted it to continue.

And there was room in the shower for two.

RALLY 'ROUND THE FLAGPOLE

Robbie Cramer

DURING HIGH SCHOOL, I SPENT A WHOLE LOT OF TIME EITHER CRAMMED inside my locker, or suspended upside down over a toilet bowl while waiting for the inevitable dunk and flush. No student at Claremont High suffered more for education than I did.

Fortunately, all that changed during the summer after my senior year. While I was waiting to start classes at the local community college, I finally managed to stumble through puberty. I didn't get gorgeous, but I did get tall, and my acne cleared up. During the maturation process, my private parts grew in a big way as well. My dick went from functional to fantastical—putting on damn near an inch in length for every inch I grew in height.

I threw back the covers and reached for the tape measure I stole from my sister's sewing basket. I laid it out on the broad, vein-gnarled back of my hard cock. I held one end firmly against the base and let the tape drape over the gleaming knob on the end. Eleven and three-quarter inches of tingling, rock-hard meat, every sweet inch of it mine.

I brushed the tape measure aside and gripped my cock, watching the blunt snout swell. It was shaped like a pink helmet. I ran my thumb down over the tip and smeared the sticky stuff that was oozing out all around the rim of the crown. I started pumping and every nerve in my body tuned in to the same frequency as my tingling hard-on. I reached down between my legs and scooped up my heavy nuts in my palm. Just the slightest pressure on the fat globes was enough to make the hairs on my body all stand on end.

I was flogging away avidly when the clock in the hall chimed the hour. I let go of my hard-on and jumped out of bed. No time to finish up now. I turned on the cold water and got into the shower, jumping around and gasping until my prick went limp. Then I slipped into my clothes and dashed down the stairs to breakfast. I was horny, but I knew I'd have a chance to take care of it during an hour break between classes at the community college, so I hurried off to school with a light heart.

I made it through chemistry and English, then made tracks for the gymnasium. The band practiced there, in a room tucked under the bleachers that shared a common wall with the men's locker room. I had discovered this one morning when I was helping the band director file some music. I kept hearing what sounded like a rainstorm, even though the skies beyond the high windows were cloudless. A little exploration had revealed a vent duct in a storage closet that looked out over the men's shower room.

For a virgin like me, this amounted to horny pig heaven. All I had to do to admire a sea of male flesh was climb up on a filing cabinet and peek through a vent. Best of all, my free period coincided with the gym class favored by the school's most serious jocks.

The humpiest jock of all was Rex Frazier, one of those charmed individuals who would always have the world at his beck and call. He had been a champion athlete in high school and it was obvious that college wasn't interfering with his muscles. Rex had the face of an angel and a body by Michelangelo. He stood six feet tall, had thick flaxen hair that fell over his broad forehead in glossy ringlets and a killer smile that melted all comers. I had long ago decided I would be content to follow him around for the rest of my life like a faithful dog. Since he didn't seem to be in need of any fawning pets, I'd been limited to jacking off while I watched him bathe his magnificent body.

I slipped into the storage closet, climbed up on the cabinet and dropped my pants. I scanned the shower but saw no sign of Rex. That was too bad, but I was more than content to lust over Mick Taggert, another guy I'd been keeping an eye on. Mick was a total contrast to Rex, but I'm pretty adaptable when it comes down to finding a man to jack off over. Mick's shoulders were a little too thick and his pecs were way overdone—but nobody's perfect. Besides, he had a butt like a couple of hard melons. When Mick turned his back to me and started washing his buns, it was all I could do not to howl out loud.

While I was working up a good head of steam over Mick, Rex walked in and took his place at the showerhead next to his buddy. They chatted about sports while Rex started washing his crack. When he dropped his bar of soap and bent over, I was eye-to-asshole with my favorite man in the world and it put me right up over the top. I laid into my stiffy with both hands, pumping it frenziedly. My orgasm was so intense that I grunted more loudly than I meant to. Rex's golden head snapped around. I was pretty sure he couldn't see me in my hiding place, but the sensation that he was staring right at me was intense. I pointed my cock at the wastebasket in the corner and did my best to fill it up. Afterwards, while I was buckling my belt and copping a last look at their assets, Rex and Mick strode back to the locker room, heads together in some kind of conspiracy.

I stayed at school late that night. It was well after dark when I started down the road that led to the subdivision where I still lived with my family. I was beginning to fantasize about Rex and Mick again, so I wasn't even aware of the car till it pulled up beside me and the driver rolled his window down. "Get in the car, Cramer," a familiar voice rasped.

"Uh, hi, Mick," I gulped. It only took an instant to recognize the shadowy blond on the seat next to him. "Hey, Rex. What brings you guys out this way?"

"Just get in the car, Cramer." Mick nodded at the back door and I reached for the handle.

"Nice night," I muttered inanely. "Thanks for the lift."

"We saw you come out of the band room today, Cramer," Rex said, turning his gorgeous head to shoot me a disdainful look. "We know about the storage closet and you watching us shower, pervert." He faced forward again and left me to stew in my own juice.

"Out," Mick ordered, killing the engine. I climbed out, then stood by the fender awaiting my fate. "Take off your pants."

I hesitated briefly, but one look at their faces made it clear that they were serious. I kicked off my shoes and fumbled with my belt. When

I stepped out of my trousers, Mick looked at my boxer shorts and shook his head.

"Suck my cock," Mick barked, popping the buttons on his fly and shucking his jeans down over his narrow hips. The moon was full, casting enough light for me to see the thick, wrinkled cock-stalk poking out of his dense bush. I couldn't see his ass, but I knew it was there and my dick started to stir at the thought.

I dropped to my knees in front of him and leaned my forehead against his hard gut. Nothing could have prepared me for the way he smelled or the effect the heat rising off his body had on me. It was incredible! The musky scent of him got me hornier than I'd ever been in my life, but that turned out to be nothing compared to the sensation when my tongue first touched his cock.

"Get it hard," he grunted. We both groaned and his dick jerked when I popped it into my mouth. It was the strangest feeling—sort of like having a small wild animal in your mouth. I'd never done anything like it before, but it must have been instinctual, because I had Mick moaning with pleasure in minutes, humping his hips against my face. I even dared to slip my hands around his waist and cup his ass and he didn't push me away. I reached down to free my hard-on from the folds of fabric it was trapped in, then got ready to settle in and suck Mick till his head caved in. At least that was my original plan.

"Holy shit!" Rex yelped, sounding genuinely alarmed. He had been standing a short distance away, waiting his turn. I guess Mick got first dibs because he was driving. Anyway, I shifted my eyes to Rex's face, careful to keep Mick's cock trapped in my warm mouth.

"What's wrong?" Mick barked, not too pleased to have his blowjob interrupted.

"Look at what Cramer's packing, man. I don't fuckin' believe this." Rex grabbed my shoulder and wrenched me around. Mick's hard-on slipped out of my mouth with a little pop and I licked my lips longingly. "Is that for real?"

I looked up into the face of my idol and couldn't help chuckling. His eyes were glued on my crotch and his mouth was gaping. I'd never even considered flashing my meat at him, but the thought suddenly made me really horny. Besides, he'd asked me to! I got to my feet and let my shorts drop around my ankles. My cock jutted up out of my crotch like a flagpole, bouncing up and down in time with my heartbeat.

"Jesus H. Christ!" This from Mick, who now stood on the other side of me. "That can't be for real."

"It's real all right," I attested, tensing my muscles, making my cock knob bulge.

"Can I touch it?" This from Rex, his tone of voice almost reverent. Could he touch it? Hot damn!

"Sure," I said, trying to sound casual. When his fingertips grazed my knob, my knees damn near buckled. My whole body spasmed and my cock rose high in the air.

"Walk over here, dude," Mick suggested, gesturing towards his car. I took a few steps, closely followed by Rex who seemed unwilling to lose track of his recent discovery. Mick flipped on the lights of his car and my cock leaped out in all its veiny splendor. What with the shadows and the angle of the lights, my dick was casting a shadow well over a foot long. It looked almost scary.

Imagine my surprise when Rex and Mick both proceeded to strip, then dropped to their knees, one on either side of me. I watched in awe as their handsome faces drew closer till they were brushing my cockshaft with their hot lips. They were mesmerized by my cock, lapping all up and down the sides of the shaft, lips and tongues darting and sliding over every inch of the sensitive flesh. Then, they both inched along the shaft to my knob. Once discovered, they went at it like a couple of playful puppies. They pressed their cheeks together and both started sucking the bulbous glans, the pressure of their silky lips setting me on fire. I pried Rex's pretty pink lips apart with my fingers and began wedging my hard cock into his mouth. He opened wide and began doing his best to swallow it. I set Mick to licking all up and down the bulging juice-tube running along the underside of the stalk, then put my hands on my hips and settled in to watch them.

In the next few minutes, knowledge of the power that comes with possessing a truly monumental cock began to dawn on me. These two foxy guys were total slaves to my big meat. I didn't flatter myself that it was me they were after, but I didn't waste any regrets over that. I was growing on the other end of my cock and I was the one who registered every lick and stroke they gave it in the pleasure centers of my brain. As my virginity began to recede into history, life became clear to me.

My philosophizing was distracted by the sudden tripping of my trigger. They'd licked my dick once too often and I was going to unload. I grabbed them both by the neck and pressed their tender lips against my jiggling balls. They licked and kissed while I blasted off a shot that flew a good fifteen feet and splashed on the grill of Mick's car. They both snorted like horny little pigs and started sliding their mouths up and down my aching love muscle, slobbering excitedly. I let fly with another shot, and another, leaving a steaming trail of white all along the dirt road from the car to my feet. While jism was still oozing out of me, I smeared my throbbing knob over their hot, wet lips. Both of them groaned and lapped my spooge greedily

"That was fucking hot," Mick said hoarsely. "Too bad it was over so soon."

"Nothing's over," I growled, startling myself with my new-found authority. "Both of you stand up, turn around, and present your asses for inspection." I'll be damned if they didn't both jump to obey me, baring their most secret treasures in the harsh lights of the automobile. At the sight of those two quivering buds of musky flesh, my cock surged with blood and pointed at the moon.

"You got a cover for this?" I growled, my voice suddenly about two octaves deeper than normal.

"Uh, I got a box of assorted safes in the glove compartment," Mick said, scrambling to his feet. He was back in a heartbeat with the box. He held a packet up in front of the headlights, then tossed it aside. He continued littering the ground with brightly colored foil squares till he finally found what he wanted.

"Extra large," Mick shouted in triumph. He ripped it open, and he and Rex set about bagging my cock. When they had it covered, I gestured and they both turned around, braced their hands on the hood of Mick's car and thrust their asses towards me.

I was frantic to fuck. It had to be Rex first—to do anything else would have constituted disloyalty to my most precious fantasies. I grabbed my hard cock and pressed against the target, giving him a tentative little poke. There was resistance, then a flutter like he was kissing me. I poked again and felt him giving way.

"Go on and take it, you horny little cock hound," Mick barked, stepping over and putting his hands on his buddy's broad shoulders. He shoved Rex backwards, and I was in. Amazingly, Rex's little rosebud of an asshole had gaped wide enough to swallow my knob. Rex was howling, but his ass channel had stretched to accommodate my huge hard-on.

"Fuck him!" Mick ordered, staring me right in the eyes. "Fuck him hard. He loves it." He shoved Rex again and his perfect ass slapped against my pelvis. Every inch of my dick felt like it was on fire, burning from the intimate heat of him. I leaned into him until my balls were crushed into his crack, and savored the tightness while I stroked his sweat-streaked flanks.

After several delicious moments, I slowly began to withdraw. Mick's eyes were focused on the bulging shaft, watching as inch after slippery inch reappeared, gleaming in the headlight beams. I withdrew till my flanged knob caught against Rex's sphincter. To pull back any further would have been like popping a cork out of a bottle of fine champagne, and I had no desire to do that. I savored the feel of his ring pulsing for a few seconds, then pounded my prick back up his silky chute. Mick clamped his hands down on his buddy's asscheeks, spreading them wide, tempting me ever deeper.

Within seconds I had established the slow steady fucking action of my sexiest dreams. These were the same moves I'd made with my cock pumping up through a collar of fingers, only this time I was probing the moist, clinging depths of the hottest wet dream I had ever imagined. It was the stuff dreams are made of—but it was as real as my big throbbing cock.

"I'm there," I gasped, realizing I was over the edge again. I popped out just in time to strip off the rubber and lay a line along Rex's spine. Glistening drops splattered on Mick's washboard gut. I looked down, watching as my hand flew back and forth along the gnarled shaft. I laid three more stripes up Rex's tanned back then reached under him and grabbed his hard-on. A couple of pumps and my palm was flooded with his wet, sticky heat. I smeared it up over his belly and chest, feeling the hard muscles jumping beneath his smooth skin. Afterwards, I stood there, dazed and panting.

"Hey, Cramer." I looked up into Rex's eyes. He was standing in front of me now, hands on Mick's heavy shoulders. "I got another big rubber right here." My thick stiffer showed no signs of subsiding. Besides, my second favorite hole in all the world was waiting for me, quivering with anticipation. I watched Rex grab my hard-on, roll the rubber down the shaft, then thrust my cock into Mick.

"Oh, shit," I groaned as Mick's succulent little ass-pucker gaped a warm welcome.

"Fuck him hard," Rex growled, his blue eyes glittering as he began impaling his buddy on my stiff cock. "He loves it even more than I do." I gripped Mick's muscular shoulders and pulled him back onto my prick. What the hell else was a guy to do?

DIRTY LAUNDRY BOYS

Bill Crimmin

I ZIPPED UP MY JACKET AND PUSHED MY HANDS DOWN INTO ITS POCKETS. Thank God it wasn't raining—that would have been the final straw. Losing my job and almost getting squashed by a human orangutan was enough for one night, I thought, as I began the long walk home.

It hadn't been my fault of course, but the manager hadn't seen it that way. Maybe I was just not cut out to sell hamburgers. Usually I managed to bite my tongue but when the redneck with the trophy girlfriend had wondered aloud for the fourth time how come a college boy was shoveling fries if he was so smart, I just lost it. I squared my shoulders, sauntered round the counter more casually than I felt and stood straight in front of him. I looked him in the eyes and told him that working in a burger joint was a way of financing my tuition, not a career choice. I should have left it there but I was on a roll. I said that when I'd finished college I'd be working in a law office and driving around in a beemer, not a beat-up pick-up with a rifle in the back and a dog in the passenger seat. I'd honestly been referring to the ratty old hound he'd left in his truck when he parked outside but he jumped to the wrong conclusion. Worse still, his date got mad. She shook her bleached curls and pouted her painted lips.

"You gonna let him call me a dog?" she squealed indignantly.

"I ain't," said the redneck, rising to his feet.

I gulped. Just my luck to pick on the only circus giant still living. Sitting down he had looked substantial, but standing up he was huge. He almost blocked out the sun. He towered over me by a head and I'm over six feet. His giant paw grabbed the front of my uniform and lifted me off the ground.

"What seems to be the trouble, sir?" asked the manager, who had heard the commotion and come out of his office.

I heaved a huge sigh of relief. I'd never been so pleased to see the weasly little creep in my life. I felt as though the cavalry had just arrived. To cut a long story short, the redneck was placated with some free meal vouchers and I was fired on the spot. Hence, I was heading for my dorm two hours earlier than usual with not even enough money in my pocket for the bus fare home.

Fifteen minutes later I was letting myself into my room hoping that my roommate was out so I didn't have to explain the whole sorry story to him. The door swung open and I got the fright of my life.

Luke was home all right. And making himself at home on my bed amidst the contents of my laundry basket.

I was so shocked I was speechless. I just stood there, eyes riveted on my roommate humping his fist. It was obvious that he hadn't heard me. He was lying naked on my bed, muscles rippling across his smooth, tanned torso and his cock thick and hard, looking every bit as edible as I had always imagined he would. His eyes were closed and the cutest little grin was playing around his lips. Tendrils of black hair clung to the sweat on his forehead. His right hand held a pair of my shorts to his nose and his left was wrapped around his straining cock. Of course, I thought, Luke was a southpaw.

His body tensed. His hand was a blur on his dick. He took a big sniff of my boxers and shot his wad. Ropes of jizz squirted all over his chest as his cock throbbed in his hand.

"Ben!" he cried as the final spurt of come spattered over his rippling chest.

I felt myself turning white. Ben! He had called my name. I guess that finding my roommate jerking off while covered in my dirty laundry was a bit of a give-away, but I swear that until he said my name I'd had no idea that his impromptu performance had anything to do with me. I just figured that he had some fetish to do with sweaty clothes. Hell, I was as broadminded as the next guy. But Luke obviously had a thing for me and was getting his rocks off surrounded by my sweaty jocks and T-shirts because it made him feel—I don't know—closer to me somehow.

He was panting now, eyes still closed. His softening dick jerked occasionally in his hand. I watched, fascinated as he used my Calvins to wipe the cum off his chest and belly. I couldn't help noticing that he had a fine set of abs. And pecs. And two hard, chocolatey nipples that I longed to nibble on.

If I'm honest, I'd always had a thing for Luke. But I'd never mentioned it because he was a member of the college boxing team and seemed as macho as any of his teammates. I kind of thought he liked me but I didn't dare risk making a move because, if I got it wrong, he might beat my brains out. But as I looked down at his smooth, sweaty body as he wiped the sperm away with my underwear I knew I had been wrong. There was a god after all.

"Hi," I said, finally. Not a great opening remark under the circumstances, but all I could think of. Luke jumped up off my bed as if his ass had just caught fire. He stood there, bobbing from foot to foot and trying to cover his embarrassment with my soiled skivvies.

"Ben, I—uh—I—didn't see you there," he said finally. I'd never seen anyone's face flush so red.

"I didn't think so. You do this often?" I asked, moving over to my bed and sitting down.

"No," he stammered, "it's the first time, I swear. I'll wash them for you," he started gathering up the clothes and stuffing them down in my laundry basket. "I'll take them to the laundry room myself. It'll never happen again, I promise." His voice trailed away indecisively. He remembered he was still naked and grabbed the wicker lid of the basket and covered his crotch with it. He smiled weakly.

"Please don't hit me."

"Hit you?" I burst out laughing. "Relax, Luke," I said when I could again control the chuckles. "Looks as though you and I are both a pair of idiots. I've been eyeing you up for weeks but didn't dare make a move because I was scared you'd give me two black eyes, then get your buddies on the boxing team to finish off the job. And you obviously thought something similar about me. I may have hit more homeruns this season than any other college player but I leave my baseball bat in the locker room. I'm not going to hit you. Not at all. Come here." I held my arms open to him and he stepped hesitantly into them. His body felt warm against mine. Our lips met briefly in a kiss and I held him close. Then I let go of him and he sat down on the bed beside him.

"You really like me?" he asked anxiously, taking my hand. "I was scared you'd hate me if you knew I was hot for you. I knew you'd be at work until midnight and I was as horny as hell. Jacking off with your dirty laundry seemed a good idea at the time. How was I to know you'd get off early?"

It seemed reasonable. I had to admit that. Except for the underwear. That part I couldn't understand.

"I didn't get off early. I got fired." Quickly I told him about the redneck and his significant other and how I nearly got squashed flatter than one of our hamburger patties.

"So that explains why I came home early and caught you canoodling with my Calvins. What it doesn't explain is why?" He blushed redder than the redneck's neck and started stammering. He took a couple of deep breaths and finally managed to speak intelligibly.

"It all started when I was thirteen," he explained. "My mom got a job, so she said that us kids would have to help out round the house. We each had a particular chore we had to do after school. My job was doing the laundry. At first, I hated it, but I quickly realized that spending hours alone in the basement could have advantages. You know what it's like—I'd just discovered my cock and couldn't leave it alone. There was a spare bed down there, which we kept for guests, and I got into the habit of beating my meat while I waited for the washer to finish its cycle. Then I'd dump the clean laundry into the dryer and go straight back to jacking off.

"Slowly a sort of link developed in my mind between sex and laundry. The smell of it got me horny. Not just the clean soap smell of the finished laundry, but the sweaty, animal smell of the dirty stuff. I'd cover myself in the dirty laundry, yank myself silly and then get on with the laundry and nobody was any the wiser. And it just sort of stuck. In high school, I even used to steal sweaty jocks from my buddies' lockers. And if the laundry belonged to a guy I liked I was even worse. I could hardly control myself."

He was looking straight into my face. His full, red lips were parted slightly and the pink, wet tip of his tongue was visible between his white teeth.

"I can relate to that," I said. "I mean, laundry doesn't do anything for me, but I can understand it. With me it's necks," I said. I pushed his hair off his face and kissed him gently at the point of his jaw.

"Necks?" he asked.

"Yeah. I have a thing about guys' necks. Sometimes I sit behind a guy on the bus, or even in class, and the sight of the back of his neck drives me crazy. There's a particular hairstyle I like. Really short at the back and getting longer on top. If a guy has that style and dark wavy hair I have to clench my fists and dig my nails into my hands to stop myself from licking the back of his neck. I can hardly help myself."

Luke smiled then. Slowly he turned away from me, presenting his neck to me. My cock, already at half mast, leapt to attention. His nape was gorgeous. I'd admired it a thousand times. I deliberately sat behind him in the one class we had in common so that I could look at it. I found it so hard to concentrate that I usually ended up borrowing somebody else's notes.

Gently, I placed one hand on each of his shoulders and nuzzled his neck. I inhaled the concentrated man scent of his hair and skin. Then stuck out my tongue and bathed his neck with it. I was in heaven. Inside my jeans my cock felt as hard and fat as my baseball bat. I just had to let it out. Reluctantly, I released my grip on Luke and stood up. I was out of my clothes in seconds and lay down on my bed, pulling Luke with me.

"I've never done—not with a guy."

I chuckled. "You mean we're both virgins?" I rolled on top of him, trapping our rigid cocks between us. His skin was hot and smooth. I pushed his sweat-matted hair back off his face and kissed his brow. He smiled and I melted inside. Our mouths met in a kiss. I snaked my tongue past his warm, soft lips.

I slithered my body downwards until one of his delicious choco-latey nipples was in reach and I swooped on it. I sucked the rubbery nub into my mouth, nibbling it. He gasped and wriggled underneath me. His nipple hardened in my mouth. I was in heaven.

I licked across his smooth chest and found his other nipple. I bathed it with my tongue, occasionally treating it to a teasing nibble. Soon, it was as stiff and proud as its twin.

I licked down the center of his torso now, pausing at his navel. I explored the shallow dimple with my tongue, relishing the concentrated Luke perfume that gathered there. His meat was as hard as anything, digging insistently into my chest. I raised myself up on my elbows and took a good look. Close up, it looked even tastier than I had thought before. Longer than my own seven inches, it stood hard and proud. A mat of curly, black hairs nestled at its base and two substantial nuts were already riding its shaft. A bead of pre-cum was glistening at the slit. I stuck out my tongue and licked the honeyed drop away.

I grasped his tool with one hand and cupped his balls with the other. I bathed his rosy knob with my tongue, poked it into the slit. I licked the sensitive underside of his cockhead and under the flange. Then I couldn't wait any longer. I opened my mouth and swallowed him down to the root.

Luke let out a sigh that left me in no doubt that he was enjoying the sensation of my mouth on his cock as much as I was enjoying creating it. His whole body was trembling. He cupped the back of my head with his hands, lacing his fingers through my hair.

"That feels so good!" he groaned, blissfully.

His cock was hard and smooth in my mouth. His skin felt like warm silk. I drank in his musky aroma, sweat and soap and the indefinable, yet unmistakable, scent of arousal. My head bobbed between his legs. My eager mouth moved up and down his dick. I took him all the way in until I could feel the nap of his pubes scratching my face and out until only his helmet was inside.

He wriggled then, rocking his hips and humping my face, impatient for me to swallow him again. His thighs were tense and quivering. He dug his heels down into the mattress. He was breathing in short gulps; air whistling between his teeth.

I reached down and stroked his taut left ass-cheek. The muscular globe rested comfortably in the palm of my hand. I cupped his other cheek in my right hand, bracing my weight on my elbows. I kept my mouth on his dick and allowed him to fuck my face. His hips moved urgently, thrusting his rigid cock in and out of my mouth.

His body was filmed with sweat. A series of incoherent syllables escaped from his lips. His rod throbbed in my mouth. His balls were hugging his shaft; the skin of his scrotum taut and thickened. I gripped his bubble butt and hung on as he humped my face. He thrust his hips forward and exploded in my mouth. I swallowed as warm salty liquid erupted on my tongue. I drank it all down, relishing its taste, its texture. Loving it because it was his.

He looked down at me and released his grip on my hair. He wiped a hand over his sweaty face, pushing his damp hair off his face. And he smiled.

"I hope you're going to fuck me now," he panted.

"If you're sure you want me to," I said.

He nodded his assent. I settled down between his legs and pressed his thighs apart. I nestled down and used my fingers to pull his bubbled cheeks apart, like I'd seen in porn videos. I buried my face between those perfect globular melons and started to rim him. He wriggled appreciatively.

I licked along his crack, wetting him. From my privileged vantage point, I could see he shaved everything south of his dick. His crevice was smooth and soft. I bathed it with my tongue then turned my attention to his crinkled ring. I circled it with my tongue, following its puckered outline. Then I began to exert a little pressure and pushed my pointed tongue past his sphincter.

He purred in delight and opened his legs a little wider, allowing me easier access. I wrapped my arms round his thighs, pulling him close. I delved inside his anus with my tongue, working it inside him. Opening him.

His dick was hard again. He gripped it in his fist and squeezed it as I rimmed him.

"Fuck me now, Ben," he begged, "I want to cum with you inside me and I can't hold on much longer."

I reached over to my night table and took out condoms and lube. I'd bought them at the beginning of term and this was their first outing. I'd been beginning to think they'd expire before I used them. I knelt between Luke's spread legs. I squirted a blob of lube onto my rigid cock and spread it around. I rolled a condom on, then applied more of the goop to my fingers and rubbed it into Luke's winking hole.

He gasped and spread his legs wider as the cold gel touched him. I spread it around his crack, making sure that everything was covered in a film of lube. Then I started to massage his sphincter. I worked the greasy stuff into him, gently pressing one lubricated finger past his puckered opening. I felt his muscles tense, then relax as my digit claimed him. Quickly I pushed a second finger, then a third into his hole and worked them around until I figured he could take my cock without hurting.

I positioned myself between his thighs and held my erect rod to his hole.

"Ready?" I asked him.

He nodded eagerly, making his black curls bob.

"Put it in me," he growled.

I pressed forward, putting my weight behind my hips. The tip of my cock slid past his sphincter and inched inside. I looked at him, making sure he was okay but his face was blank and his eyes were glassy with arousal. I figured he liked it. I pushed with my hips, slowly, oh so slowly, relishing the feeling of every millimeter of my cock sliding into his guts. His ass felt velvety-soft and hot. So hot. Soon I was buried up to my balls in him, my pubes pressed up against his ball-sac.

Luke's eyes were closed. He was panting. Carefully I lifted each of his legs in turn until his ankles rested on my shoulders. He gripped his twitching cock in one hand and pumped it furiously. I braced myself on my hands and began to fuck him. Slowly at first, I slid my latex-covered manhood in and out of his tight, slippery hole.

My plums rode my shaft. I plowed his sweet ass. He swayed his hips, lifting his ass off the bed. He met my thrusts with powerful lunges of his own. My aching member slid through his hot bowel. I moaned in delight. I circled my hips, relishing the sensation of his muscles gripping my cock. Sucking me inside.

I picked up speed, pounding his ass with a rhythm dictated by my ardor. Between us, his dick was engorged with blood. He pumped it frantically, squeezing his taut balls with his other hand.

His eyes were closed. His mouth formed into a rictus of delight. Sweat poured off him. His entire body was stiff and quivering. He groaned—a rich, deep, throaty rumble which betrayed his arousal.

I fucked him hard. Pistoning my hips, I tensed my thighs and buttocks as I rode him. A ball of fire pulled at my nuts. My dick felt as though it would burst. Luke was panting and grunting, his hand a blur. I reached down to the floor and quickly scooped up the briefs I had removed earlier. I put them over Luke's face, forcing him to smell them.

His cock exploded then; volleys of jizz shooting all over his chest and mine. He reached up his free hand and held my jocks over his face. I could see him inhaling as he came. His dick jerked in his hand, pumping out spunk onto his smooth belly as he sniffed my shorts. The expression on his face was rapturous. His body was jerking so much I had a hard time staying on top of him.

His muscles relaxed slightly and he opened his eyes. Wordlessly, he smiled at me and wiped all the sperm off us both with my underwear. I continued to pound his ass. Then he brought the jizz-smeared garment up to his face and sniffed it again.

That was enough for me. The sight of such a hunk as Luke getting off on the smell of my briefs while I fucked him, tipped me over the edge. I shot my wad inside the latex buried deep in his sweet guts. I grunted as wave after wave of orgasm crashed over me.

I thrust my hips forward, pushing my throbbing cock as deep into him as I could. I spasmed inside him, filling the condom. His muscles gripped me, rippled around my rod, pulling me inside. Milking me. It was incredible, coming inside of him as he lay there inhaling the smell of my cum-covered shorts. And the sight of him was so cute that I just couldn't resist bending down to kiss him.

After that, we lay in each other's arms for a while. When we'd got our breath and our energy back we went for an encore. Several encores.

Luke and I have been an item since then, although we've been careful to keep our liaison secret from his buddies on the boxing team. I got a new job waiting tables at a restaurant near the campus with a better hourly rate than my old job and better-mannered customers. I still occasionally catch Luke rolling in my dirty laundry with his dick in his fist and, to tell you the truth, I find it kind of cute.

I'm not tempted myself but, in a way, I can understand why it arouses him so much. After all, it's my smell that's turning him on and knowing he's so hot for me that just getting a whiff of my undies can get him horny makes me feel kind of special. He particularly enjoys sniffing my sweaty running shorts while he comes and, for my part, I make sure he has plenty of dirty laundry to play with.

Sometimes I ring him up from the restaurant during my break to tell him how hot and sweaty I am and how I'm going to make him sniff my Calvins when I get home. It's guaranteed to get him hot and horny.

And if I ever run across the redneck who lost me my job at Bettaburgers, I'm going to walk straight up to him and shake his giant hand until his teeth rattle.

JOCK ITCH

Grant Foster

IT WAS THE TYPICAL MIX-UP. A FUCK UP REALLY, BUT THE UNIVERSITY wasn't about to admit to that. When some heifer in admissions finally found my paperwork, the only dorm space left was in Kane Hall, the jock dorm. I had a strong premonition that I wasn't exactly going to fit in.

I was the kind of guy who'd get carded in a candy store. At five-foot-six and a hundred and fifteen pounds, I was nobody's idea of a jock. My stature, coupled with my pale blond hair and rosy cheeks, made me look like I was pushing puberty instead of nineteen. I was strong academically, but I suspected that my brains would not be appreciated at Kane.

I unlocked the door and looked inside my new home for the next semester. My roommate was settled. His bed was a tangle of sheets and the floor was strewn with athletic equipment. In one corner I saw a barbell with enough weights on it to sink a large boat. The shelves above the desk on his side of the room were full of balls—soccer, football, baseball, basketball—but no books. My heart sank and I sat down on the floor, feeling more alone than I ever had.

"Hey, Squirt. You the new rommie?"

I looked towards the open door. The first thing I saw were long, bare, muscled legs. I had never seen calves that thick or thighs with that degree of definition. My gaze rose and I quickly discovered that the legs were the least of this guy's endowments.

His torso could have appeared in the reference books as the standard by which all others would be judged. The belly wash-boarded, the lats flared, the pectoral muscles jutted out like a shelf, and the shoulders loomed broad enough to block my view entirely.

His upper arms were thicker than my thighs and his forearms were, in the words of my younger brother, totally awesome.

The last thing my roommate needed was a model-handsome face, but he had one. It was all planes and angles, high cheekbones, strong chin, startlingly blue eyes and lashes so long they almost created a breeze when he blinked. His thick black hair was plastered to his skull. Sweat gleamed on his tanned skin and beaded the hairs that feathered the expanse of his massive chest. He was incredible—and totally intimidating.

I gulped. "Yeah, I'm just moving in," I mumbled as I watched him cross the room.

"I'm Mark," he announced, his huge hand engulfing mine.

"Keith," I replied.

"My last roommate flunked out. You don't look like the flunking type."

"I—uh—I hope not," I stammered, doing my best not to drool on his shoes. He raised his arms over his head and stretched, knotting up muscles in places where I didn't even have places. After tickling the ceiling with his long, thick fingers, he bent over and planted his palms on the floor. More muscles jumped and knotted, making me feel warmer than the temperature warranted.

"Maybe you could give me a few pointers, Squirt. Math doesn't like me very much."

"Sure, Mark. Any time."

"Gotta go to football practice now," he said, glancing at the alarm clock on his desk. "See you later, Squirt."

"See you, Hercules," I blurted without thinking. He turned at the door and gave me a quizzical look. I stood there, hoping the first punch would be enough to do me in so I wouldn't suffer. He grinned, winked, and was gone.

I stood there, my heart pounding, looking out the window at the lawn in front of Kane Hall. A couple of minutes later, Mark came bounding out of the front doors and loped across the expanse of green. He turned, looked up, and waved at someone. I waved back, pretending it was me. Once he was out of sight, I locked the door, stripped, and jacked off while sitting on his bed.

For the first time in my life, I wanted another guy. Consciously. Knowingly. Feeling and touching. Whatever guys did together. I had a feeling it was going to be a very long semester.

"God, my neck hurts. How about a massage, Squirt?"

I put my hands on his shoulders and began kneading his incredible muscles. I was helping him with his calculus again. It was slow going, but he was beginning to absorb the concepts. We'd been working together a couple of hours a night for the past month and I had to admit that explaining it to Mark was helping me as well. Of course, I would have happily spent the same amount of time standing knee-deep in dog shit just to touch him as I was now doing. I pressed my thumbs into a knot above his right shoulder blade, and he sighed.

"I'm afraid I'm about ready to give it up for the day, Squirt," he stiffled a yawn. "Practice was rough this afternoon."

"Sure, Mark. You're ready for that test tomorrow. I've got total confidence in you. Just don't freeze up."

"Thanks. You've been a great help." He grabbed his toothbrush and towel and headed down the hall to the bathroom. When he returned, he stripped down to the buff like he always did, sprawled out on top of his unmade bed, and was snoring softly in less than a minute.

I read to the end of the paragraph in my history text, closed the book and looked over at him. I let my eyes follow the contours of his upper body—contours I had committed to memory weeks ago—then focused on his crotch. In the past month, I'd come to know that I was gay. I wasn't totally comfortable with it—I sure as hell wasn't going to tell anyone—but I wasn't going to freak out either. The object of my affection—my lust—was, of course, my roommate.

In addition to all of his other physical attributes, Mark was hung like a horse. I'd known that some men were hung bigger than others, but I had never imagined anyone with a cock like his. When it was soft, it looked like a big, wrinkled Italian salami—hard, it became an incredibly long, immensely thick club. It was hard a lot at night—I guess he had hot dreams.

The first week or two, I tried to ignore his nudity, turning my chair so that I sat with my back to his bed. I knew he was there though—his dick was there—and the temptation to look was strong. The last two weeks, I'd been holding out for an hour or two, before I'd let myself cop glances at it. Tonight, I was staring—I couldn't help myself—watching the veiny cylinder hover above his belly. He leaked a lot when he was hard. It oozed out of his gaping piss-hole and drooled onto his gut.

I'd been jerking off looking at Mark's dick since that first night, getting so excited by his monster meat that I could shoot it three times in a row without even losing my hard-on. One night last week, I got brave and caught a drop of his lube on my finger, then smeared it on my stiffer. I came instantly, shooting my wad up over my shoulder, onto the wall. After that, I wanted his juice on my rod every time I jerked it.

After our study session, when he was asleep, I really lost my mind. Mark was in deep sleep, and his dick was levitating big time. I had pulled my clothes off, put my books away, and sat naked, in my chair, facing his bed. His dick looked bigger than ever, the knob swollen, the tip glowing a delicate pink. The veins lacing his cockshaft were bulging and he was leaking like a broken pipe.

I reached over and held my fingertips under his knob, getting them sticky. I touched my dick, then raised my fingers to my lips. I sucked his slime into my mouth, felt it on my tongue, slippery against my teeth. The taste was an aphrodisiac, making my dick flex against my palm. I reached again, scooped, then sucked my fingers clean a second time.

The next thing I knew, I was kneeling beside his bed, close enough to smell his musky sweat, close enough to feel his body heat. His prick pulsed when I breathed on it, rising a fraction higher above his belly. His eyes were closed, his chest rising and falling steadily, his enormous balls twitching in their low-hanging bag.

With one hand firmly on my cock, I leaned closer, finally daring to brush his dick with my lips. The sensation was like getting punched in the gut. My face got all hot, sweat began trickling down my sides, my skin began to tingle. I touched his cock again, then began licking his knob. The honey smeared my lips and dribbled off my chin.

I wanted to put his dick in my mouth—so I did. Hell, if he woke up, Mark was unlikely to make a distinction between licking and sucking. I opened my mouth wide and wedged his glans between my lips. Everything about it was incredibly hot—the taste, the silky texture of his dick skin, the pulsing hardness of him. I ran my tongue over the spongy surface, felt the blood pounding through the swollen veins. My teeth slipped over the rim of the crown and raked the massive shaft.

I don't know how I did it, but I began to swallow—not even gagging when his knob slid past my tonsils. I could feel the muscles in my throat stretching, flexing around the hot shaft I was struggling to engulf. Mark kept snoring, muttering gibberish, and rubbing his fuzzy chest.

When I was halfway down on him, his hips pumped suddenly, ramming his dick deeper into my throat. I grabbed the side of the bed and hung on tightly.

By the time I was face down in his pubes, I was so turned on my whole body was throbbing. I was a heartbeat from coming, but I wasn't jacking myself. Instead, I sucked Mark's dick, bobbing my head up and down, licking, stroking, probing in his deep, salty blow-hole for more of the juice that kept bubbling up from his monster nuts. The flow increased, then he began whimpering. His balls snapped up and bumped against my nose. I pulled mostly off of him and began working on just his knob, feeling his cock get ready to erupt.

Mark humped deep into my throat again and cried out as his cream began blasting my throat. I didn't have time to think; I swallowed as my mouth filled. I swallowed again as the next load filled me again. I tasted his cum on the third load and knew I was going to want it always. I reached out and grabbed him, then milked his stalk till he was drained dry and going limp in my mouth. I sank back on my haunches, smeared his cum on my cock and got myself off.

I walked over to the window and stood looking out into the darkness. I had betrayed Mark, my Hercules, a man I genuinely liked. I had sneaked around like a thief, violating his private space and his body while he slept. I told myself that I had every right to admire him—even to lust after him—but I had no right to do what I had done. Tears welled up in my eyes and within moments I was sobbing uncontrollably.

"Hey, Squirt, what's the matter?" Mark was behind me, close behind. I felt his hands, heavy on my shoulders, then his big body, hot and hard against my back. His cock was half-hard and pressed against my spine at my shoulders.

"I'm sorry, Mark. I—" My voice failed me, as I sobbed again. What was I going to do? He'd kill me if he knew what I'd done. How could I ever even look him in the face again? I knew I was going to have to move out immediately. It was the least I could do.

"I wasn't asleep, Squirt." His hands gripped my arms gently.

His words rang in my ears. The feeling of him vibrated through every fiber of my body.

"Y—you weren't?" My heart slammed up into my throat and my stomach began to churn. Dread and relief flooded through me in equal measure.

"Hey, I told you I was tired, not dead. That was one hell of a blowjob."

"Huh?" He didn't sound angry and he hadn't folded me in half and stuffed my head up my ass. His fingers began to gently knead my arms.

"I said you give great head." He turned me to face him. His big dick pressed against my ribcage, still moist with the remains of his jizz and my spit. He raised his hand and wiped the tears off my cheeks and smiled down at me. "You're a sexy little fucker, Squirt." His fingers latched onto my left tit and gave it a pinch. I jerked against him like he'd stuck an electrode up my butt. "If I've got a type, I'd have to say you're it." He pinched my tit again and winked at me.

Mark moved back, drawing me with him. He sat in his desk chair and pulled me down on top of him, straddling him, face to face. My cock and balls nestled against his belly and the hairs on his thighs tickled the backs of my legs. I just stared at him, too dazed to speak.

"Go ahead, Squirt. Feel me up to your heart's content." He clasped his hands on top of his head and his biceps swelled to monumental proportions. I watched, fascinated, as he flexed. His pecs bulged and the ridges of his abs were etched clearly beneath his belly fur. He was obviously serious—all this full-blown masculine beauty was mine to enjoy.

I began with his arms, stroking from wrist to armpit, savoring the solid strength of him, feeling his blood pulse in the prominent veins that snaked over his forearms. I pressed my fingers into the mossy hollows of his armpits, then trailed them down his sides, following the fan of his lats. When I rubbed his belly, his silky fur curled around my fingers.

I touched his ribcage; then, at last, his chest. He lowered his arms, clamped his hands on my waist and took a deep breath, swelling the rock-hard shelf of his pecs to the max. I leaned forward and pressed my face into the furry hollow in the center of his chest. I inhaled. The scent of him—very sexy, very male—tickled my nostrils and made my cock go hard.

"Pinch my tits," he growled, his voice a husky rumble. I rubbed the mounds of muscle, found the thick nubs and applied a gentle pressure. "Harder!" I obeyed, squeezing my thumbs and forefingers together tightly.

His cock rose up from between his thighs and smacked my ass-cheeks, sliding easily into the crack. "Oh!" I looked up at him, wide-eyed.

"You like that, Squirt?"

I nodded. I pinched again and got another smack. Mark watched me through the fan of his eyelashes as I went to work on his nipples in earnest.

He lifted me and his dick rose up like a fleshy monolith. "God, I want to fuck you, Squirt. Will you let me do that?"

"I—I don't think that's possible." I eyed his mammoth prick doubtfully, even as part of me was demanding I go for it.

"You got it down your throat easily enough. Please let me try. You've got such a pretty ass." I swallowed noisily and nodded.

I knew then that I wanted it. I wanted to feel him in me. I wanted that as much as I'd wanted to taste him earlier. He smiled at me, then reached into one of his desk drawers and pulled out a rubber and a big bottle.

"Bag it and lube it up. Then we'll see what happens." I unwrapped the rubber and unrolled it down his dick with trembling fingers. Then I took the bottle from him, popped the top and squeezed. A huge dollop splattered out, rolled across the broad dome of the head and down the shaft. I kept on squeezing and smearing until his entire cock gleamed. I tossed the bottle aside, wiped my fingers in my ass crack, took a deep breath, and nodded to Mark. He put his hands on my hips and lifted me until I felt his immense knob press against my hole.

"I feel like I'm sitting on a flagpole," I quipped, trying to hide my misgivings. "Uh—don't ruin me for future encounters, Hercules. Okay?"

"Hey, Squirt, I wouldn't do anything to hurt you. Just relax and trust me." I put my arms around his neck and laid my head on his shoulder. His chest pressed against mine and I could feel the beating of his heart. His strong fingers curved around my ass-cheeks, kneading them gently. I felt the throbbing heat of his cockhead as it pressed against my asshole.

It was amazing. I had felt no pain. None at all. There was this incredible feeling of fullness in my bowels, then an intense sexual rush that made me feel like I was going to lose it. I struggled to control the impulse, digging my nails into my palms, holding my breath, willing myself not to shoot. "Aaahhh!"

"Am I hurting you?" His voice was soft in my ear.

"No, but I think I'm gonna cum."

"Not yet, Squirt. Not yet."

"I'm okay," I panted, still teetering dangerously close to the edge. "I think."

"Your ass feels good, Squirt. So hot and tight." He put his big hands on my chest, then his thumbs pressed down hard against my nipples. I jerked around in his lap like an out-of-control puppet. "That's it, Squirt. Ride my dick. Bounce on it."

I braced my palms against the solid wall of his belly and tensed the muscles in my thighs. I rose up, then sank back down into his lap. I rose up a second time, relaxed, slid back onto him. A ball of heat began to grow deep in my gut, radiating out along my limbs.

"That's good, Squirt. That's real good." He pulled my head down onto his chest. The rubbery point of his tit rubbed against my lips. I caught it between my teeth and started sucking it.

Mark growled and thrust his hips up off the chair, raising me into the air. I stayed still when he started to pull out. I felt his huge dick slide out of my chute till the head of it pulsed against my sphincter. I started to sit down on him again, but he thrust up hard, driving deep into me. I locked my hands behind his thick neck and held on tight, sucking his nipple frantically as he started to fuck me.

Within moments, my whole body was vibrating. My hard-on was hugging my belly, squirting clear juice every time Mark thrust his cock into my body. I looked up at him, still sucking. He moaned, his eyes closed tight, sweat glistening on his forehead. A flush of pink was rising in his neck, staining his cheeks crimson. His mouth gaped open, his full, sensual lips pulled back from his teeth. His breathing was ragged.

His prick was jerking and flexing inside of me, getting harder and bigger as he got ready to blast off. The muscled wall of his belly was rubbing against my cock, making control impossible. My body began to spasm as I started to cum. I felt my muscles tighten and go rigid, felt my balls snap up tight between my legs as my orgasm began. My jism gushed out onto Mark's belly, hot and thick and sticky. He looked at me one last time, winked, then threw his head back as he blew his load deep up my ass.

I lay there on top of him, not wanting to move. His prick slowly deflated and slipped out of my hole, leaving me feeling empty and incomplete. Mark rose from the chair and carried me over to his bed. He dumped me on top and climbed in beside me. I snuggled up against him and drifted off to sleep, thinking that the semester wasn't going to seem so long, after all.

FARM BOYS

J . L . G o r d e n

I STOPPED AT THE CEMETERY LONG ENOUGH TO PAY MY RESPECTS TO MY parents then headed towards the farm. The Harley purred as I drove along the country roads I had tried to forget. Roads that were as familiar now as they had been then.

The sweet scent of lilacs drifted on the air as I parked at the foot of the steps. Her lilacs.

My gaze went immediately to the freshly painted barn where my life then had come to a crashing halt. Memories tried to break through the barriers I'd erected against those last moments seven years ago.

Tears welled in my eyes as I climbed the steps to the porch. I wiped them aside roughly with my shirt sleeve as I stepped up to the front door and found the key in its usual place.

"Lucas?"

Who—? I dropped my bike helmet as I whirled around, and saw the boy standing beside the Harley, looking up at me.

"I'm sor—sorry," he stammered. "I didn't mean to startle you."

I saw what I thought was a flicker of fear in his eyes as he stood watching me. I knew I looked rough—my long hair tangled and a three days growth of beard on my face. I ran my fingertip down the scar on my cheek and tried to still my pounding heart. I was bone tired and in no mood for company. "Who are you and what do you want?" I demanded as I bent to pick up the fallen helmet.

"My name is Ben," he answered. "I've been taking care of the place since—"

I quickly turned away, not wanting him to see how the mention of my parents still hurt.

"They were good people and I'll miss them."

I shot him a brief glance, saw the tears running down his cheeks, and nodded. "Thank you, Ben. Why don't you come in and I'll pay you."

His brows furrowed. "I don't want money. I owed your dad—if it wasn't for him I wouldn't have graduated." He paused to wipe away a tear from his cheek. "He was the father I never had."

"Yeah?" My old man? The son of a bitch who'd kicked me out of his house seven years ago? What was it about this guy that would get him to act like a father?

I studied him now. Blond, blue-eyes, boyish face accented with a pug nose with freckles running across its bridge. Tall with a slim, hard body.

Ben's eyes boldly met mine. "Your parents took me in when I was sixteen, right after my mother kicked me out when I told her I was gay."

"How long ago was this?" I asked, allowing myself to become curious. The old man taking in a gay boy? The irony of it made me smile.

"Three years ago."

So, Ben was nineteen. And queer. "You live here?"

"Yes."

"Grab my saddle bag before you come in," I told him, entering the house and taking a seat at the table.

He laid the bag on the floor beside me, then leaned back against the kitchen counter, watching me.

I studied the bulge in his pants for a moment before reaching down and taking the bottle of Jack Daniels from my bag. I uncapped it, took a healthy swallow, then held it out to him.

He shook his head.

I shrugged and took another drink. "So, what happened to your own father?"

A tinge of red crawled up his neck. "He ran off before I was even born."

"Ah, that must have been rough," I said, lighting up a cigarette and looking around for an ashtray. There weren't any.

He placed a tin lid on the edge of the table, then leaned back again.

"I got by."

I yawned, drank some more and stubbed the cigarette out. I started to get to my feet. "I'd like to sit and chit chat with you but I haven't slept in three days," I said, my words slurring. The room tilted.

Ben was instantly there to steady me.

I leaned against him. "You smell good enough to eat," I mumbled, while nibbling on his ear lobe. I felt him tremble.

"You're drunk," he stated, pushing me away.

I fell back into the chair. "It's my usual state," I told him, finishing off the bottle before climbing clumsily to my feet. "I really would like to fuck you," I added, leering at him as I groped his crotch. He was rock hard.

"I'm not about to lose my cherry to a drunk," he said, gripping my wrist.

His fingers felt like bands of steel, a fact that impressed me. I reluctantly stepped away from his hot body. "Are you saying you're a virgin?"

His cheeks flamed red. "Yeah, so?"

"So what the hell have you been waiting for? A hunk like you could have his pick of any faggot in the county."

"I haven't met anyone who I really wanted—until now."

His statement jolted me clear down to my toes. "Until now?" I asked, trying to shake the cobwebs from my brain.

He turned bright red. "I've lusted after you ever since your mom showed me your high school pictures."

"Fuck!" I muttered, staring at him in amazement.

"Perhaps tomorrow, when you're sober, we can do something about it," he said, his eyes twinkling as he grabbed my arm and guided me toward the stairs leading to the bedrooms.

"I don't want to wait that long," I grumbled as he helped me to climb the stairs.

He chuckled. "Yeah? That's too bad. I want my first lover sober." He guided me into my old room. "Sleep well," he said, closing the door.

The room was spotless. It looked the same as the day I left. My books were on the shelves, a poster of a hot-looking model was on the wall, and my old stereo stood in its usual place. On the bedside table was a framed picture of my parents and me, taken the day I graduated from high school. It was the last picture we had ever taken together as a family.

I sat on the side of the bed and kicked off my boots, wiping the fucking tears from my eyes. I groaned as the room began to spin.

I thought of the fight I'd had with my last lover. He had yelled that I was incapable of any kind of commitment, that I didn't know the meaning of love. Yeah, right. He was like all the rest of the gay boys out there—his ass riding my big dick. Where was the love in that?

He was also tired of my drunken, whoring ways and was glad to see me go. Hell, I was just as happy to leave. Fucking him had begun to get boring. I pulled a pillow over my head and forced that memory out of my head. I just wanted to sleep. To forget.

My head was pounding relentlessly, but I was used to that. For a moment I lay staring at the clock on the nightstand. I swung my long legs over the side of the bed, went to the window, and looked out. The sun was coming over the distant mountain peaks. I thought it was one of the most beautiful sights I'd ever seen.

I wondered where Ben was as I left my old room. I was horny and fucking his sweet ass would start the day off right. I glanced into the extra bedroom; but it was empty, the bed neatly made. "Shit," I muttered, heading for the bathroom.

I got rid of the road dust and washed my hair. I shaved with my father's razor. I used my mother's hair brush to untangle my hair. It was then that I noticed a ribbon laying on the shelf and lifted it to my nose. It held a faint scent of her and I smiled. I tied back my hair and took another look in the mirror. The ribbon did look better than just a rubber band.

Rested, clean, and dressed, I went exploring. I hoped to find Ben. I rubbed my crotch and grinned. I was sober now.

I stood just inside the barn door, letting my eyes adjust to the dim interior. I smelled freshly cut hay and heard the meow of a cat and the answering whimpers of newborn kittens. My gaze shifted upward to the hayloft.

It was where I began. Where I'd learned how shitty life really was. Unable to resist the impulse, I climbed the ladder and found a hay bale to sit on.

There, in the middle of the loft, was where it happened. I'd been after the hired hand most of the spring, wanting to lose my virginity to the student from the nearby agricultural college who the old man had hired. What was his name? I couldn't remember and it didn't matter. He was just another body, the first in a long line of hot bodies.

He'd let me catch him the day after I graduated from high school, two weeks after I'd turned eighteen. Right there. In the middle of the loft. "You want my dick, don't you?" he'd said as we stacked hay bales.

He stood before me in just his jeans and work boots, sweat glistening on his chest. I'd nodded, suddenly unable to speak. He grinned. "I haven't had any in a week. This can work out for both of us." He opened his jeans and pushed them over his butt. He wasn't wearing underwear. He was hard. "Come and get it, boy."

The old man caught me with the hired hand that morning. Caught me with cum sauce dripping from my face. I lifted my hand to my cheek, remembering how it felt when his fist hit me for the first time in my life.

It was his eyes that I still had nightmares about. They were like icicles that pierced my heart and my soul. I felt my throat tighten.

"I thought I'd find you here."

I glanced at Ben as he walked toward me, thinking of how innocent he looked. I frowned. "Please Ben, if you don't mind, I'd rather be alone."

He ignored me, pulled up a bale of hay and sat down, facing me. "You have the same expression on your face that he did."

"Who?" I asked, confused.

"Your father."

I stared at him.

"I found him here one afternoon. He was sitting on a bale of hay with a lost look on his face. I almost asked him what was wrong but sensed that it wasn't the thing to do. I sat down and waited. After a few minutes he started talking."

Ben paused, picked up a piece of straw and stuck it in his mouth. "He told me about that day, the day he found you here with the kid from ag school. He said he had never told anyone about that day, not even your mother."

He chewed on the straw for a second, then continued. "Perhaps he knew I was the same as you, that I found men attractive and that I was fighting with myself over it, I don't know. All I know is that he took my hand into his and he told me never to be ashamed of what I was. Never to let anyone make me feel like a freak. Then he took me into his arms and started to cry."

I couldn't picture my father crying.

"He told me how much he missed you, how sorry he was that he had driven you away. He wished that he could go back in time and change it all. I think that was the week he gave your mother all the letters he had hidden from her. The ones you had sent over the years."

"It took over a month for her letter to reach me," I mumbled. "It was the only one I got before I heard of the accident. She asked me to come home, that they missed me and wanted to see me. I came as soon as I could, but it was too late." Our eyes met and held. "I never had the chance to tell them that I loved them, that I was sorry."

"They knew you loved them, Lucas," Ben said, taking my hand and giving it a squeeze. "Your dad told me that he wanted to tell you that he wanted your forgiveness, that he didn't understand, but that he still loved you no matter what."

I didn't realize that I was crying until Ben reached out and wiped the tears from my face. "I never thought I was worthy of his love," I croaked out, my throat tight. "I wasn't the son he deserved to have."

His fingers tightened around mine.

We sat in silence for a moment, then I moved over beside him, and kissed him. I felt him tremble as I slipped my tongue into his mouth and pulled him close.

"I knew I wanted you to be the one," he whispered huskily when we finally came up for air. "I knew even before I saw you standing on the porch."

"I thought you were afraid of me," I said, running my hands up and down his muscular back.

"Only afraid of what you were making me feel."

"You've never kissed a man before?" I asked, aroused by the idea of it.

"No. Never—nothing."

The thought of shoving my hard prong up his cherry butt made my pulse react. The temperature in the loft went up a few notches. "Perhaps we should go into the house. I don't have a rubber with me."

He gave me a shy grin. "I have a couple in my pocket," he said. "I brought them along hoping that you'd be interested—now that you're sober."

"Drunk or sober, a man would have to be crazy not to be interested in a hot stud like you," I told him. I smiled as his cheeks turned scarlet. "And," I murmured, "I'm not crazy. What I am is hard and hot." I guided his hand to my crotch, letting him feel my engorged cock.

His eyes widened. "It feels huge."

"It's eight inches—but don't let that scare you off."

"I'm kind of nervous," he said.

I chuckled. "Believe me, I remember what it's like. We'll take it slow and easy and, if you want to stop, you just tell me."

I brushed my lips across his as I reached for the buttons on his jeans. I wanted to suck his virgin cock more than I had ever wanted anything in my life. I wanted to make his first time special. I licked my lips as I pulled his jeans and underwear onto his thighs. I leaned down to flick my tongue over the cum-oozing slit. He gave a low moan as I pulled his pants down to his ankles, spread his legs wide, and made myself comfortable between them.

"You have a nice piece of meat here," I told him, trailing my tongue up and down the blue veins while fondling his sac. He trembled. Remembering how quickly I had shot my wad the first time someone sucked my dick, I backed off, letting him gain control. Tenderly, I kissed the inside of his thighs.

"Jesus, I almost lost it," he told me, shivering as I nuzzled his balls.

I smiled up at him, wrapped my fingers around his swaying rod and slipped my free hand under his ass-cheeks. As I took his prong into my mouth, I probed his tight ass with a finger.

He squirmed and soon began to breathe hard and fast.

Sensing that he was on the edge, I clamped my mouth down harder, sucked him all the way in, and felt the pulses under my lips as he erupted. Eagerly, I swallowed the man juice that filled my mouth.

"Fuck!" he wailed, jerking like a man being struck by lightning. "I didn't know—!" he managed to gasp out as bullet after cum-loaded bullet blasted my tonsils. I swallowed greedily.

I lifted my head, wiped a few stray drops of cum sauce from my lips and gave him a shit-ass grin. "The next time we'll make it last longer, I promise," I told him and quickly shed my clothes.

His eyes roved up and down my naked body. "You're beautiful," he mumbled as he reached to his pants and found a condom packet. He tore it open and handed it to me.

The obvious admiration in his eyes made my heart skip a beat. "Thank you, Ben," I said, rolling the rubber down my fully aroused shaft. Then, seeing the uncertainty on his flushed face, I reached out to touch his cheek with a fingertip. "We don't have to do this if you don't want to."

He met my eyes. "I want to. It's just that I'm a little scared."

"That's natural, we're all scared the first time. And I won't lie to you and say it won't hurt, cause it will." I leaned over him, nibbling on his nipples as my hard rod trailed along his thigh. "I want you, Ben. I want you real bad," I told him, rubbing my cock under his balls.

"I want you, too."

I covered his face with kisses, then claimed his lips. The ache between my legs was intense; but I forced myself to take it slow. I wanted his first time to be one that made him smile when he thought about it. I wanted him to remember this loft better than I did.

My mouth made its way down his body, stopping to lick, to kiss, and to touch every inch of his flesh. By the time I got down to his crotch, he was again hard. I wanted his ass but, instead, took his prong into my mouth again, tantalizing it with my tongue. I delved into the slit, licked it like it was my favorite treat, then sucked his balls until he was squirming.

Each moan he made excited me. Each little shiver that cruised up his body made me work harder to please him. Sweat poured off my face as I buried my head between his legs, sucking his dick deep into my throat. Each time he came close to erupting, I would back off, let him catch his breath, then start all over again.

"Please," he whimpered.

I took pity on him. Deepthroating him, I rammed a finger up his tight ass.

"God almighty!" he screamed, jettisoning his hot spunk into my mouth while his body gave a violent shudder.

I couldn't wait any longer. Lifting his legs upward, I smeared his chute with his own cum, then began to inch into him.

"Oh shit!" he groaned, gritting his teeth.

"Let your ass muscles relax, Ben," I said, watching his face.

He took a deep breath and relaxed.

Slowly, I slipped another inch into him, feeling him clamp down. "Easy, Ben, easy. Relax."

"I'm trying," he groaned, beads of sweat rolling down the sides of his face. "It feels like you're shoving a log up my ass."

"Do you want me to stop?"

He shook his head. "I want it all, Lucas."

I smiled at him. "I'm glad to hear that cause I want to give it to you, every last inch," I told him, carefully sliding deeper into him.

"Oh," he cried, a startled expression on his face as I hit that special spot. "Oh, oh, oh."

"I told you it would be worth it," I said, beginning to plow his ass with long, even strokes.

Wonder glazed his eyes as I worked his prostate. "Fuck me," he whispered.

"Your ass is so tight I won't be able to control myself much longer," I warned, embedding my shaft to the hilt, then pulling back until only the knob remained inside. His eyes held a wild gleam as he contracted his ass muscles.

Caught by surprise, I gave a strangled gasp as my spunk shot up my prong and into the rubber. I held him tight as my body shook with the intensity of the orgasm that ripped through me like a tidal wave.

"Who taught you to do that?" I finally managed to ask, when my heart slowed down to a more normal rhythm.

"No one. I read about it," he replied, grinning.

"Yeah well, you sure the hell milked me like a pro," I said, beginning to pull my wilting shaft from his ass. His hands grabbed my butt, holding me still.

"Leave it in me, Lucas—please?" He looked up at me and all I could see was the pleading in his eyes. I pushed back into him. He smiled. "Kiss me, please."

I was lying on him, his thighs riding my waist and his heels lying on my asscheeks. We kissed—our tongues exploring each other's mouth. My cock remained hard enough to stay inside him.

I'd never felt more comfortable, not with any of the guys I'd whored around with. I didn't even want a drink now that I'd fucked him. All I could smell was fresh hay and Ben's scent. I could almost sense Dad patting me on the back, giving me—us—his blessing. I felt alive.

And I knew this was what I wanted. What I had always wanted. I wanted Ben. I had wanted him in every boy I ever fucked.

I broke our kiss and reached up to kiss each of his eyelids.

His fingers caressed my face. "Lucas?"

"Um?"

"Can I sleep in your bed tonight?"

"Absolutely," I agreed, my heart singing.

"Are you going to be leaving soon?" he asked a moment later, a sad expression in his eyes.

I gazed down into his face. "I had no intention of staying when I first arrived," I admitted. "But, now I think I might like it here." I paused to kiss him again, just a peck on his lips. "Would you be willing to work the farm with me? We could be partners or something—"

His smile was radiant. "I'd love that."

I hugged him. "Let's go into the house. I need to shower."

"Can I shower with you?" he asked as we both looked down at our coupling, a hungry expression on his face.

"Absolutely," I told him, laughing as I pulled out of him, rose, and helped him to his feet. "I think you and I are going to make a great team."

PHI BETA SUCKA

Dak Hunter

IT WAS ANOTHER HOT AND HUMID DAY AT SOUTHERN BAPTIST University as Kappa Omega Kappa prepared for the first night of freshman rush.

"Billy, where's the slide projector—and that picture of your sister?"

"Fuck you, Red," Billy said, punching his carrot-topped frat brother in the arm. "You know I took that of your mama the last time the circus came through Dallas."

Red threw a can of beer across the room at Billy, who snatched it from the air and popped it open. He raised it up high for a toast.

"To the first night of the freshman fry. Those poor bastards have no idea what a hell their pathetic little lives are about to become," he chuckled.

Red raised his beer and clicked his heels. Stewart and Ryder were glued to the big screen TV in the back room, but managed to scratch their guts and belch their approval.

Billy gulped his beer and pounded upstairs to his room. It was a collage of jockey shorts, encrusted socks, and bowls full of technicolored gunk that had long since cemented. He kicked his deflated basketball to the corner, and bent down to search underneath the bed.

"I know that damn photo is around here somewhere."

He strained to reach farther under the bed, when from between the mattress and box spring, a corner of glossy paper poked at his eye. He sat back and stared at it. Then he pulled the magazine out from the crevice. His eyes focused hard on the blond muscular man on the cover. The surfer in the magazine was wearing very tight shorts and a giant erection bulged from his groin. Billy flipped to the well-worn center pages and took in the blond again, this time bare and stroking his giant cock. On the facing page the surfer slid the cock between the pink lips of a fair-haired Marine. Billy closed the pages and fell forward on the bed, burying his face in the blankets.

"Fuck. Fuck. Fuck."

He shoved the magazine back beneath the bed and rolled over, looking up at the ceiling. "What the hell am I doing?" he whispered.

Sounds of the Red Hot Chili Peppers blasted from the windows of KOK house. From the top floor of the three-story plantation-style mansion, Billy and Red looked down on the line of freshmen meandering its way towards the front porch. Ryder and Stewart screamed obscenities from the balcony and poured beer on any kid who wasn't paying attention. Bonfires raged on either side of the yard with thirty or so half-naked men dancing around, their chests and legs clothed in various designs of greasy body paints.

"You bitches better get ready!" one red and black painted frat brother bellowed, as he unzipped his pants and swung his dick about.

Billy surveyed the freshman class. They all looked about the same as last year. Except one. About halfway down the line, a face was calmly studying the frat house. The spiked dark hair and light eyes stood out from the crowd. The freshman took in the sights around him, and seemed neither scared nor secure. He just looked. Then he trained his eyes on Billy. Billy forgot himself for a minute and stared back—then looked away quickly.

"Well, shit, Red, we better get to it, I guess," he mumbled, and cracked open a beer. They had started downstairs when Billy caught his reflection in the hall mirror. He ran his fingers through the front of his sandy brown hair to even it out, and then realized what he was doing. He messed it back up and hurried downstairs after Red.

"Arooh Arooooh!" Stewart cackled in his best rooster crow.

The spotlight in the foreboding main room of the KOK house reflected off the fearful faces of the freshmen pledges.

"All right, you bitches." Stewart walked down the line up of young men like a sergeant. "If you want to be part of the best fucking house on campus—in the state, soldier!" he screamed into one shivering young man's face. "You're gonna do everything—and I mean EVERYTHING—I tell ya to do! Got it?"

Timid responses squeaked from a few boys.

"WHAT? What the hell was that, you damn pussies! I can't hear you!"

"Yes, Sir!" the young men said in unison.

Stewart turned to Billy and the brothers who all stood with arms folded in the shadows. Billy's gaze was trained on the hunky youth he had spied from the balcony. The odd thing was, even though Billy knew there was no way the kid could see him, it still seemed like he was staring straight back at him.

"Billy," Stewart whispered again in irritation. "Get that fucking cock suit on or we're gonna lose the fear, buddy."

Billy shook his head back to reality. "What?"

"It's your turn to wear the suit—hurry up!"

Billy's eyes bulged.

"Stewart, I don't think I should—not this time."

Stewart left the troops and huddled with Billy. "Man, you're the president of the house. How do you think it looks with you never taking your turn?"

"It's just that I—"

"Billy, people are gonna start thinking something, buddy." He looked into Billy's eyes. Billy had no choice. "Fuck it. All right. I just didn't want to choke any of those bastards with my torpedo is all."

Stewart grinned an evil smile and patted Billy on the back as he went off to put on the suit. Stewart turned to the potential recruits.

"OK ladies, here's the deal. Everything that happens inside these walls stays here—got it? If even one of you candyasses makes a peep to anybody, you'll have your butt chewed by this whole goddamn house. Understood?"

The young men nodded, more fearful than ever. In the backroom Billy slipped into a giant rooster suit. He looked into the mirror and straightened the crest of his crown. His green eyes were masked, but his lips were exposed. Then he unzipped the crotch and slid his cock out.

"OK, line up and get on your knees!" Stewart bellowed to the cadets. "Now in just a minute, our kingpin's gonna come out here, and I want all you girls to show him some hospitality. If you don't, your ass is outta here!"

Billy's heart was racing. How was he gonna get through this? Don't get hard, don't get hard, he kept telling himself. He walked into the room and into the light. From the shadows his frat brothers grinned with glee. Billy walked up to the first lad and stood in front of him, his cock lightly brushing the boy's lip.

"Open your mouth," Billy said in a deep voice.

The freshman's eyes clamped shut. Slowly he opened his mouth. Billy slid his cock gently in. It filled the blond surfer boy's mouth and poked at the back of his throat. "Suck it," Billy said.

His head whirled. Oh fuck. Don't get hard, don't get hard! The blond youth pulled on the cock twice and then Billy removed it. He walked to the next pledge, a stocky, freckle-faced boy. He was trembling. Stewart plodded from the darkness in the back of the room screaming. "Aw, what's the matter, baby? You suck that cock or you'll suck two!" Stewart said, grabbing his own package.

Billy gave Stewart a look and motioned him to get back in the shadows. Billy looked down at the quivering eighteen-year-old. "Just open your mouth, it'll be over soon," he whispered, almost kindly, to the boy.

The boy opened his mouth and began to slide back and forth on Billy's shaft. The freshman cupped his hands over his own crotch to hide his erection. Again a hot swirl filled Billy's head. Oh fuck. I don't think I can do this. He shook it off and moved to the next pledge. It was the hunk he had seen from the balcony. Billy closed his eyes. Oh, shit! I'm done for. "Open your mouth," he said in an even lower voice than before.

The hunk opened his mouth and slid the slab of meat down his throat. Billy looked down at him with desire. Then, the hunk looked up—straight into Billy's eyes. Billy's heart jumped. He can't know it's me.

The hunk rode Billy's shaft. His lips felt like velvet. Inside the hunk's mouth, his tongue played with Billy's head. Billy couldn't take it anymore. His cock rushed with heat and filled the hunk's mouth. Oh god, what am I gonna do? Suddenly from behind him, Red rushed up.

"OK, gentlemen, that's it for now," he told the plebes. We have something else in store for the rest of you."

Stewart walked over into the light and whispered: "What the funk are you doing, Red? This ain't over."

Red shot a look at Stewart. "Yeah, it is fucking over. C'mon Bill, zip yourself up."

Red walked a stunned Billy into the hallway. Behind them he heard Stewart yelling at the freshmen to strip and do the chicken dance. Red sat Billy down and removed the rooster headcap. Billy's face was scarlet. He glanced over at Red. "I tried not to get hard," he groaned. "Fuck!"

Red patted him on the back.

"Hey man, anyone of us would have," he looked around quickly. "I mean, it's just a physical thing, you know?"

"But it wasn't just a physical thing, Red. I wanted him to do it. That freshman out there made me get hard, and I wanted it to happen!"

Red looked around cautiously. "Shh. Shut the fuck up, man. Christ! Billy, you don't think some of the guys feel the same way? Just shut up about it."

Billy wiped his eyes. "Really? What about you?"

Red looked down and pursed his lips. "I'm engaged."

They were both silent.

Billy stood and walked to the curtain that divided the main room from the hall. He pulled back a corner and watched as Stewart made the freshmen eat plate after plate of raw hot dogs. "Yeah," he said finally. "It's probably just a phase."

His eyes trained on the hunky freshman shoving handfuls of raw meat down his throat. "I'm going to bed," Billy said without looking at Red, and ran up the stairs.

Billy plopped down on the bed and stared at the ceiling. All he could think about was the freshman. The feeling of his cock in that mouth. His groin began to throb. This was no phase. But he knew his brothers would not receive the news very well that their president was a queer. How was he going to keep a lid on it, but still get what he needed? Most of all, how was he going to get that freshman alone? There was a knock on the door.

"Yeah?" No one answered back. Billy got up and opened it.

"Yeah, what do—?" He stopped. There stood the hunky freshman.

"Hi," the boy said, his jet-black spikes and crystal blue eyes shining.

"Uh, hi," Billy stammered, his cock kicking to life.

"Can I come in?" the pledge looked quickly about the room.

"Uh, sure." Billy looked down the hall, didn't see anybody, and let the hunk in. "Have a seat," he said and pointed the youth to the chair next to the bed.

Billy sat on the edge of the bed and put a pillow in his lap. He stared at the boy in front of him. His beauty. Those ruby lips. All he could think about was his cock sliding between those lips. Perspiration beaded on Billy's forehead. He wished they could take up where they'd left off. There wouldn't be anybody to disturb them now.

"I just wanted to thank you."

Billy was puzzled. "What do you mean?"

The youth dropped to his knees before Billy, his hands resting on each of the KOK president's knees. "But I'd like to finish the job."

The hunk pulled the pillow from Billy's lap and put his hand on his bulge. "Sweet Jesus!" Billy moaned. The hunk opened Billy's pants, spreading the panels to release his cock. Lowering his head, he slid his lips down the shaft. Billy's cock surged, swelling to the corners of the boy's mouth.

The freshman rode the shaft, taking the beast deeper into his throat. He pulled back until only Billy's cockhead was still in his mouth and ran his tongue over the knob. He plunged back down towards the balls and held on tight with his lips moving the bursting cock in and out of his mouth, faster and faster. Billy was on the verge of climax, his moaning barely stifled by his clenched teeth. Suddenly the freshman stopped.

"I want you to fuck my ass," the hunk whispered, lifting his head up, his bright eyes boring into Billy. "It's been waiting for you."

"What's your name?" Billy asked, his voice quivering.

"Frank."

"Sweet fucking Christ," Billy gasped. "Are you sure you're just a freshman?"

Frank laughed as he stood up. "You're my first, but it seems like I've wanted you forever."

"Did you know this would happen?"

Frank smiled. "I didn't," he said. "But I'm glad I was right. There wasn't much chance of me becoming a KOK if you'd been straight."

Billy frowned and sat up. "Me?"

Frank walked to the other side of the room. The wall was covered with pictures of Billy and his football buddies and drunken nights at keg parties. "I've wanted you since high school," Frank said and turned to look at Billy.

"What?" Billy forced himself to study the freshman's features, trying to place him.

Frank moved along to Billy's trophies. "You came and gave our team pointers one day during Phys. Ed," he said over his shoulder. "I knew then that I had to have you. I saw you later that day in the shower." He turned to Billy, his cock stiff as a board. "You haven't changed," he said, looking down at Billy's hard cock.

Billy remembered him then. "You were the quarterback for the freshman squad in high school."

"And you were the first string quarterback," Frank answered and grinned.

He pulled off his T-shirt, revealing a deeply tanned, rippling torso. He took a foil packet from his pocket and dropped his pants. His cock shot out from trimmed black curls. He took Billy's hand and led him to the desk, brushing books and papers to the floor. He smiled and tore the foil and held up the condom. "Let's get this sucker on you."

Frank bent over the desktop when Billy was suited up and gripped both sides of the desk. "C'mon, Mr. KOK President. Fuck my ass."

Billy stood behind the boy, his mind reeled. He looked down at the two melons jutting out at him, at the crack that separated them, at where the hole he knew was there had to be. He wanted it, he wanted it more than he ever wanted anything in his life. He slapped the youth's cheek and slowly slid his cock along the crack between the bronzed melons. Frank moaned.

Billy's knob breeched the freshman's sphincter and Frank groaned but didn't pull away. Billy stared down at his dick as it slipped deeper into the boy. He had never felt such pleasure. He humped against the ass, pushing his cock all the way into Frank. He began to move then, slowly at first and then faster.

Vibrations shot through Billy's balls and abdomen. It was all he could do not to blow right then and fill the boy with his cream. He pulled out and turned the youth around. They stood eye to eye, sweating. Billy brushed the boy's fallen spikes back. "I want to see you when I fuck you," he gasped and raised Frank's legs to his shoulders.

Billy grabbed the boy's face and pressed his lips against his as his cock reentered Frank's gaping chute. Its warmth again engulfed him, pulling him into its center. Their tongues dueled as Billy began to ride the freshman's ass.

Frank reached around his raised legs and grabbed Billy's buns, his hands guiding the older man's flexing ass-cheeks, directing Billy's cock in him through them. Billy's fingers found the hunk's chest and began to tweak his nipples as he moved in and out of him in a steady rhythm. Billy could not remember doing anything that felt as right as this. Not the girls he'd had. Not his solo efforts. He stopped trying to think and gave himself up to riding the waves of pleasure that ripped through him.

Before Billy was ready, a familiar stutter began at the center of his pleasure. His dick pounded Frank's ass faster. His thrusts immediately grew shorter. The stutter quickly grew to blot out the pleasure and his body stiffened as his balls let loose with the most powerful orgasm he'd ever experienced.

His cock stayed in Frank's ass even after he'd blown his load. Their tongues entwined and licked lazily; sucking lips led to biting necks. Frank raised Billy slightly to look up at him. He smiled. "That was everything I hoped it would be."

Billy's gaze went to Frank's cock. It was hard—so big, jutting straight out at him, demanding attention. "You didn't come?" he asked in surprise. Pulling out of the freshman's ravaged ass, he knelt and licked the head before his lips traced the length down to the boy's balls.

Frank moaned. Billy returned to the cockhead and his mouth slipped over it. He tasted Frank's pre-cum as his lips learned the size of the freshman's rod. He was quickly hard again. He wanted it to fill him up. He wanted it to fill up every part of him. Just like Frank had done.

He was finally home, and he loved it. Billy enveloped the shaft, making his lips tight around the cock possessing him. Frank pressed his nails into Billy's back—then pulled him up so that they were both facing each other.

"I want you," Frank whispered. "I want your ass."

Billy had never even thought about being on the receiving end. But his desire for Frank wiped any hesitation from his mind. He wanted this new pledge—every bit of him. "Not on the desk," he mumbled and looked around the room. "There. On the bed." He looked down at Frank's hard cock. "I don't know if I can handle you pushing that into my tight ass."

Frank chuckled. "I've heard it's easier if you sit on it—that way, you take what you can at each step instead of having somebody else feed it to you."

"Yeah?" Billy's cock jerked in anticipation and he felt an itch way up his ass. "Okay. The bed then—" He started across the room.

Frank knelt beside his trousers and retrieved another condom. He sat on the edge of the bed, unfurling the latex over his mushroomed cockhead and down his shaft as Billy watched with anticipation. He looked up and smiled, his hands reaching out to Billy and pulling the KOK president towards him as he lay across the bed. Billy held his own cock and climbed onto the bed, straddling Frank's waist. He looked down into that face and was lost in the eyes that watched him.

He began to lower his ass slowly until the head of Frank's cock pressed against his butthole. He gasped as Frank's knob pushed through his sphincter. He stopped as he fought the pain. He wondered how Frank had managed, but just the memory of the freshman taking him drove him on. He gritted his teeth and inched further down the hot dick now inside him. He smiled down at Frank when the pain lessened.

Lower and lower, he squatted. Billy felt Frank's pubes scratch the insides of his thighs and knew he had taken it all. Pleasure flooded him. Frank stroked Billy's cock and, bending forward like a gymnast, put it in his mouth. Frank's hands held Billy's cheeks, raising and lowering him on his cock, all the while raising and lowering his own head on Billy's erection.

Billy's eyes crossed. He was being flooded with more pleasure than he could even imagine. He lost his moorings and went where the waves cresting through him carried him. "Oh, shit! Yeah!" he groaned and began to ride Frank's cock fast, ignoring the freshman's hands there to guide him. He wanted the boy's cock, all of it, as fast as he could get it—to increase the pleasure spreading through him from his ass.

Frank grunted and moaned beneath Billy and the KOK president felt the dick inside him thicken. "I'm shooting!" Frank groaned.

Suddenly, the door flew open. "Hey, Billy, when are we gonna—?" Red stopped short. His eyes bulged.

Behind Red, the blond surfer boy pledge peered over his shoulder in amazement. Billy sat down hard on Frank's pubes and panicked.

"Ah … Hey, buddy," he grabbed a pillow to cover his midsection. "We were just—uh—well …"

Everyone was silent.

Red looked at Frank and Billy and then down at the floor. A moment later, he turned to look at the surfer over his shoulder. "Well, what are you waiting for?" he growled. "Get in here and strip."

The blonde did what he was told. Smiling, he walked to Billy's desk and took off his clothes. Billy was still dazed as Red shut and locked the door. Red walked past the surfer and sat in the chair. He unzipped his pants and his thick meat pushed through the slit in his boxers and into the surfer boy's mouth.

Billy pushed off Frank and was surprised at how empty his ass was. That was something he knew he didn't like much at all. "Want another piece of me?" he asked the freshman as his feet found the floor.

"Yeah," Frank answered and watched as Billy jerked his head towards the blond surfer giving Red head. "I'm fresh out of rubbers, though."

"In the nightstand," Billy told him and started towards the desk and the head job going on there. "Get me one, too."

He massaged the surfer's ass-cheeks and the boy wiggled them in greeting. He slid his pulsing cock between the surfer's cheeks, dry-humping him a couple of times. The blond moaned and began to suck Red harder and faster. Red's head was tilted back, a look of ecstacy on his face. He opened his eyes slightly and peered at Billy.

"Becky and I were thinking of breaking up, anyway," he said with a contented look, and nodded his head for Billy to join in.

Frank handed him a condom as he stepped behind him. "You go in first, Billy. I'll follow, okay?"

Billy nodded his head and raised the surfer's ass so he had an easy shot at it.

"Good evening, gentlemen!" Ryder announced into the crackling microphone. "It gives me great pleasure to present to you the new freshmen class of KOK house!" He swept his hand across the room of tables covered in white linen and pointed to the makeshift stage, complete with technicolored spotlights. Lined up were ten smiling freshmen. Billy sat at the president's table with Red at his side and surveyed the young men. The stocky redhead was there. So was the blond surfer. At the end of the line, his blue eyes shining and his black spikes trimmed, was the new Pledge President.

Everyone of them had sucked and fucked their way into the frat-brothers' acceptance. Billy was pretty sure some of the brothers had gotten around to returning the favor. Nobody minded Frank sleeping with him or the blond surfer with Red.

"Yes, it's gonna be a good year at the KOK house after all, Red," Billy said patting the man on the back. "A real good time."

THE BOYS CLUB

David MacMillan

"WANT TO GO UP TO THE CABIN WITH US THIS WEEKEND, DIETER?"

I glanced across at my roommate of two months. He still sat at his desk, leaning over his textbook. He wasn't looking at me.

"Who's going, Alan?" I asked, nearly drowning in the wash of suspicion sweeping over me. It was nearly Halloween—a time for tricks and treats. I had learned that Americans were enthusiasts for these tricks. Alan especially. There were far too many times I'd found myself the brunt of his and his friends' jokes.

"Barry and Jordan—and me." An image of Alan's two friends immediately formed in my mind. Barry the red-head and Jordan, whose hair was the color of the sand on an Adriatic beach. They both had bodies nearly as perfect as Alan's. I blushed, but the image would not vanish.

Alan sat back in his chair, sighed, and slowly turned to face me. "Are all Germans like you, Dieter?" he asked, a puzzled look in his eyes.

"Like me?" I shook my head. "No, many are red-haired or like Jordan—what you called sandy-haired—few are this blond. And few run five miles a day, Alan. Too many of us have become lazy."

"Bullshit!" he growled and pushed himself out of his chair. "Dieter, why don't you ever lighten up?" he demanded and took a step towards me.

"Lighten up?" Did he want me to become lighter, to levitate? Only magicians did that—with tricks. That was not logical.

"Loosen up. Let your hair down. Be one of the boys—just once, will you? Relax, Dieter."

"I—I thought I was," I stammered, watching his hand at his side

9 2

where his fingers were making a fist and then extending straight out before they again became a fist. I wondered if he wanted to hit me. Why? I had been so careful. Could he possibly know how much he excited me?

Black curly hair, tall, a slim-yet-athletic body that was so smooth I imagined it to be tanned alabaster. Yes, the American excited me as no other boy had in my nineteen years, as did his friends. I had come, in two short months, to imagine doing with him what only Schwuelen do. I was not Schwuele, I was not gay—I did not think. Yet, Alan and his two friends were the most beautiful boys I had ever seen. With them I could easily become Schwuele.

"You know, my history prof says that the Germans don't have a sense of humor—that's why you guys went for Hitler rather than laughing him right out of the country."

I coughed. Discretely. My parents and grandparents had spent most of their lives trying to live down the twelve years of German fascism that gave the world its second war this century. Hitler remained an uncomfortable subject to Germans, even fifty-five years after his death. We wanted to think we were just like the Englander and Amerikaner. Germans were not murderers—that was the Nazis, like the American Klan.

"We'd like you to come with us, Dieter, but you've got to promise to let your hair down if you do. You've got to promise to go with the flow. We want to know the real Dieter Haas."

"Where is this cabin, Alan?"

He grinned. He knew he had me. Just as he always did. I did not understand how he did so, but he could always manipulate me. "It's up where Georgia, South Carolina, and North Carolina come together. You'll love it."

"In the mountains?" I yelped. "Alan, I am a Berliner. I know nothing about mountains."

"What about those Alps where everybody yodels from the mountaintops?"

"Those are in Bavaria. In Austria—more than nine hundred kilometers from my home."

"We're going to fish. Cook out. Swim. Drink. We're going to be just us boys, doing boy things. It's a boys' weekend, Dieter."

"I will go with you," I told him and returned to trying to understand the American Civil War. I succeeded in not imagining Alan's cock as I studied Robert E. Lee's move into Gettysburg.

I had imagined something rustic. Something like the one-room cabins on the shore that professional Finnish families use to get back to nature in the summer. Alan's cabin was a house with electricity, running water, indoor toilets, and heat. There was nothing primitive about it. I didn't know if I was pleased or disappointed. I wondered if I would finally explore my strange curiosity about Alan and his friends, and the thought frightened me.

We drank beer and sat outside under the night sky and the full moon. We talked of school and even memories of growing up as the night grew colder around us. Alan and Jordan went inside, retreating from the night's chill. I remained under the stars, enthralled by the shadows of the mountains around us. Barry Anders stayed with me and I was happy to have his company.

"I gotta take a major piss," he announced and stood up. I continued to sit beside the red-head and watched as he fumbled with his zipper and then struggled with the slit in his underpants to claim his dick.

"Fuck it!" Barry growled and opened his waist button. A moment later, he had pushed his underpants beneath his balls with one hand while possessing his dick with the other. He pointed himself towards the dark slope below us and began to piss. I watched and thought that he had such a large cock. Virile. I wondered what it would taste like. I wondered if Barry and the others would respect me if I gave myself over to these strange interests that had plagued me most of these past two months. If I would respect myself afterwards.

"You all right, Dieter?" Barry asked, pulling my thoughts back to our side of a Georgia mountain in late October.

His zipper was still open, his underpants still rode the underside of his balls, and his dick was hard. It was also only centimeters from my lips. My face burned with my embarrassment. His hand moved to grasp my shoulder.

"We have a bet on between us, Dieter," Barry said quietly. I was staring at his dick and my mouth was dry.

"Yes?" I managed.

"Yeah. Which one of us three can get to you first." He was watching me when I looked up.

"Get to me?" I mumbled, thinking I understood him and hoping I didn't. I did not want any one of the three of them to think I was Schwuele. I did not want to think I was, either.

"Yeah. The three of us have something of a sex club, Dieter—even back in high school. Jordan and I have pretty well paired off; but Alan doesn't have anybody. Not anyone we could trust; someone who's mature. Like you." He smiled. "You want it, don't you?"

I stared at his cock, unable to pull my gaze from it. It looked at least twenty centimeters long and thick. His hand on my shoulder moved me imperceptibly closer to it. It touched my chin and I jerked.

"Nein!" I moaned. I tried to explain that I was not that way but realized I was speaking in German. I tried again in English. The mushroom head of his cock caressed my jaw as I spoke. "Suck it, Dieter. I want you to. I need you to."

I stared at his pubis, dark red even in the moonlight. He swiveled his hips until the head of his cock touched my lips. "It is too big," I groaned through clenched teeth.

"So, let just the head in and lick it."

I shook my head. His hips moved forward until his cock pressed against my teeth. "Come on, man. You want it and I want it." His hand moved from my shoulder to the back of my neck. My lips pressed harder against his knob, its tip was hard against my teeth.

I looked up at his face again. "Come on, Dieter. Do it," he said and smiled again. I wanted Alan's dick, but I also wanted Barry's—and Jordan's. I shut my eyes, sighed, and opened my mouth.

Centimeter after centimeter of cockhead entered, stretching open my jaws and filling my mouth completely. Then came the slightly slimmer shaft of Barry's large dick. I felt his head press against the entrance to my throat as his other hand found the back of my head. Together, his hands pulled me further onto him, spreading my throat. I gagged. My eyes watered.

Barry loosened his hold on my head and I pulled off five centimeters of him. "Sorry," he mumbled, his fingers coming up to my cheek to caress it. "I got carried away there. We'll take it slow, okay?"

I began to wash around his knob with my tongue, my lips tight against his shaft. I reached out and grasped his buttocks and slowly pulled him towards me. I bobbed on his cock as he stood in front of me. There were no more inhibitions left to stop me; I wanted his cock. And it was now mine—as I hoped those of the other two would be.

His hands slid beneath my sweater at the neck and explored my shoulders through my shirt. "I wanted you the first time I saw you," Barry said, conversationally, from above me. "Your lips, your dick, your ass. All three of us did. Alan couldn't wait to tell us about you; he practically dragged us over to your room so we could drool, too."

Barry continued his monologue, but I wasn't listening and his voice was only a buzz in my mind. I wanted to experience this act of fellatio I was performing. I did not want to hear his past history or how much he and the others wanted me. I was doing something I had never imagined doing before I came to America. This was my first time doing schwuelisch things. I wanted to remember all of it.

I became aware that my nose was buried in his pubic thicket. I had his cock buried in my throat.

"Hum, Dieter. You have no idea of how good that'll feel," he told me as I sucked his scent into my lungs through my nose. I hummed and he twitched, rising up on his toes. "Yeah!" he mewled.

He again began to fuck my face. Slowly at first but becoming faster, more insistent. I hummed. My fingers slipped under his flannel shirt and felt his hot skin. His tight, washboard belly, his hair in just the middle of his chest, his smooth back.

My fingers slipped beneath his underpants and gripped his buttocks. "That's Jordan's, Dieter," he growled, reaching down and taking my wrists. "Not even Alan gets that any more." He placed them again on his belly. "I'm close. You're going to get your first spunking real soon." His hands returned to the back of my head, guiding me as I bobbed on his cock.

Spunking? I did not know the word. I tried to associate it as he continued to fuck my mouth. I had already learned how to suck a cock. It no longer required conscious attention.

I realized suddenly that his dick had grown thicker as he pounded my face. Now, he shoved himself into my throat and I was held against his pubis. Barry seemed to have become rigid before me. His hips pulled back, his cock again retreating from my throat. I tasted something salty, sour, and viscous.

"I love to cum in a guy's mouth," he groaned distantly as a large dollop erupted from the head of his cock. "Swallow it, Dieter. Swallow my cum."

I swallowed. Each load of his cum. I tasted it, my tongue worked it into the mushroom head of his cock, and I swallowed. There was so much of it.

"What is spunking?" I asked after he was through and had pulled away from me. My gaze stayed on his glistening cock even as it lost part of its erection. Its taste was still on my tongue, haunting me.

"Cuming—shooting your jizz," he told me and arranged his underpants before zipping up his trousers.

I followed Barry to the cabin. I held back as he opened the door and stepped inside. I did not know what to expect.

I knew what he had told me about our companions. But I reminded myself that was during the sex act itself. Men lied often at that point; I knew I had.

Would Alan and Jordan accept me, once they learned that I had done a Schwuele thing? Would Barry, even though it was his dick I had sucked? This was America with preachers belching hatred from the television every day. I entered the cabin's lounge slowly, finding the location of each man as I did so—ready to run if I had to.

Alan and Jordan were giving Barry high fives before the fire. My heart sank; he had already told them. I mentally counted the money I had in my wallet and knew it was not enough to take a bus to Atlanta.

"You finally let your hair down," Alan said when he saw me. I watched as he broke away from the others and started towards me. He was smiling. I smiled back—tentatively. Still unsure. "Did you like it?" he asked, as his arm went around my shoulders.

I stiffened but instantly relaxed. "Yes. I never thought... I have wanted you since I first saw you—"

Alan chuckled. "Just as I've wanted you, Dieter." He pulled me into the center of the room with the others, his arm still thrown across my shoulders. They were smiling at me.

"Here's the deal," Jordan said. "Barry and I are off-limits except for blow jobs. We've worked it out with Alan—"

"What is the meaning of that?" I asked.

"They're lovers," Alan explained. "They've included me because we're good friends. They're willing to include you, too—but only for the oral stuff."

"So, Barry and Jordan will be happy to let us suck them—?"

"And they'll suck us, too. It's also all right to watch them fuck when they get into it—only, we can't join in."

"That leaves you and me," I mumbled, unsure of the situation.

The smile bled from Alan's face. "You don't want me?"

I turned to face him. I felt all three pairs of eyes on me, watching me. Waiting for me. It was time for more than four horny youths to have sex together. It was time for truth. I understood the moment without thinking about it.

"I had never thought of having sex with another man," I told them, "not until I was in America and saw Alan the first time. After I met the two of you, I found you in my fantasies, too—but Alan was first there and his role is always the largest. I wanted Barry's and Jordan's friendship, the thought of sex with them is just an extra pleasure—" I looked down at my hands, unable to meet Alan's gaze. "But I have wanted Alan from the first moment I saw him—not just as a friend with whom I could play sex games. But—" I forced myself to look into his face then. "As more. It has taken me until now to understand this—and to accept it."

Alan's face swam towards mine and I realized my vision of him had beome blurred. His fingers wiped tears from my eyes. "We're going to do just fine together, Dieter," he said just before his lips touched mine.

Barry and Jordan were gone to their room; Alan and I sat before the fire. He held me to him and my face pressed against his smooth, exposed chest. I was happier than I had ever been with a girl with whom I had just had sex. I felt complete—and safe. And loved.

Alan and I had not made love yet. But there was no hurry. We both knew we would and that it would be good.

His lips nuzzled my ear. I suckled at his teat. His fingers slipped inside my underpants and gently kneaded my buttocks. Mine worked his zipper down and freed his cock.

"Gehen wir jetzt nach Bette," I mumbled, forgetting to translate I was so relaxed.

"Did you say we ought to go to bed?" Alan asked. I nodded against his chest. "Are you sure, Dieter? We don't have to—I'll understand."

I sat up and fixed him with my gaze. "We don't have to? What? Make love?" I took a quick breath. "Alan, if we do not join now, then when? Until we do, until we give ourselves to each other, what I feel now is only half complete. It can only be half true—and I do not live lies, Liebchen. Not with myself."

We undressed before the fire, each of us exposing himself completely for the first time to his lover. Each of us looking and seeing our lover naked for the first time. Alan pulled me to him and kissed me, our cocks caught between our bellies and dueling each other. His hands reclaimed my buttocks, grinding me against him.

I wanted him. I had no more doubts of that; my bout with Barry had left me clear of those. I wanted to give him my virginities and feel his possession of me. I knew with total certainty that I had come to love Alan Moore in the two months I had known him.

He took my hand and led me to his bedroom, our bedroom now. I crossed to the bed as he closed the door behind us. He came to me then, and I watched him do so with a smile that I knew covered my face.

How I wanted him. To feel his touch. To join with him. To feel our union.

He knelt before me, his fingers reaching out to caress my bollocks. My erect manhood touched his face, its skin pulled all the way off its knob. "I've wanted to touch you since the very first time I saw you in the dorm, Dieter," he breathed.

"I too," I told him, my fingers stroking his hair. "But I did not understand then. I was frightened by the feelings I had—"

His fingers traced my ball-sac up to my shaft and began to move out along it, encircling it. My foreskin moved to cover my helmet, and I felt weak under his manipulation.

"You're uncut," he mumbled against my shaft as his fingers reached my skin-covered knob. "This is going to be interesting." He looked up at me and I knew he was smiling. "You're my first natural man, Dieter." With that, he leaned back until my 17 centimeters were aimed at his lips.

He nibbled at the skin bunched at the tip, his lips riding higher, half-way up the glans. Gently, he milked my cock as if it were a teat, his tongue worrying its way beneath the pucker of skin to lave the very tip of my manhood. I shivered.

He swallowed me then. All of me, until his nose was buried in my pubis—both of his hands finding my buttocks and pulling me into him. I gasped.

His fingers began to explore the crevice between my ass-cheeks. His index finger quickly found my rear entrance and began to massage the puckered, wrinkled skin there. I moaned at the new sensations his finger brought me. At what his mouth was doing to my cock. My ball-sac tightened and my balls rose to ride the shaft of my manhood.

Alan's finger eased through my entrance and began to explore what I knew at that moment would always be my love-chute. "Gott!" I cried as that finger found my prostate. I erupted.

I felt Alan's throat milking my cockhead, volley after volley of my essence crashing out of my balls into his gullet. A second finger joined the first to work my hole. I collapsed on the bed, my legs spread to permit him between them, his mouth still on my 17 centimeters and his two fingers deep in my hole. I had never experienced an orgasm as powerful as the one he gave me.

"I want you to—" I looked down my chest at him looking up at me, all of my cock still in his mouth. "I want you to make love to me, Alan." I smiled. "Fichst mir, bitte," I told him and wiggled my hips on his fingers.

Alan chuckled. "Does that mean what I think it does?" he asked and nuzzled my balls. I jerked.

"Yes," I groaned. "Please, Alan. Do it. Make me complete," I told him. "Make me yours."

"This is a part of you I've never seen," he mused. "Have you done it before?" I shook my head and concentrated on the pleasure his fingers were generating in me. I remained erect, my skin pulled completely off the knob of my cock. He chuckled. "Well, I guess you've loosened up nicely, Dieter."

His fingers left me and I felt suddenly empty. I watched as he pulled out the drawer of the bedside cabinet and took out a foil packet. Smiling, he held it up for me to see. "Protection always, Dieter," he explained. "Put it on me." He climbed onto the bed, straddling my chest and bringing his dick close to my hands.

I tore open the packet and flattened the condom against his knob. "That tickles," he giggled as I rolled it down his shaft.

"If that tickles what will being inside me do to you?" I asked.

He grinned down at me and said: "Don't know, but let's find out." He climbed back off the bed and stood before me. "Get all the way up on the bed, Dieter. If you're going to lose your cherry, you might as well be comfortable when it happens." He reached back to the cabinet and picked up a tube of something.

I pushed myself to the center of the bed and watched as he followed, crawling across the sheet towards me on his knees. My attention concentrated on his erect, sheathed cock pointing the way to me.

It was bigger than mine, at least Barry's 20 centimeters and perhaps more. I thought it was wider too. I wondered suddenly how we were going to get it inside me comfortably. Even as I doubted, however, I knew I wanted Alan to possess me, to claim me. To make me his.

Reaching me, he raised my feet and placed them on his shoulders. I felt the coolness of the October night caress my buttocks as they rose from the mattress. He bent over me and my feet moved down his back. His lips found mine and our tongues were immediately dueling for supremacy. His two fingers found my entrance and worked their way into me.

I gasped when they again found my prostate. I ground my hips against his hand in pleasure, trying to get more of him into me. He worked a third finger in with the others. I no longer wondered how he would get his manhood inside me; I just wanted it there, plowing me with its length.

"Do it!" I commanded as I broke away from our kiss. Never had I known the pleasure coursing through my body like a flooding river. I was beyond thought. I only wanted more pleasure and, then, even more.

He nibbled at my teats and I felt movement beneath me. Moments later, his fingers left me and I felt uncomfortably empty. He pressed a dollop of something cool and greasy against my entrance and shifted his body between my legs. His lips returned to mine and, as we began to kiss, I felt something large press against my hole.

I grabbed his buttocks and pulled him to me. The pressure increased until it was almost painful. My sphincter surrendered then and his knob pushed into me. I felt each centimeter of his knob, of his shaft, sliding into my belly. It felt strange, even uncomfortable, but not painful.

His cockhead reached my prostate and I bucked as it pressed against my gland. I grounded my hips against him as each new centimeter continued to massage me. My own dick erected proudly and rode our bellies. I was washed away on the waves of pleasure spreading through me.

"Feel good?" Alan asked from above me. In wonder, I realized he again sat on his haunches, my ankles crossed behind his neck and the edge of his pubis scratching at my ball-sac.

I smiled up at him and ground my buttocks against him. "Make love to me," I told him.

He began slowly to pull from me and I felt each centimeter. My hands went to his buttocks to stop him before he left me completely. As slowly, his 20 centimeters returned to fill me. He developed a steady, slow rhythm that allowed me to learn to clutch at him with my anal muscles as he pulled from me and to raise my buttocks to greet him upon his return. I watched him as he fucked me, my own cock bouncing across my belly with each movement.

I watched Alan Moore, my new lover. I watched him make love to me.

My hands slid up his back to pull him down to kiss me as I raised my head to meet his. His cock continued to move in me, possessing me, as we kissed.

We groaned as each new pleasure crashed over us. We humped and clenched and held each other. The bed creaked beneath us and we did not care that it announced our lovemaking to anyone listening.

I rode the waves of pleasure growing in my love-chute, reveling at the knotting in my balls as they flattened against the shaft of my cock and made ready to erupt. I held Alan tighter and gave the last of myself to him.

I again became aware. Alan's cock still plunged freely into me, but harder, faster now. His lips were still on mine, his tongue still dueled mine. The bed groaned and squeaked louder than before. My still erect manhood bounced across my belly, but now it plopped in puddles of my sperm. "Cum in me," I groaned around his tongue and into his lips.

Again, I rode the pleasure coursing through my body, pulling away from him even I drew closer to him—as we ground against each other. I knew with certainty I could never do without dick in me again; but I wanted it to be love and not just sex. I wanted it to be Alan's cock.

He grunted and pushed away from me. I realized he was pounding my love-chute. His breathing was labored. He shoved his whole manhood into me. I felt his cock thicken as it held deep within me. He was cumming. I was his.

"Somebody got fucked," Barry said as I walked into the kitchen the next morning. I was as naked as he was, as they were—for I saw Jordan then. Barry was sitting on his lap.

"We made love," I answered as I headed towards the coffee pot. "And you?"

"We're still doing it," Jordan grunted. I looked towards them then. Barry was raising and lowering his buttocks. His face was slack, his cock bouncing from thigh to thigh.

"Enjoy," I told them and poured two cups of coffee. I started back to our bedroom, wondering if Alan would be as good in the morning as he was at night.

FRISKY FRAT BOYS

Howie Marshall

MY ACCOUNT WAS OVERDRAWN AGAIN. THE NASTY LITTLE FORM letter the size of a # 10 envelope kept telling me so every time I read it. How the hell could a bank be so fucking snide with such bland words?

I looked around my bedroom, trying to figure where the money had gone. My room was trashed, of course. I'd been thinking of bringing a maid service in once a week before I got the overdrawn notice.

I needed every CK, Polo, and Eddie Bauer piece of clothing I had. I had a reputation to maintain—I mean, I was the best-dressed sophomore at Gulfstream University, Mississippi's university for young gentlemen, facing the beautiful Gulf of Mexico. It just got a little hard to remember to hang everything up after I had stripped off and was drinking the last Beefeater gimlet of the day.

That reminded me, I was almost out of gin and the weekend was coming up. I read the notice again. The bank had paid the check. Thank God. That'd left me twenty overdrawn and they'd tacked on another thirty for the rubber check. So I was fifty short. But I still had another month to go before the holidays. I also had another month of rent due before the holidays. I couldn't understand what I'd done wrong. I hadn't had this problem when I was living in the dorm last year.

I knew better than to ask dear old Dad for another handout. He'd already bailed me out three times since the semester started and was sick of looking at me. I thought of good old Mom for a moment but knew I couldn't depend on her. Every dime she spent went through Dad, with his personal stamp of approval on it. She was worse than old-fashioned; she was an unliberated woman. The folks were both out, all right.

My stomach growled. I tried to remember what was in the fridge but knew there wasn't much. I just wasn't much for cooking. I went through every pocket in every pair of pants, shorts and even my five pairs of sweats (yeah, I know they're all Calvin Klein, but they feel so good on my butt). I found twenty. My eyes bulged and my hands got sweaty as I realized it was the last twenty I had.

I decided I could have a medium everything pizza and save a couple of slices for breakfast. I called Pizza Man and checked to see if I had enough German beer to get through dinner. My nose wrinkled in disgust when I saw I was out of Rose's. Fuck!

Most of the guys I knew were just poor assholes who loved it when I gave a party. If anything, I could maybe get five or ten off of any one of them.

I remembered Marc DuBois then. Good old Marc and only a year older than me. He was the son of Dad's business partner. He was why I was at this backassward college in the first place. It was good enough for him, it was good enough for me. My dad could be real strange at times. I didn't hang with Marc. He was fraternity row all the way. The fact was that I didn't like him much. And there were those rumors from high school. But he had money, and that was a commodity I needed fast.

I rummaged around through the clothes on the floor and found my cleanest Ralph Laurent shirt and CK sweats. I debated underwear but if those rumors about Marc were true... I decided to let myself hang loose down there and slipped on my Bass wejuns. I studied the effect in the mirror—six feet and buff. Brown hair with bangs that came down to the tip of my button nose. My last girlfriend had told me I had the face of a Greek god. If Marc really was queer, I should bowl him over good. I started for the TKG house.

A pledge showed me right up to Marc's room.

"Johnny, what brings you here?" he said, rising from his desk and stretching before crossing the room to shake my hand.

I was gym-buff, but Marc was pool-tight. The boy had been on Gulfstream's swim team the past three years, and he looked it. My height, Marc was blond with chiseled features. He was old money from Natchez. I had to admit he was a handsome devil.

"Come on in, John," he said, smiling at me, my hand grasped in his, his other hand going around my shoulders. "Gammies don't bite."

I was getting cold feet, the real clammy kind. I mean, asking the son of Dad's business partner for a five hundred dollar hand-out was beginning to sound like not the best plan I'd ever come up with.

"What's the problem?" he drawled ever so softly as he sat me in his chair and went to the cabinet under his sound system. I watched his butt spread as he pulled out two crystal glasses and a bottle of Courvoisier. I felt my face flame as I realized his ass was really nice and round. He glanced over his shoulder and said: "I'm sorry I don't have a better brandy to offer you." He poured drinks, brought one to me, and sat down on the bed facing me.

"Come on, Johnny. Spit it out, boy."

"What makes you think there's something wrong, Marc?" I asked, and gave him my best little boy grin, adroitly sidestepping his direct approach. I thought.

He laughed. "One, you've avoided me the year and a half you've been at Gulfstream. Two, Daddy's laughing at how your father is bitching about how frivolous you are."

I gulped.

"How overdrawn are you?"

I stared at Marc DuBois, my eyes bulging. Either he was psychic or he read my mail before I did. "Only fifty," I admitted and downed my brandy. I hardly coughed, its burn felt so good going down. "But there's rent and just surviving this next month."

"Think five hundred will do it?" I stared at him, my eyes really bulging now. He was psychic.

"Y—you can loan me that much?" I stammered. "This late in the semester?"

Marc got up and poured me another drink. I didn't see a smile anywhere as he sat back down on the bed. "John, I don't make loans. No DuBois does."

"But you said—" I groaned seeing the speculation in his eyes. "The five hundred?" I figured right then that the rumors I'd heard about Marc were true. I was a hundred and ten percent heterosexual but I was already figuring getting a blow job might not be so bad a deal. I probably would even be willing to pork him. He did have a fine looking butt.

"You're nineteen. It's time you become a businessman, Johnny boy. Pretty much like your daddy did—"

"I don't understand." At that moment, I was facing not having a pot to piss in, and Marc was talking about me becoming a business-man. It didn't make a damned lick of sense. I took a big swig of the brandy and stared at him, waiting for him to pull a rabbit out of his hat.

He laughed. "Twenty years ago, maybe a little more, your father was driving big rigs for one of Daddy's businesses. He got up north and out west, but he was still living with your grandparents he was so poor. He came back to Mississippi with a bad back and couldn't drive any more. He also came back with an idea. He'd seen all these 7-11's in every little town—some with gas pumps, some without. To make a long story short, Daddy advanced your father enough money to set up one of the stores that have made you Joneses so rich."

"Dad and Mr. DuBose are partners—"

"Not really, Johnny. It's your father's business—every one of those Perky Panda convenience stores in Mississippi and Louisiana. He makes the money. His deal with Daddy is that he pays him ten percent of the profits. Eucle Jones makes the money he makes be-cause he's a good businessman. He pays Daddy ten percent as a royalty for investing in him."

Marc leaned back against his pillows and smiled at me. "I'd like to make the same investment in you. It's my idea, but it's your product. I'm a fair man, I'll guarantee the first five hundred from your little business for a measly fifteen percent of the profits—if you start now. How does that sound?"

"It certainly sounds fair enough," I told him, latching onto the idea that I was going to have the money I needed before the end of the night if I played my cards right.

"Good!" He sat up and pushed himself off the bed. "Let me see if the Gammies are game. Stay here, I'll be back soon."

I watched Marc start for the door. Something wasn't exactly right about this. It took me until he was opening the door. "What's this business I'm starting?" I asked.

"One you'll like when you get into it. Let me find out if the boys are interested. Help yourself to the brandy while I'm gone." He grinned. "And loosen up, Johnny." He was out in the hallway and I was sitting in his room staring at a closed door.

The more I thought about it, the more I didn't like this shit one bit. Inside of ten minutes, Marc DuBose had moved right in and taken over my life. Now I was waiting for him to find out if his frat brothers liked his idea for a little business for me. Hell! I didn't even know what the business was. I could run a cash register and stock a store; dear old Dad saw to me learning that—every goddamned summer.

I got up and poured myself another brandy. A real stiff one. I told myself to get the fuck up and leave. Only, I knew I couldn't. Marc had me by the balls now, and good. He was dangling five big ones in front of me. I could survive until the holidays when I'd get enough from presents to finish up the semester. I knew I'd do just about anything Marc DuBois came up with to get my hands on that money. I just didn't want to find out just how much.

I hit Marc's liquor supply twice more and was feeling no pain when he returned with another guy. "You're on, Johnny," he told me as he put one gigantic mixing bowl down on the table beside the door. His buddy shut the door behind them, and both dropped several bills each into the bowl. "What's that for?" I asked, nodding towards the bowl but staring at the new boy. Man, was he big!

"Johnny, I want you to meet Tommy. He's on Gulfstream's wrestling team and won State for us last year."

I looked at Tommy as he came into the room. He was a full head taller than I and thick. Not fat—just thick everywhere. I sure as hell wouldn't want him putting a half-Nelson on me. He'd probably rip my head off. I gave him my best smile and stuck out my hand. "Hi, Tommy," I said politely as you please. "Nice to meet you."

Tommy's paw engulfed my hand. He grinned. His other hand plopped down on my shoulder, shoving me back down on the bed. My eyes were suddenly level with his bellybutton. I felt prickly all over when I realized he had an erection under his gym shorts that was tenting those shorts even out at the hip.

Jesus Christ! What the fuck had Marc set me up for? Nervously, I looked to Marc and my gaze followed him around to the other side of his bed. "What's up?" I asked; it came out as a squeak. I was looking at him over my shoulder, unable to take my eyes off him until he explained things to me. My body was covered in goose bumps. Talk to me, I wanted to demand.

He did. "The boys liked the idea of your little business, Johnny. So, what we're going to do is give you two at a time tonight, right here in my room."

"W—what're we going to be doing here?" I stammered. I didn't know why I asked, I had a sinking feeling I knew.

Tommy's hands were on my face before I could even think to re-act, turning me back to him. I knew what my new business was about then; it nearly slapped me in the face. Tommy was standing in front of me butt-naked. His boner was rock hard and was the biggest dick I'd ever seen. He had to be nine inches. "I want you," he told me and grinned as he ground his hips and his monster pole jumped from hip to hip. I gulped.

"Johnny, it's the only way to get you the money," Marc said in a soft voice near my ear. I felt his hand touch my back, under my shirt. "Just go with the program tonight and you've got the cash you need. Your father won't know."

"I ain't queer!" I moaned and watched Tommy's mushroom jerk with the beat of his heart.

"You want your father pulling you from school, Johnny? Daddy said he was talking about sticking you in one his stores—down on some bayou."

"No—" I groaned. I couldn't let that happen. I belonged at Gulfstream.

"Nobody's going to know, Johnny. You just have to do what you have to do. You'll be able to live like you want to, when you want to."

I felt my face being pulled towards Tommy's crotch. Towards that one-eyed monster. I couldn't take my eyes off it. And I couldn't resist. My brain blanked out on me.

I focused on Tommy's tightly curled black pubes and figured them to be maybe eight inches from the tip of my nose. My jaw felt unhinged and my lips were stretched tight behind the corona of the helmet of his dick in my mouth. I wondered if I would ever get my nose down in those pubes.

"Lick that big thing," Marc whispered at my ear. "Make Tommy feel good, Johnny." I did what I was told as he undressed me.

"Get up on the bed, Johnny," Marc told me, one hand on my six pack, the other on my fanny, guiding me. "Get on all fours and suck that big thing. Give Tommy the time of his life."

I couldn't think. I could barely feel. Nothing mattered except that I bury my face in Tommy's short curlies. I had to take his whole dick in my mouth. I had to prove to myself that I could. I had to.

With Tommy's hands on either side of my head guiding me, I was soon bobbing up and down most of his thick pole. "Feels good," he grunted from above me and pulled me down onto another couple of inches of his meat.

Behind me, Marc's hands caressed my back and butt-cheeks. His knee spread my legs as he settled between them. My shirt rode up my back and my sweats moved over my spread cheeks. I continued to suck Tommy off, my hands holding onto his hips.

A light clicked on inside my head when I felt Marc's finger push into my butthole. I could feel the cool grease all along the walls of my chute. He was going to butt-fuck me.

I started to pull off Tommy's dick. Somewhere along the line, I had decided I could suck dick this one time. It was sort of like adding more weights to the barbells at the gym—pushing myself and seeing how much I could take. But getting my ass porked like some girl's twat? I didn't think so. Not for all the tea in China.

Tommy's hands tightened on the sides of my head, holding me on him. Marc's finger found my prostate. My lips jumped down the length of my friendly giant's pole and my nose was buried in his pubes and his knob was past my tonsils and halfway down my throat.

I blew my load on Marc's bed without even touching myself.

My eyes bulged as I stared at the shiny dark curly hairs that ran up to tickle my nose and then ran back down inches and inches of the thick tube that was Tommy's dick. Marc's finger continued to fuck me. No! I'd suck dick for five hundred, but get butt fucked? Oh, Jesus, no! Marc pulled his finger out of my rectum. I relaxed. I told myself that a little humiliation wasn't so bad. I could survive it. I'd be chuckling to myself tomorrow as I refilled my account.

Something hot, thick, hard, and sort of oval wedged against my hole. I felt both of Marc's hands grasp my hips. It took until he had a hold on me to figure what was behind me. Lord God above! I almost got off all nine of Tommy's inches before he put the brakes on my head and started pulling my face back down into his crotch. Sweet Jesus!

I didn't think to shut things down back there to try to keep Marc out. He just jabbed all the way into me with his first thrust. Pain shot out of my ass and spread over my body like a wildfire. I screamed, but it only came out as a moan.

"Yeah!" Tommy moaned happily above me. "That feels so good. Just keep humming on my dick, little buddy."

"I'm covered, Johnny," Marc said and his dick stayed buried deep in my gut, giving me time to adjust to its being there. The pain ebbed and I just felt full.

"Come on, boy, hum on my dick again. I want to give you my load," Tommy told me. I hummed. Marc started grinding his crotch against my fanny, his dick moving around in my gut.

It felt good. His dick touched off sparks of electric shock every time it rubbed over my prostate. I started to grind against him. And to bob on Tommy's dick, humming each time it went past my tonsils. Marc started to fuck me then. I was hard and my dick bounced off my six pack every time his balls hit mine.

A small part of me remembered the crazed faces of preachers ranting from their pulpits about the abomination that I was now enjoying. I kept telling myself I wasn't queer even if I was getting fucked and sucking dick.

Most of me, however, did what my body was already doing, it

went with the flow. Mindlessly, I sucked on Tommy big dick. I bucked back to greet Marc's dick slamming into my hole. My dick was hard and leaking. I was having sex and enjoying it. I accepted that it didn't matter what kind of sex it was, it was good as long as I was an active part of it. And, boy, was I ever a part of this fuck.

Tommy blew his load into his rubber down my throat. I could feel his dick flexing and expanding down around my adam's apple. That set me off again. I erupted, my dick bouncing around and spewing slime everywhere. My butt muscles clenching got Marc good. He slammed into me one last time and held me hard against him as he groaned and unloaded in the rubber up my ass.

Tommy shuddered and stepped back, pulling his hose out of my throat. I smiled as I watched each thick, slick inch appear under my nose. Marc collapsed on my back and left himself connected to me as he caught his breath.

"You're just what this fraternity needed, boy," Tommy told me, patting the top of my head. Marc pushed off my back, pulling his dick out of my butt. I felt empty. I also felt ashamed because I'd gotten so into our sex. I didn't know the etiquette that went with the aftermath of getting fucked by a man.

"You were damned good, Johnny." I felt Marc get off the bed behind me but wasn't ready to look up and see in his face what he thought of me now that I knew I liked man-to-man sex. Marc's hands found my butt-cheeks and began to massage them. "Time for us to get out of here, Tommy. Johnny here has more customers waiting at the door for him."

His words sunk in. I looked up into his face. "More—?" I gulped.

He smiled down at me, he moved a finger down to trace the valley of my ass. "Just relax, boy. They're going to love you. You're a natural at this."

The next morning, I debated whether to skip classes or not. My jaw ached and I wondered if I was ever going to be able to clench my butthole shut again. I was sore as shit down there, too. For some fucking reason, I was staying half hard. I was wearing just a pair of Calvin Kleins and didn't know if I even wanted them on. The doorbell went off like an alarm clock and wouldn't quit. I opened the door.

"Hi, Johnny," Marc DuBois said. He was dressed like a GQ model and wearing a smile. The thumb and index finger of one hand were stroking the very obvious tube in the crotch of his trousers.

"Fuck off!" I grunted and started to shut the door.

"I brought you your money, boy," he said and shouldered his way around me into the living room.

"And I wanted to see how you were doing after that impressive show you put on last night."

I felt all the blood drain out of my face. It drained out of arms and chest, too. Every goddamned pint of it went straight to my dick. I was so hard, the head of my dick just snaked right up under the elastic of my CKs and started drooling.

Marc grinned. "You're happy to see me." His hand left his tube and made its way into his pocket. I wasn't watching him and didn't even see his grin. My gaze was glued to that long, thick ridge tenting his trousers. His hand came of out of his pocket and he laughed. "We'll get into that, Johnny boy—just as soon as I give you your money."

"Money?" I pulled my gaze from his pants with difficulty. I focused on his hand. There was one hell of a roll of bills in it.

"You made seven hundred last night and I didn't hear one complaint." He handed me the cash.

"I took out my fifteen percent, that leaves you with $595, which is what's right there."

I stared at the roll of twenties and fives in my hand. His hand returned to the tube stretched across his crotch. "I could use a quickie, Johnny—" He took my free hand. "Let's go to your bedroom."

I followed after Marc DuBois as we entered the hallway, clutching the money hard in my hand. "I've got you lined up with the Delts tomorrow night. They didn't even bat an eye when I told them they had to guarantee seven hundred for you to come."

"You what?" I yelped as I stepped into my bedroom and turned to stare at him in shock.

"Just look at it this way, Johnny—just the two frat houses and you're earning fourteen hundred a week—that's almost a twelve hundred net. I think I can line up at least one more—that'd make twenty-one hundred a week." He grinned. "Now slip those things off, boy. I've got a class in an hour."

I put the money on top of the dresser and turned to face Marc. Both hands slipped under the waistband of my underpants.

He licked his lips. "On second thought, don't rush it, Johnny. Make your strip sexy for me." He grinned. "It'll get my dick good and ready for your butt."

I began to grind my hips as I watched his face. I pivoted to show him my suddenly hungry butt as I eased the soft cotton over my cheeks.

CHERRY BOY IN THE BIG APPLE

Roddy Martin

I SLIPPED OUT INTO THE HALLWAY. NERVOUSLY, I LOOKED BACK AND watched Dad for any sign that he knew I was going out. He slept peacefully in the far bed of our hotel room. I wondered if I should forget about my plans. I didn't have to prove anything. Not to me, not to anybody. I eased the door shut then, being extra careful that it didn't make any noise when it locked.

I was 19 and bound for my first gay club—in the Big Apple! My heart pounded as I walked towards the elevators. I punched the button. I punched it twice. Unable to wait, I dashed down the six flights to the lobby. My excitement had been building in me all afternoon, I couldn't wait to get this show on the road.

The night smelled like life. I booked up 42nd Street in my jeans and black T-shirt, my crisp jockey shorts—hoping I looked good. At 8th Avenue, hot neon lit up the block. Cars honked. Vendors' grills sizzled. People dodged one another. Sailors, tourists, panhandlers.

In minutes, I was among them. It felt scary, good scary—like climbing the board at a swim meet. Now all I had to do was find the place.

Show Guys. Two Screening Rooms! Live shows daily! Special guest star—Jason Flipp! Purple light glowed in the doorway and, beyond that, a poster of Flipp, with tawny hair, broad shoulders and bare buns. It looked like a dive! I slowed and stopped.

I attended a college without a gay student union in a Pennsylvania town without a gay bar. What did I know about male burlesque?

Could I go in there? Should I? Did I need to come out this way? Or should I sneak back to the hotel, keep the *Unzipped* buried in the suitcase until I was back at college? I'd spent the term wrestling with my identity, but I couldn't wrestle any more.

Flipp grinned from the poster like showing his ass was the most wholesome fun in the world. My legs carried me past him, up the stairs. Admission was $12. I passed the man a five and a ten, and waited. My grin felt like granite. My dimples ached. I just knew he was going to card me, possibly call the cops.

At last he asked, "Problem, boss?"

"My change?"

I pushed through the turnstile, into a wall of air-conditioning and cheap disinfectant. And something else. I figured this was the adult male smell I'd know the rest of my life. It grabbed me by the balls.

The place resembled a faculty lounge, but real shabby. There were soda machines, a video game. More naked posters. And there were patrons. I glanced at one and saw nice calves and teal shorts, perfectly cinched with a belt. His V-neck shirt clung perfectly too, and his face—

Our eyes met. We both looked away.

I went for the door in the middle, into the dance beat and colored lights. I was almost shaking I was so excited!

And self-conscious. I felt so young and inexperienced, like I didn't belong. I inched by the knot of men just inside the door and stepped into the auditorium. I thought it weird how they hung back.

The stage was a platform with seats on three sides and mirrors behind it. It was bathed in pink and blue and gold, but no one was showing his stuff there.

Still, the knot by the door acted like a show was on. My eyes focused. I saw a hunky figure in the middle of the third row. The pink light outlined his rich, brown skin. He was on top of a scrunched-down man, moving against him. Glancing away, my face hot, I saw another hunk under the blue light opposite the stage with someone squatted before him. And, way over there in the shadows, some guy with broad shoulders and bare butt cheeks—someone's hands were squeezing those butt cheeks, prying them apart as the guy leaned over to give him better access.

I looked around and sank under a wave of dismay. Anonymous sex. In front of anyone, everyone. This wasn't what I wanted.

I'd been so sure in the afternoon when I bought the *Unzipped*—I mean not before, but after. The newsstand lady sold it to me without a blink. A block later, I slid the bag off and walked with the cover showing, proclaiming myself for anyone to see.

It'd been awesome, sitting in the park up near Lincoln Center. The sky was blue. The sun was high. Joggers passed, and roller-bladers. And who I thought of as accountants with chests—I couldn't believe the chests. I'd find the blandest, most unassuming face, look down, and—wow! All New York men were beautiful and I felt like one of them there in the park with my copy of *Unzipped* clearly in view.

I didn't feel that here.

For sure, I was scanning just the backs of heads, but these men seemed different. They were scattered around the auditorium—pairs of them fucking and sucking. Or standing there, pants down, watching the men at the door.

Where was the fun?

My brows were getting higher—and my eyes rounder—by the second.

I fled.

I got as far as the exit. A wipe-off board hung beside it, a dancer schedule. It put "Flipper" at 8, 10 and 12. The clock said 11:45. I thought: well—I did pay $12 to see him, didn't I?

I was in Screening Room 1. It was about six rows of folding chairs and a TV, which showed an Australian masturbating in a plush white bathrobe that made his tan look great.

"Feels unbelievable," he said huskily. "Want to have a look?" The robe was open only enough to show a hip and a pec, a flat stomach and pubic fluff.

He'd made the offer already, in the exact same words and the exact same tone, as if the same film clip ran over and over.

"Right-O!" said the Australian.

I was panting for that look, but I'd somehow developed an equally great need to know what was going on in the auditorium I'd just left and in Screening Room 2. I needed to know about the patrons, nervous as they made me.

"Want to have a look?" The Australian threw off the robe. "Can you fucking believe it?"

I stared at the screen. No. The beauty of that smooth, ivory thing was—

"Unbelievable," said the Australian. He grabbed the sofa, humped the air with his rod. "I'm gonna fucking blow. Can't hold it. Why would I want to?"

I felt my butthole rise to meet my balls.

"Shit, here it comes. Here it comes. Gonna blow a fucking monsoon. Oh yeah, oh yeah! Argh!" A look of naked surprise crossed the Australian's face. He grimaced and groaned, screwed both fists. "Look at that blow," the Australian sighed, sinking back.

I couldn't see anything.

It was 11:58. Time to move. The ebony hunk I'd seen humping earlier carried a red G-string out of the auditorium. His cock swung before him. "I'm on break," he called into the admission booth.

"What break?"

The knot at the door of the auditorium had thinned when I got back, and there was no sign of Jason Flipp. I took a seat. One in the path of one of the hunks, a show guy. It seemed I decided to do this, without knowing I'd decided.

He was a short Italian, about my age. Gold chain, white baseball cap, white socks and sneakers. Nice shoulder blades. I tried not to drool. Would he come to me? Would he?

"Hey guy."

He did. His jock undulated in my face. He was tan everywhere. What abs!

He reached into his jock pushing his cock out the side.

I felt the heat of his erection, saw his slit and his foreskin pulled back behind his crown. It was too much. I didn't know where to put my hands.

He turned, flexed his ass. I touched it. It was heaven—so firm, so silky. Not like mine. Though actually I didn't know how mine felt. I'd have to check that out. I reached around his hip and pushed his foreskin over his knob and pulled it back. He moaned.

"Sock," he muttered a second later and straightened.

"Excuse me?"

"Tips go in the sock."

Oh. All I had was the three dollars change from admission. They were crumpled and smarmy. I poked them in the sock. The show guy left.

I felt sick with embarrassment. I hadn't known you had to pay to cop a feel.

The clock said 12:25. Jason Flipp was nowhere. I left the auditorium. Screen 2 showed a story about a freshman with smooth balls, a hard perineum and the dean's cock halfway up his pink slot.

"Fuck my ass, sir," the freshman with smooth balls grunted.

"Yeah, your ass feels so good on my dick."

The man in teal shorts sat down three chairs from me. I remembered him from every room I'd been in. I caught him glancing over me at me. I decided he was following me around. He smiled. My stomach lurched, but I felt good, too, that someone was interested in me.

I wandered into the lobby. "Strippers," the admission man was shouting through the glass. "You like strippers?"

"Streepers?" asked a French voice.

"Studs with big cocks?"

"Cocks?" There was a barrage of French curses. After it trailed off, the admission man remarked to no one in particular: "He knew about cocks."

"He knew," agreed a show guy with him in the booth. "Hell, this is New York City."

I studied the naked posters. Chance Caldwell was a coming attraction. Chad Knight and Johan Paulik also. Porn stars, I guessed. If I ever got out of here, I'd never look at another bit of pornography.

But I was going to see Jason Flipp first. I wondered if he was a porn star too.

In his poster, he looked as if he'd been caught unawares, cupping his butt cheeks, grinning from molar to molar. He had wonderful teeth—wonderful gums, even. He tapped into my dream, which was to have gay friends and a very special boyfriend and to grin at him that way.

I approached the admission man. "Jason—?"

"Coming, boss. Coming."

On Screen 1, a shirtless miner swung a pickax way over head. His torso became a sweeping line of muscle—arm to shoulder, shoulder to chest, flank to abs. Oooh. I popped pre-cum. By now I was soaked, due to lots of close calls.

"Whew." The miner mopped his brow. "This is hard work. I gotta do something to relieve the tension." He opened his jeans and shoved his hand inside. "Oh yeah—Oh yeah. Oh God, yeah!"

"What's up?" asked a second miner.

The first miner grabbed a hard-hat, covered his crotch. "Shit!"

"Looks like you're working a—mother load. I'll give you a hand."

The miners kissed. I almost blew. I mean, Adam's apples! Underarm hair, chin stubble, hooked shoulders! Men with men. I wanted it. How could I live without it?

The second miner stepped behind the first miner, ran his tongue up and down the cord of his neck. Caressed his ribs.

I could unzip, make it quick and quiet. Lord knew others were, even if it was gross.

I heard a noise in the corner of the room. I saw butt-crack. Patrons wrapped together, doing unspecified things. I wheeled away, scrunched my neck down like a turtle.

On the screen, the second miner yanked down the first miner's jeans. "Man, you got a good ass," he said, sinking his teeth into it.

"Fuck yeah," the first miner gasped and frigged himself. The second miner's face was up his lightly-haired butt. "I hope you're as good at sucking dick as you are at eating ass."

"Better."

My eyeballs shifted in the butt-crack's direction. Slowly, slowly my head followed. The butt was humping. These men were having sex. Men came here for sex.

Duh…

Now the screen showed the view from over the first miner's shoulder—down the sweeping torso, to the stomach. And the hips, which pumped the long cock all the way in and all the way out of the second miner's mouth.

"Oh yeah."

"Umph."

"Fuck yeah."

Meanwhile the pair in the corner had gained spectators. The spectators were pairing up. I got a mental picture of cherries floating in cream. I'd been a virgin for 19 years and that was a long time. But did I want to lose it in the porn world?

I found myself drifting over, standing beside a spare body. Any old body. I looked at his knees, felt him look at mine. It was teal shorts. I looked higher. He looked, I looked. His knuckles touched mine.

I hated this. I wanted out.

The loud speaker cracked then. "Gentlemen, now on the"—buzzzz!—"stage, superstar of Falcon, cover man of *In Touch, Torso, Playgirl*, and *Unzipped*. Please experience—Jason Flipp!"

I waited in the front row, hiding my socks. There was a pre-cum spot on my jeans. I just wanted to go to bed. See Jason Flipp and go to bed. See Jason Flipp, beat off, and go to bed.

And toss the *Unzipped*.

I heard applause. Clomp! Jason Flipp hit the stage in hiking boots. Awestruck, I realized how bad the view from my seat was.

His hips started to twitch. He slithered the belt out of his split-side shorts, undid his fly. Clomp, clomp, clomp! The moves weren't slick, but they were happy.

Now he faced the mirror. Down came the shorts. Up went the shirt. He had a pert butt. Sideways, at least. Swinging the shirt flag-like from his dick, he smiled the poster smile all around. I wanted to clap. That smile was everything. He tied the shirt around his waist, did a hula, and hopped from the stage.

Right to me. "Are you having a nice time?" His breath tickled my ear.

"No," I said stupidly.

"Ahhh."

Next thing, he was on my lap. His chest smooth and square. It looked beautifully, impossibly close. I gulped. "Sorry, I can't tip you."

"No problem."

He stroked my cheek. His dick bobbed under the T-shirt and he put my hand there. It was the softest, strongest thing.

I peered up at him. "Better?" he asked.

"Uh-huh."

"Good." He brushed my cheek and smiled. I returned it. He moved on.

At last, I could go. I had gotten what I paid for. I felt so happy, floating through the crowd. I felt whole. I turned for a last look, and bumped into my fate.

"Hi," I said, gaping. He was one of those accountants with chests I'd seen in Central Park across from the Lincoln Center. He was also the man in teal shorts.

"Hi."

He was kissing me, tugging at my shirt. Such sure hands. They held me up, them and the wall, except now the shirt was gone—who cared where?—and he had my pants down to my knees. He knelt, massaging the space between my navel and the base of my cock. He jerked the head with his thumb and forefinger. I'd have cum, but he pinched me off.

I pulled him up. I just wanted to kiss and kiss and open his shirt, feel his chest. I'd forgotten we were at Show Guys.

His tongue was in my ear. "What do you want?" he breathed.

"You." He looked like a Disney prince. He had the hair, the jaw, the soulful eyes.

"Do you want everything?"

"Yeah."

He dropped to his knees and sucked. I never thought—I never dreamed—Thank God for the shadows and the partition. I ignored the fact that it was made up of guys standing next to each other watching us. I didn't want to see people watching.

He brought me to the brink again. While I was gasping and shuddering, I wound up bent over a chair and what he'd been doing in front, he did in back. I felt lips. I felt tongue. He spread my cheeks. He jabbed. My underwear was around my ankles along with my jeans.

It felt so good that I surrendered, wiggled my bottom on his handsome face. Presently he moved up. I felt his cock and oily latex at my entrance.

Ungh!

His cock was an endless slab shoving into me. The partition dissolved into the individual men who made it up. I bit my tongue, consciously telling myself I wasn't going to cry out. I wasn't going to let these men know I was virgin, that I didn't belong among them. The seat of the chair I was bent over blurred and I realized my eyes were filled with tears.

An intense pleasure suddenly flared up right behind the balls. My butt did spasms. It sucked in the rest of the man in teal shorts. Ten, twelve strokes and I began to cum. I didn't stop and neither did he.

I humped back to meet his thrusts. "Dick that ass good!" a voice close to me said loudly. I heard it as a tiny buzz. I was riding the pleasure building again in my ass and my balls. There was nothing real but that.

I rode his dick as it possessed me. Someone knelt beside me and worked his face between my thigh and the chair. I felt lips close over my knob and slide towards my pubes. I started to hyperventilate. I saw stars.

Just as my balls erupted, I realized teal shorts' thrusts had gotten short and fast. He slammed into me as my jizz hit the back of the throat sucking me. His dick pulsed inside me as my muscled clutched him

"Thank you," I told him when we were done and he was holding me by the chest, his dick still buried deep inside me. The men had left us, searching for another show to experience.

"No. Thank you."

As I walked back to the hotel, I thought about sitting down with Dad in the morning and telling him in a very adult way that my sexual status had changed. I tried to imagine him smiling back at me asking if I was sure. I'd tell him I was. "It doesn't change how I feel about you," he'd say.

Sure. And the moon was made of green cheese.

Two hours later, I couldn't sleep. I was back in the hotel room, in my bed, staring at the ceiling. My butt felt sore, like a muscle after a grueling workout. But it was still spasming and my dick was hard.

I tried to ignore both of them. I was ashamed of what I'd done. Of what I'd let happen. But I was glad, too. Getting screwed in public— in front of an audience watching me take it. Jeez! Only, I was already planning on going back tomorrow night. I wanted Jason Flipp, but, if he wasn't free, I'd take somebody like teal shorts. There had been a lot of good looking men there.

"Dad!" I growled, letting my frustration show.
"Huh?"
"Roll over. You're snoring."

THE COMING OUT PARTY— SPENT YOUTH

Alan W. Mills

I DIDN'T KNOW WHAT TO EXPECT. MY SECOND DAY IN L.A., AND MY best buddy was taking me to not just a porn party, but what he called the biggest fucking porn party of the year.

"What are you here for?" asked the huge guy at the door, his black skin darker around his menacing eyes.

I waited.

"Dada's birthday," said my friend Alex, and the guard let us pass and enter the unassuming studio on the dark, quiet street somewhere in the middle of a city so huge I couldn't see the end of it from my friend's sixth floor apartment.

"How do you know Dada Cherille?" I asked.

"I don't," said Alex. "I tricked with Bobby Godrod last week, and he invited me."

"Bobby Godrod!" I exclaimed, a bit awed. The one porno Alex sent me once was my only connection to gay life back in Sioux Falls, South Dakota. Four scenes directed by Dada, and just one with Bobby Godrod. Bobby Godrod and Carl Cumson—I jacked off to it over and over, no matter how familiar it got.

I stared at Alex as we followed a crowd through some corridors and emerged in a large, open room, roofed by what looked like silky, colorful tents.

From several points in the tented ceiling, rich fabric flowed to the ground, sloping gently and cascading down the studio's walls. Inside these walls were men, beautiful men. I'd seen an occasional cute guy on Santa Monica, but here they all were, all perfect, all giving off a sweet, musky scent, like gods.

Alex was off, saying hi to several of them as he pulled me through the tight sea of flesh and led me to a long, heavily stocked but make-shift bar. "Do you trick with a lot of porn stars?" I shouted over the powerful noise.

Alex looked at me like I needed sympathy. "Cape Cod, dear?"

"What's that?"

"Vodka and cranberry."

I glanced over at the tall, handsome bartender. "Aren't we gonna be carded?"

"Not here, Billy. Not here."

I'd noticed how different Alex had become from the moment I stepped off the plane. Even when I called him and told him I'd had all I could take of Sioux Falls and had saved enough to fly out West, he seemed so unlike the small town boy I had grown up with. "Oh, it's fabulous out here," he said. "And you'll do well."

I didn't fully understand what he meant, but I missed him and I hated Sioux Falls without him. So... I quit my job, said good-bye to the folks, and took off for the big city.

A year out of high school, I felt as if I could do anything. I was scared though, but Los Angeles held lots of possibilities. I could go to college, learn a trade, wait tables, get discovered. Who knew what could happen in a city that massive.

"I don't do more porn stars than anybody else in this town," he said as we lost ourselves in the crowd.

I studied him for the moment. He was still just as beautiful as he was all through school. Captain of the track team, star science student, son of a wealthy internet geek, Alex was every girl's dream. He was my dream, too, but I spent all of our high school years not telling him.

"Right! You're a handsome guy, Alex. I bet you do all of them."

He smiled, making me feel like a school girl, and whispered in my ear: "What can I say, they all go to my gym."

I turned away and, suddenly, there was Bobby Godrod, in white lycra and leather pants, standing right next to us with a video camera and a bright light just behind him. Obviously drunk, Bobby threw an arm around Alex and shoved a microphone near his lips. "Hello, everyone," he said to the camera, "this is a guy I met last week, and he has the hottest ass. Show them your ass," he ordered, pulling on Alex's belt.

Alex laughed, opened his pants, turned, and bent slightly to show off the smooth, firm, fuckable flesh with which God had blessed him.

As Alex buckled up, Bobby looked deep into his eyes. "Um, um..."

"Alex."

"Yes, Alex! Is this cute blond over here your boyfriend?"

Alex glanced at me and said into the microphone, "No, he's just an old buddy, fresh in from South Dakota, of all places."

Bobby stabbed the microphone in my direction. "So, wanna be a porn star?"

"Um, I haven't even unpacked yet." I felt flush, my face warm and my body uncomfortable. I tried to look away from the glaring light, but it seemed to be coming from everywhere.

"You're totally hot," said Bobby, moving Alex aside and stepping closer to me. I felt his crotch press against my leg and looked right into his beautiful face and shallow blue eyes. Only his disheveled golden bangs hung between us. I couldn't breathe, and it seemed as if the whole universe was just moving way too fast.

"Are you even old enough to be here?" he whispered, and before I could get indignant and say, of course I am, he kissed me, hard and deep, his arms around me, his huge, fat, world famous dick pressed firmly against me, held off only by his leather and my jeans. His lips were strong, and his breath smelled like my uncle's at Christmas.

It was unlike any kiss I'd ever felt—totally unlike Suzy Wallace or Maggie Rogers. I felt possessed, and when he tasted my lower lip before pulling back, I could still feel his faint stubble burning my lips, even as his fingers dug into the crack of my ass. Grinning like a demon, he said, loud enough for the microphone to pick up, "Boy, I'd love to fuck the shit out of you!"

I was, I was—overwhelmed. "Excuse me," I said, pulling away and pushing through the crowd.

"What's up his ass?" shouted Bobby after me.

I heard Alex laughing, "Nothing yet. Nothing yet."

Nothing yet! What a shitwad! I'd spent last night on Alex's couch unable to sleep, thinking about him in his bed, in just his underwear—I imagined—and he, like before, never touched me, even though I'd secretly wanted him to. It was like when we were teens, when I'd sleep over. His body was amazing, even back then, and I was always excited by him, even though I didn't know why.

After he left for UCLA, he still called once a week and sent me stuff and still felt like my best friend. When he told me he was gay, we had a long talk. It was late and my parents were asleep, and what I told him made me tremble with fear. I felt the same way, maybe—I didn't know. That's when he sent me the porno. "Maybe you are, maybe you're not," he said. "Never hurts to find out."

But now, I was in California, away from Sioux Falls, and now I could find out, and Sioux Falls might not ever know. I was staying with Alex, living in his high-priced apartment, paid for by Daddy, and Alex told me not to worry, said I could stay as long as I needed, said he was thrilled just to have me around again. "It's too late for this semester," he said when I looked down on his college from his balcony, "but maybe you can apply for the spring, and it'll be just like it used to be." I wasn't sure I could take that. I wasn't sure what I could take.

I made my way deeper into the party, bumping up against stud after stud, every now and then feeling the attention of the occasional old, rich man and the weight of his lecherous stare. Beyond the tented space was the actual studio, a huge cube-like room that was filled with loud music and shirtless hunks and drag queens of every size and shape. I stood there, at the entrance, getting shoved around by people walking in and out.

Taking a sip of my Cape Cod, half of it already sticking to my hand, I tried to relax, to accept, not to be afraid. And as I looked from my right to my left and turned around, I saw her, Dada Cherille, making her way toward me. With every step, she said hello to someone new, and the crowd opened up for her and her entourage of close friends—friends like Rod Icon, Kirk Angel, and even Tina Crystal. I'd seen them all in a couple of magazines I bought once, and here they were, the nasty elite of this illicit industry.

Dada was more outrageous than I thought. Tall and heavy, she separated the room with a pair of large breasts that had the illusion of exploding out from her strapless leather teddy.

As she moved past me, she looked down and smiled, and even though I couldn't figure out if I was nothing to her or the most important guy in the room, in that one, brief moment, I felt blessed. Still, she walked on, stopping to sit on a couch at the opposite end of the room while her close friends surrounded her, positioning themselves like slaves in a harem.

"What could we have here?" said someone next to me. I turned my head and saw another drag queen, short and scary-looking, starring back at me, her pale skin, green lips and excessive eye shadow making her look like a nightmare beneath a dark red wig. "Hello," she said, "I'm Amy Nitrate. What's your name? Stud!"

"Billy."

"Oooh, really—? How innocent of you." She quickly grabbed my hand and pulled me with her toward Dada.

In moments, we were standing before the queen of porn. "Happy birthday, Dada. Look what I brought you." Suddenly, I was pushed forward and guided to sit next to the legend herself.

"Gee, Amy, what on earth is it?" said Dada, touching my arms and my cheek.

"It's a Billy, Dada, and they're very, very rare."

"I'll say," said Dada. "What does it do?"

Amy Nitrate grinned evilly, her green lips sparkling from a thick coat of glitter. "I don't think even it knows that."

"Really," said Dada. "Let's find out." Dada looked me in the eye. "Billy, what do you do?"

I looked around. Kirk Angel was staring intently. Rick Icon simply looked bored. "Nothing, yet," I said, and Dada laughed robustly, and all her friends laughed with her.

"Oh, that is a clever answer. Thank you, Amy, I think I'll keep it." And with that, Dada stood and pulled me along. I thought to protest or escape, but it just didn't seem like something that should be done. I was in L.A. now, and, well, when in Rome...right?

To say L.A. was different than Sioux Falls wasn't even near the mark. I had never met a drag queen before tonight. Hell, I hadn't even heard the term before I was in high school. Alex told me about them one time while we hid out in a rehearsal room during drama class. He was talking about Mr. Bender, our school's drama teacher. Alex said, "You know he does drag, don't you?"

"Drag?" I said.

"Yeah," he said. "He's a big fuckin' faggot, and he dresses like Patty Duke in a drag show on weekends."

"You mean he—?"

"Oh yeah," said Alex, "and he takes it up the ass, too."

My stomach turned at the image, and my skin felt warm. This new information confused me. I had always thought that Mr. Bender was such a nice man.

Back in what I guessed was the VIP room, Kirk asked me more about myself. Where I was from, where I was going—that sort of thing. As we talked, he played with a small brown vial that had a pink plastic top on it, making the thing look like a bullet. Putting it to a nostril, he sniffed something out of it.

"Is that—?" I asked.

"No," he said with a smile, "it's just coke. Want some?"

He set himself up with another hit, and then prepared one for me. I looked at the plastic bullet and wondered if this was the right thing to do. A bit amused, Dada looked at me and asked, "Have you ever done drugs?"

"No," I said.

"Have you ever been with a guy?"

"No, not yet," I said.

"Hmm, well, they feel almost the same."

"Really?"

"Yes, Billy." Dada paused as she blatantly studied me. "Billy, how old are you?"

"Nineteen."

"Well, considering that it's my 34th birthday, I have two words of advice for you… Do. Everything."

Kirk went to put the bullet under my nostril when Bobby Godrod slammed into the VIP room pulling Alex behind him. "Oh, there you are," shouted Bobby. "We've been looking all over. You didn't think you could get away from me that easy, did you?"

Alex looked perplexed. "Bobby, what are you doing?"

"Nothing." I pulled away from Kirk's bullet and rubbed my nose.

"Are you doing drugs?!" asked Alex, surprised, laughing.

"No, Alex, I didn't do any."

"Whatever," said Alex just before Dada bellowed: "Goddamnit, Billy, I want to see you suck some cock!"

"Excuse me?" I yelped. Even Alex looked shocked.

"Alex, is it? Whip out your cock!"

Alex stared at Dada in disbelief.

"Bobby, you whip out your cock, too. This boy's never tasted it, and tonight's his night."

From the sofa on which I was sitting, I looked straight ahead to see Bobby Godrod open his fly and let his cock fall out. Half hard when it hit the air, it grew within seconds, and by the time Bobby gripped it in a fist, the fucker was fully erect and ready to go.

Alex stood next to Bobby, his eyes turned downward to that famous cock. I stared at it, too, thinking about how it fit up Alex's ass. Up close, it didn't seem possible. "What are you waiting for?" shouted Dada. "Get down there and suck some cock!"

Bobby was looking right into my eyes. He smiled, stroking his thing just two feet from my face. Alex turned to Dada. "I can't do this. Billy's my best friend."

"I don't care if he's your brother. Whip out your cock and let him suck it, motherfucker, or get the fuck out of my party!"

Alex laughed and started undoing his black jeans. "Alright, whatever," he said, but when he finally exposed himself, he was hard and beautiful and leaking from the tip.

I just stared at it. I'd been wanting to see Alex's stuff since puberty, and here it was, right within reach—not as oversized as Bobby's, but still substantial and, well, just about perfect. Bobby stroked it a bit, pulling me out of my trance. I looked up to Alex's loving, I'll-always-be-there-for-you smile. "Go ahead," he said. "I don't mind."

Feeling like none of this could be real, I mindlessly did what Dada ordered. "Get on your knees, bitch!" And I got on my knees. "Put that cock in your mouth!" I looked from Bobby to Alex, from ultimate porn star fantasy to my best friend from back home, and I did it; I put it in my mouth; I opened up and let it slide in, so caught up in the intensity of the moment, I went all the way down and didn't even gag. And it was love, I could tell. It was love.

And he tasted like something wonderful, like something you've craved your entire life but never gotten to try, until now. And now, it was like heaven, and as I worked the cock in and out of my throat, back and forth, over my tongue, across my wet lips, I didn't even have to think about what I was doing or how to do it right. I just did it, and I don't know if it felt good for him, but it felt amazing for me, and I must have been doing something right, because Dada kept yelling things like, "Yeah, work that cock, bitch!" and "Go all the way down on that fucker!"

I pulled off of it to catch my breath, and as I licked up the shaft and tasted the thick fluid leaking from the piss hole, I opened my eyes and saw Alex, my friend, flush and excited, grinning expressively as if his whole body had been dipped in pure joy. "Oh, man, Billy, you're good."

I smiled proudly as he held the base of his cock and rubbed the head of his prick on my wet, sloppy lips, the smell of his sex now sticking to my nose.

Feeling Bobby's cock bat up against my cheek, I turned toward it, realizing I had been ignoring him. I opened for him and let him enter, and even though he was bigger than Alex, I did my best to make him feel just as good.

Trapped in my jeans, I think I was harder than I had ever been in my entire life. I was painfully hard, but I kept sucking cock, just like Dada ordered.

"Okay," the drag queen shouted, "enough! Boys, put your cocks away. I've got to go back to the party. I stood up only to feel Dada's fingers wiping the spit from my chin. "You're a good cocksucker, Billy," she said just before handing me a small card. "We're having a small party. I'd love for you and Alex to attend."

I reached for the card, and she pulled it away from me. "This is just for you and Alex, understand?"

"Yes," I said, and she handed me the card before walking past me and out into the party. I turned to see Alex tucking in his shirt. Bobby kissed me as he walked out. "We're still friends, right?" I said to Alex as soon as everybody left.

"What?" he said. "Oh, don't even worry about it. This was nothing." And with that, Alex walked from the room and gestured for me to follow.

When I was a little kid, about eight or so, I followed Alex home for the first time to play his new Super Nintendo that his dad bought him.

It was fun and we were a good match for each other at the various games we played. We grew closer, doing Cub Scouts and baseball. For awhile, when I was twelve, Alex's dad was thinking about moving to New York. I almost stopped being Alex's friend the day he told me, the idea hurt so much. I felt I'd never have another friend like him. It's a good thing his dad decided to just expand his business in Sioux Falls. I still have yet to meet a guy like Alex.

It was after three in the morning when we pulled up to the Asgard Hotel on Sunset, high above West Hollywood. Alex handed the keys over to the valet, and I let Bobby Godrod and Davy Bottoms out of the backseat. "This is gonna be so cool," said Davy, and I suddenly understood why Alex called boys like him tweakers. As we stood in front of the hotel, Davy's dilated eyes took in everything as if he had to see the entirety of the hotel all at once. As we walked through the posh, well-lit, marble-floored lobby, Davy had to check out everything, and it all seemed so fascinating to him. I can only imagine what was bouncing around inside his head.

When the doors opened to Dada's suite, it was like stepping into another world. Hot guys walked around shirtless. Drag queens did lines off the dining room table. And, over in the bedroom, I could see men sucking cock and getting fucked, their clothes still on but their jeans pulled down past their muscular thighs.

Not a few feet into the fray, I was instantly abandoned by my new and old friends. Dada sat on a sofa with three apparently new porn stars and looked up at me. "Oh good," she cheered, "somebody remembered to bring my Billy to the party!" The other drag queens and gorgeous hunks around her at the time followed her pointing finger with lackluster interest. Tina and Kirk were among them, but it seemed that they didn't remember meeting me.

Taking a stab at proper after-party etiquette, I walked up to Dada and gave her a kiss on the cheek. "Happy birthday again, Dada."

Dada smiled up at me. "Never mind that, darling. Let me see your cock." I was stunned. I was speechless. I had everybody's eyes on me.

"Oh," sighed Dada, "enough of the innocent crap. Let's see your cock." And my fly was ripped open and my cock was pulled out. As all the guys and drag queens stared, I grew hard. Dada grinned like the Cheshire Cat as fluid leaked from the tip. Nervous, I glanced from face to face. All eyes were focused on my crotch.

Dada took it in hand and I felt her power. She was the queen of all she surveyed, and if I wanted to belong, I had to do as she decreed. I grew fully engorged within one or two strokes. This whole thing excited me like I had never been excited before. It was sinful and decadent and I had spent my entire adolescence in a small town dreaming of an orgy just like this.

Slowly, all the while looking up to gage my reaction, she bent forward and licked the dewy tip. I didn't flinch. Refusing to be intimidated by this city or its queer elite, I gripped the base of my cock and slapped the head against Dada's extended tongue.

Dada moaned and wrapped her mouth around my cock, letting her garish lipstick smear as my shaft sank down her throat. Now I was the one grinning as all the guys around me, including Alex, stared.

I may have been a country mouse, but I was quickly learning how things were done in the big city, and they weren't all that different. Sure, costumes were more extreme and modesty less apparent, but when it came to sex, everyone was basically the same. And that was a theory I was ready to prove.

Drawing from a story I once heard in the locker room, I thrust my cock forward and spit out: "Yeah, suck that cock!"

Dada pulled off and looked up at me. Everyone's jaws dropped. Dada chuckled a bit. "What?" she said, with a slightly indignant smile.

I started to lose my nerve. "I said—um…"

Dada put my cock to her lips, which, for reasons I couldn't figure out, still looked perfectly painted. She touched her teeth to the underside and the hole, still grinning, but this time she looked even more mischievous.

Suddenly, she slapped my cock away from her mouth. "Get the fuck away from me, you nasty bitch!"

I stepped back.

"And put that cock away!" she yelled before laughing along with her entourage.

I looked over at Alex. Laughing like everyone else, he took my hand and led me to the bedroom. I was a bit stunned. "What the fuck was that about?" I asked.

"Don't stress over it," he said. "She's just teasing you."

I glanced around and realized that Alex had led me into the middle of an orgy. We were surrounded by porn stars and other hot studs, and before my eyes could even adjust to the darkness, Alex was on his knees, heaving my hard cock out of my jeans.

"What are you doing?" I asked.

"Just getting a closer look," he said before closing his eyes and sucking down my cock despite it being coated from head to base with Dada's spit. I can't even begin to describe how it felt. It wasn't just the sensation. There was a whole wave of backstory that hit the moment his lips touched my cock. Just the sight of him was an image I'd already jacked off to over and over again. The understanding of being on his lips, in his mouth, was a familiar part of my dreams. He reached up and held my nuts, rubbed my groin and inched a finger closer to my hole. It was unbelievable, not because this was new, but because it wasn't. It was déjà vu.

"Turn around," Alex whispered, and, without questioning, I just did what he wanted. He pressed down on the small of my back as he pulled my jeans down to my ankles, and I bent forward slowly and put my hands on the bed. Before me, a mass of about eight bodies writhed and throbbed, and as I felt Alex's tongue lick along the crack of my ass, hands reached out to me and tugged at my shirt.

It was dark and it was hard to make out details, but the bodies in front of me were like one huge flower, its tendrils pulling me in. As I fell, Alex opened my ass with his fingers and dove in with his tongue. I'd never experienced anything like this. I was lost to it, filled by it. It was like floating on a cloud and sinking into the grave, and as I gasped out for breath, lips closed on mine, and mouths kissed me, and hands covered my skin and pulled on whatever they could grip.

I opened my eyes and recognized Davy sucking Bobby's cock, and I felt anchored by Bobby's friendly smile as he handed a condom over my back. I panicked for a moment, but the tongue kept washing my insides, and Bobby kissed me before I could begin to voice my fear.

When Alex's tongue was replaced by his cock, my hole was soaked with lube and was wet and aching to be filled. This was the moment. I pulled away from Bobby and looked back at Alex standing behind me. He was looking down at my ass, rubbing his cock up and down my crack and slapping his shaft against the small of my back. His shirt was gone and his body was as perfect as I remembered it. He looked up and met my eyes. Grinning like he had when he first asked me over to play Super Nintendo, he aimed his cock at my ass and pushed a little bit, only enough for me to feel the pressure, the tension, the understanding of what was about to spread me open and use me for its pleasure.

When Alex had walked toward his plane to fly to LA and UCLA, I stood in the airport with his father. It was the strangest moment. I wanted to cry, but I wouldn't let myself do it. It was hard and painful and it felt like dying. Everything I had was gone and I was left with emptiness. It was like my whole life, at that point, had been for nothing, and still, I didn't even understand it at the time. I could only express my feelings for Alex, even to myself, in terms like "friend" or "buddy." So much had changed, and now I had a whole bunch of new terms; but, still, I didn't know how to describe what Alex meant to me and, for some reason, the word for me and Alex seemed important. In that one single moment, as the pressure increased, I wanted a word for what was going on. I wanted a means to encapsulate it, examine it, understand it, a way to control it and give it to the world. And then, like a bullet, the next moment exploded into my life, and suddenly, words didn't seem so important anymore.

"Fuck!" I shouted, and Bobby's arms held me as I slammed forward, desperate to pull myself off of the tremendous cock that had just pushed only a few inches inside. "Shit! Shit! Shit!" I pounded, each breath fired out like shells from artillery.

"Easy," whispered Bobby, stroking my back. "Just relax."

Davy looked straight into my tearing eyes. "Oh man," he moaned, "this is so fuckin' cool."

Alex eased out a bit and eased in a bit more. "FU—!" Bobby kissed me before I could shout any more, and Alex took the opportunity to claim another inch while gently stroking my ass and sides.

Still, I couldn't open up to it. My ass burned and clenched down on the cock that threatened it. My eyes were wet as I forced air in and out of my lungs like I was a woman giving birth. I was dizzy with pain and barely noticed Bobby reposition himself, shoving his cock in my face. He rubbed it against my lips and, for some reason, just the smell opened my ass enough for Alex to sneak past some hidden ring and bury himself all the way to his pubes.

I gasped, but Bobby rubbed his cock on my tongue. "Open up," he ordered.

"No!" I pushed my head away, too overwhelmed by the fire in my ass. "Suck my fuckin' cock, boy!" shouted Bobby, grabbing my face and pushing his cock past my tongue. I gagged on the thickness and pushed back, slamming myself on Alex's cock and opening up even more.

"Yeah," said Alex, "suck that cock and give me your ass. Oh, yeah, you fuckin' like that, don't ya?!"

Suddenly, it was like I wasn't even there. There was just my body and two cocks going at it. I gave Bobby full access to my throat and glanced down for a second to see Davy lapping at Bobby's low-hanging nuts. My ass was looser now, but it still burned. I didn't even care, and Alex was free to fuck me, thrusting his cock forward and pulling it out. Each movement, in and out, hurt like a motherfucker, but it didn't seem to matter. Somewhere, deep inside, it felt good, really good, and I loved the taste of Bobby's cock and the musky scent of his crotch and the gentle tickle of Davy's tongue on my lower lip every time Bobby filled my mouth full of cock.

Other guys started joining in, and I felt a mouth on my cock and could, for a second or two, see Bobby sucking the dick of a guy who stood on the bed, his foot just below my chin.

Alex was pounding my ass by now, and as some guy's mouth worked my cock, I felt close to squirting down his throat. I held back and held back, not wanted to be the first to go and, thank God, it wasn't me.

It was Bobby, and I tasted him get salty just before he pulled out and pelted my face with his warm, sticky cum. It dripped down my forehead and neck, down to the foot on the bed, and the guy at my crotch quickly pulled off and let my own jizz explode from my slit. My ass tightened on Alex's cock, and I could feel Davy's convulsing body vibrate the bed. Alex pulled out and turned me over with rough hands. I watched as he ripped off the condom and stroked his cock between my legs. "I want you to see this," he said but, just then, the standing guy let loose, and his cum rained down on my chest. Alex didn't even noticed as his cum erupted and rocketed over my stomach and chest to smack me in the face. Two, three, four, five loads of cum burst from his cock, each wad landing on a different part of my body.

As he finished, his body shook and he fell forward, his sweat sliding on my skin. Weak and vulnerable, he kissed me. It was soft and wet and felt like it contained the only strength he had left. It was an interesting image, like he had walked here, to West Hollywood, all the way from Sioux City, just so he could kiss me.

After a long pause, Alex looked up past my chin. "I guess we should get cleaned up."

I grinned shyly. "Yeah, I guess."

Alex stood and helped me up. Taking my hand, he led me to the bathroom as more guys moved in to take our place. Naturally, Dada was bent at a corner of the bed with a burly porn star's cock buried in her throat. As we stepped around her, half naked and dripping with cum, she pulled off and looked up.

"So, slut!" she said with a wicked grin. "Did ya get enough cock?"

"More than enough," I said politely, "thank you."

With that, Alex and I stepped into the bathroom and shut the door.

We stood before the sink, side by side, washing cum off our skin. "So," said Alex, "did you have a good time?"

"Yeah," I said, "it was great."

Alex kissed my shoulder, and some piece inside me suddenly twisted out of shape. "I did too."

Alex took a washcloth and started wiping off my face. "Maybe we could fuck again tomorrow."

"No," I said, "that hurt way too fucking much."

Alex smiled and kissed me briefly. "Okay," he said before kissing me again and putting his arms around my waist. "I'm sorry I hurt you."

"I'll be fine," I said, pressing up against his chest.

"How 'bout we stay in all day and play Mario Kart, and I'll wait 'til you're ready."

I kissed him more passionately. "Or," I said, "I could fuck you."

Alex chuckled a bit. "Yeah, we could do that, too."

THE SUMMER BLOW JOB

Bryan Nakai

"BRYAN, YOU PROMISED YOU'D GET ME MOUNTED BY DINNERTIME!"

Okay, before you go thinking this is one of those stories, let me explain that I work summers at the Lazy Q Dude Ranch. Actually, to be honest, it is one of those stories, but Mr. Spencer was just tired of practicing on the mechanical pony. I saddled Molasses for him, hoping she'd live up to her name this afternoon.

Once I had Mr. Spencer happily ambling around the corral, I left him to the trail guides, and started on my chores in the barn. I bent over the feed bin, scooping up oats.

My ass got hit hard—like a swarm of bees.

I jumped, dropping the bucket of oats and clapping both hands to my ass and trying not to howl. Tears stung my eyes.

Ben grinned at me from the nearest stall. The bridle he'd been cleaning hung from his fingers, and I knew he'd slapped me with those long reins. My ass felt like I'd sat down on a branding iron. I swallowed hard, so I wouldn't let him know how much it hurt.

"I thought nobody could ever sneak up on an Indian," he joked as he hung up the rest of the gear.

I gritted my teeth and returned to the feed bin. This time, though, I didn't turn my back on the self-styled King Jokester, but shoveled sweet feed with one hand while I kept watch on my backside. Ben only chuckled. He'd been working outside that morning; his arms and face were nearly as red as his hair. No amount of sunscreen ever seemed to prevent him from reddening. When I could talk without showing hurt, anger, and everything else, I mentioned that fact aloud.

"At least I'm red on a place I'm not ashamed for anybody to see!" he retorted.

I gave up and went to fill the feed troughs. Ben wasn't worth it. So what if his blue eyes twinkled like the sky just after sunset? So what if his lean, muscular body had been the subject of far too many of my late night fantasies? Just because I knew I was gay didn't mean I had to jump at every man I passed.

Well, okay—I had yet to jump at any man. I hadn't exactly grown up in the big city, after all. I wasn't really sure how a gay man was supposed to act. And how did they ever find one another? I could never tell if the man I was drooling over was likely to drool back or reach for a shotgun. Maybe real gay men had some sort of signal, something I hadn't learned growing up out in the country. Not even a year of college had taught me anything about real life.

I finished my chores. Ben might've been cute, but he was probably as straight as all the rest of the guys on this ranch. I wasn't about to risk what little status I'd gained by branding myself as gay in addition to being one of the new guys.

At least, I was in the majority when Ben tried his tricks on me. His jokes were pretty much the stuff of legend among the regular staff. They ranged from the garden-variety prank, all the way up to the Jokester Special. The latest Special, I'd been warned, had involved a new hire; a wheelbarrow full of manure, quick-drying cement, and a camcorder hooked into the ranch security cameras.

The staff had sworn revenge—of course, my cabinmates freely admitted to swearing revenge every summer without success. Now, my ass throbbing like it was on fire, I joined the others in the dinner line. They needed only one look at my face to see that I was the latest victim of Ben's attempts at humor.

"Somebody needs to put that guy into his place," Craig muttered. Craig, a lanky blond, had the top bunk to my bottom, and a tendency toward late night chats. I merely nodded grumpily. Fine words, but who could out-joke the Jokester?

The line fell silent suddenly. Ben appeared in the doorway, then strutted inside. I pretended not to see him as he strolled up the line. He never actually had to break in line—nobody wanted to wake up with itch powder in their jockey shorts, so most anybody would offer him a place.

"Look out!" Ben shouted at a novice who'd just reached for one of the "authentic" tin trail plates. "Those just came out of the oven!"

The greenhorn yelped, knocking an entire stack of plates to the floor with a loud clatter. Ben slapped his knee and let out a guffaw, then slid in line before the blushing newbie—who was trying to gather the cold plates and return them to the counter.

That did it. I elbowed Craig.

"War meeting, our cabin, after lights-out," I ordered. I watched Ben load his plate, completely unaware of the plot spreading down the line behind him.

The next morning, we set Project Payback into motion. I got up early, then waited until I saw Ben head to the shower room. I high-tailed it after him, waving to Craig to assemble the guys at the corral.

Pasting a scowl onto my face, I strode into the shower room, shedding my shorts as I entered. Ben averted his eyes as I approached. I paused for an appreciative glance at his pale, muscular body.

His thighs bulged with muscle from hours of horseback riding. His chest and upper arms were wirier, with sparse red hair that matched his carrot-colored head. His body was covered with freckles—so many that in places they fused into pale brown spots. His cock was especially nice: not enormous or anything, but well proportioned, with a nice, firm set of balls beneath. As though it knew somebody was watching, it began to harden in front of me, thickening to half-mast.

Ben flushed a bright red, and turned away, trying to hide the evidence of his arousal. I was amused that his blush didn't stop at the neck, but crept downwards to cover the chest and back as well. I couldn't spend the morning admiring him, though—I was here to teach him a lesson.

"This is all your fault!" I shouted, closing the distance between us. "I was finally going to get to lead a trail ride but, thanks to you, I'm stuck back in the stable today!"

The latter was true, but only because I'd traded with somebody. I just couldn't face the thought of spending the day with my ass bouncing up and down in the saddle.

I got right in his face and yelled. "Look at what you did!"

He tried to turn away, but I'd backed him against the wall. He dropped his eyes, then flushed deeper as he found himself staring at my cock, which was (I'm not modest) quite a bit thicker than his own. I smothered a grin at his expression.

"Not that, you asshole," I growled, whirling away to shove my ass towards him. "I'm talking about that!"

The stripes had ripened to a rich, dark purple, swollen into a perfect outline of each bridle strap. I turned back, to see a horrified expression on Ben's face.

"I didn't—" he stammered.

"Yes, you did! You always do! And you think it's so damn funny."

I grabbed him, twisting one arm behind his back. "The rest of us are going to show you just how funny you can be," I said in as threatening a voice as I could manage. My cock was enjoying the feel of his wet, slippery body against mine, and I was having a difficult time concentrating on our revenge.

He bellowed as I shoved him out the door. I tightened my grip as he struggled frantically to free himself. The sight of the staff gathered around the corral did nothing for his self-confidence. Two of the others rushed forward and helped me wrestle Ben to the fence.

I explained things to him as they lashed his wrists and ankles to the posts. "We've decided we're tired of your little jokes. Nobody enjoys them but you—and you're not important enough to run our lives."

"Guys—" Ben said, twisting in his bonds. He tried a nervous giggle. "Okay, okay, I get the point. I'll cut out the practical jokes, honest."

"Yes," I informed him. "You will." I gestured, and two of the guys dragged the charcoal smoker from the gate to Ben's side. We'd started it burning about an hour ago, and the coals were white-hot. The branding iron resting inside caught Ben's attention immediately.

"Wait a minute, guys!" he yelped. "You can't do that! This is crazy!"

"So are your stupid jokes," I said, pulling the iron out of the fire. Ben twisted to watch me, his face as white as the snow on top the nearby mountains. He struggled against the ropes, bucking against the fence. I nodded.

This was the signal for three guys to "hold him down" for me. Actually, they were just blocking Ben's view of me while I switched the hot iron for the one we'd kept in the freezer all night.

"This should teach you to have more respect for other people's feelings," I shouted, pressing the icy metal to his quivering asscheek. Ben screamed.

"What the hell is going on out there?!" a bass voice bellowed from the cabin across the corral. Oops. The foreman must have slept in—usually he was in the barn by this time, posting the day's chores. We must have interrupted his shower, for his burly body was dripping wet. He strode out his door wearing nothing more than a pair of boots and the thick coat of hair that covered him from the neck down.

Everyone spoke at once. "Y'see boss—" "It's like this—" "We were just—"

"QUIET!"

Fixing his eye on the only other naked bodies on the ranch, the foreman crossed the corral in ten swift strides to stand before us, his brawny hands resting on his slim hips. The guys parted before his anger like the Red Sea before Moses.

"What the devil are you boys doing with my brands?" he bellowed. "Those are not toys!"

He snatched the iron from my hand, tested the metal with one finger, then glared at me. "If you ruined this iron, so help me—"

Ben squealed. "They burned me! Call the cops!"

The foreman gave him the same glare I'd gotten. "This iron's colder than a witch's tit, you asshole. Quit whining and get to work."

The guys scattered as the foreman cast his glare over the crowd. I hung my head and untied Ben's arms and legs. His face was red again, but this time it was probably anger instead of embarrassment.

"We—er—we didn't mean to bother you, boss," I started to apologize. Then my gaze fell on the foreman's doorway, and my voice died in my throat. The ranch owner had appeared on the stoop. He was zipping his trousers. His hair dripped water onto his naked chest. I watched him cross the corral, unable to make a sound.

"Would anyone care to enlighten us?" the owner asked, his voice a soft purr.

I swallowed hard. My mind was no longer on Project Payback—it was on the shocking image of the owner and the foreman sharing a shower. I felt my face flame as the images flashed through my mind: two furry chests pressed tightly together—brawny, masculine hands and arms entwined—bearded lips kissing! Through the fog, I heard Ben's voice.

"It was just a practical joke, sir."

The owner glowered. "Practical jokes are juvenile, young man. And they're not funny."

"I know that, sir," Ben replied. Then he added, so softly that only I heard, "now."

The owner and foreman turned away, the latter retrieving both branding irons before leaving. I heard the owner ask softly, "Dinner tonight?" and saw the foreman's nod. My head was spinning.

I vaguely noticed Ben feeling his ass for marks. He had a sheepish expression on his face, and his upper body was bright red with embarrassment. I somehow stumbled back to the cabin, dressed, and found myself in the barn doing my chores. Suddenly, Ben was beside me.

"I'm—I want to apologize," he said. "I never meant to hit you that hard."

I turned a glare in his direction. He looked down, scuffing his sneakers against the floor. His face was still bright red.

"I just wanted you to—to notice me," he muttered. "Everybody always laughs, but nobody ever really sees me—the real me."

"Maybe if you'd quit joking long enough—"

"I know," he said. "I promise, no more stupid jokes." He looked up, and I saw fear in his eyes. "Do you think we could be friends?"

I shook my head. "I'm not sure. You never let me get to know you before."

He grinned. "What do you want to know?"

I swear, it slipped out before I could stop it. "What's going on between the foreman and the owner?" I clapped a hand to my mouth, but it was too late.

Ben let out a laugh. "Where are you from, Mars? Those two have been an item since Day 1."

"You mean—?" I could barely get the words out, I was so excited. "You mean they're gay?"

Another guffaw. "No, the foreman's just a real hairy woman—of course they're gay!"

Ben's eyes suddenly narrowed. He stepped close. "Why?"

I found myself taking a step back. "I—er—I just wondered…"

Ben looked pointedly at my crotch. "Looks like you were doing more than wondering, pal."

My face flamed. I could hardly deny that the front of my work pants bulged as though my cock was trying to rip its way out. When Ben lowered one hand to gently cup the bulge, I nearly jumped out of my skin.

"You want to find out what it's like?" he asked, his voice barely above a whisper. His face was only inches from mine, and I stared into his twinkling blue eyes in shock. Almost without my knowing it, my hand moved to his face, to trace the high cheekbones and angular jaw. He closed his eyes and smiled.

"I'll take that for a yes. Shall we borrow the hayloft while everybody's on the trail ride?"

My heart thudded like a drum as we climbed the ladder to the loft. Either I was about to make the stupidest move in my life—or all my dreams were about to come true.

Ben gently peeled my T-shirt over my head. He paused, with my arms trapped in the shirt, to kiss me roughly. My response startled me. I leaned against him, mouth open. He tasted so good—I had no words to describe his taste, but I knew instantly that I liked it. I couldn't get enough of his mouth.

I struggled out of the shirt and wrapped my arms around him. I had no idea that a kiss could be so wonderful. He broke off long enough to shrug out of his shirt, and the feel of his bare chest against mine took my breath away. Our hands wandered over each other, sliding over hard muscle. Both of us were sweating, and the smell of his body was intoxicating. Soon, Ben lowered his head. His lips moved over my chest, tweaking electrical surges from my nipples. I shifted from one foot to the other, not sure that I could stand the sensation. My fingers balled into fists in his short hair. I felt his fingers at my buckle, and my legs trembled. He slid my pants slowly down my legs. I stepped out of them, and he caught my hand and tugged me down beside him on the hay.

We kissed again. Time stood still for me—we might have kissed for only a few moments, but it seemed like hours. My cock throbbed between my legs. At last, Ben stood up and wriggled out of his pants. The sight of his hard cock underneath his white jockey shorts was too much for me. I reached out to run my hand over that thick bulge. He shivered beneath my touch, and dropped to his knees beside me.

"I've wanted to do this ever since they hired you," he whispered, burrowing his face in my hair. "You're so hot."

I couldn't think of anything to say to that, so I ran my hands down his back and slid them underneath his shorts. His ass quivered, and he shoved his hips forward against me. I squeezed gently, enjoying the sensation of another man's ass beneath my hands. Ben had just enough hair to let me know he wasn't a girl. I decided I liked that better than having to dig through a thick pelt like the foreman had. I worked my fingers into his crack, and he spread his legs.

When I felt the tight pucker of his asshole, I nearly passed out from excitement. It was time to 'fess up, though. I hadn't a clue what would make him feel good.

"I don't have any idea what I'm supposed to do," I whispered shamefully.

Ben pulled me into a tight embrace. "That's okay. I'm a good teacher. Why don't you just lie back and let me give you a few lessons."

Feeling the flutter of an army of butterflies in my stomach, I did so. The hay prickled against my back. Ben worked my shorts off and tossed them to one side. He slid down until he knelt at my waist, then pushed his hands beneath my ass.

"Spread your legs and relax," he urged. I gasped as I felt his fingers slither into the crack of my ass, but I spread my legs.

Ben moved to a position between my legs. He moved his hands around so that his arms supported my legs, lifting and spreading them even further. I clenched my fists in the hay beneath my head as his fingers explored my ass. I'd never felt anything but my own hands down there, and the flutter of strong, male fingers set my cock to throbbing again.

Ben ran his finger all around my puckered hole. I could feel his breath on my cock and balls, and knew he was watching my asshole spasm with delight. Suddenly, a hot mouth closed over my balls. I nearly leaped straight off the floor.

"Whoa, there," Ben said. I could hear the laughter in his voice. "Settle down, now, you bucking bronco."

"Sorry." My face was flaming again. "I—"

"You're new at this, I know. I'm not going to hurt you, though. Just relax and let an old hand break you in—gently."

I stretched back out on the hay and tried to follow his instructions. Every muscle in my body trembled. Ben lowered his head again, and I felt his tongue on my ball-sac. A moan slipped past my lips before I could stop it. Damn, I'd never felt anything so good in my life!

As Ben's hot tongue lapped at my balls, I felt his finger slide gently inside my virgin hole. At first, I wanted to tighten up. It felt like I had to take a crap. Then, his probing finger hit something deep within my ass that had me jerking around like I was hooked up to electricity.

My hips gyrated against the hay, grinding my ass down on Ben's finger. I wasn't sure if I could stop, even if I wanted to—and I sure didn't want to! I felt a second finger press against my hole, and tried to relax so it would fit inside. With a lot of squirming, Ben managed to fit both fingers up my ass.

"We're gonna need some lube," he muttered. "Reach behind you and grab that jar off the shelf."

I stretched out one arm to the makeshift shelf tacked onto one wall of the loft. After I fumbled around and knocked down a spool of baling twine, a utility knife, and a bottle of sunscreen, I clamped my hand over a tube. I pulled it down and looked at it.

"KY Jelly??" I squeaked. "You keep a tube of KY up here?"

Ben chuckled. "Why do you think I'm late for dinner 'most every night? There ought to be some condoms up there too."

My eyes widened. This was it, then—I was about to lose my

cherry. I fumbled on the shelf until I located a foil packet, and handed that and the KY to my partner. Then it hit me. "There are other gay guys working here?"

Ben laughed so hard I saw tears in his eyes. "Man, you are so green I ought to put you back on the tree to ripen! Tell you what: just let ole Ben break you to the saddle, and I'll introduce you around after dinner."

My eyes nearly popped out of my head, but I nodded. Ben slowly lowered his head. His tongue shot out, leaving a hot, wet trail up the shaft of my cock. My legs quivered. Ben slurped at my cock like a kid with a candy cane, until the entire shaft was dripping with saliva. Then, he closed his lips over the swollen, throbbing head. I leaned my head back and closed my eyes, groaning with pleasure.

Ben slowly worked my cock into his mouth. My breath came in short pants by the time he got the entire thing inside. I barely kept myself from thrusting hard into his throat, but I was afraid I might hurt him if I was too rough. When he started a gentle rhythm, my hips bounced against the hay. I whimpered, like a puppy that wanted a treat.

I barely noticed Ben's hand working the KY into my ass. Suddenly, his mouth was gone, and I felt his strong hand close over my cock.

"Don't want you coming too quick," Ben muttered. "Not your first time, anyway."

I raised my head. He'd ripped open the condom packet, and was rolling the sheath onto his cock with his other hand. I could smell the KY now, and the latex, mixed with the scent of my pre-cum and the sweat dripping from both our bodies. I wriggled against him, eager for him to enter me.

When I felt his hard cock pressing against my hole, I tensed a bit, anticipating the pain I'd always read about. But Ben didn't shove inside like they always did in those smut stories. Instead, he pressed slowly forward—just a tiny bit—then paused. After a moment, he pushed forward a little more. It took a minute before the head of his cock was completely past my sphincter. His hand stroked my cock as he entered me—just enough to keep me squirming, but not enough to bring me to climax.

Ben was right—he was breaking me in gently. I felt almost no pain, only a sense of great pressure. I felt like I wanted to crap too, but I knew that was just because my asshole was getting stretched so wide. Once he got the head inside, the KY coated his shaft so that he slid the rest of the way without difficulty. Before I knew it, I had a big, hot cock right where I'd always wanted one.

I felt his pubes brush against my ass, and he paused for a moment. I looked up, and our eyes met. He grinned down at me. "You ready to get ridden, bronco?" he asked, and I nodded breathlessly.

He pulled slowly back, his cock sliding out of my hole. I really felt like I had to crap now, and almost said something. Then, he thrust forward, and that fat shaft caressed my prostate, and I forgot all about everything else. I closed my eyes, spread my legs, and shoved up against him. He let go of my cock, slid both his arms beneath my legs, and started fucking.

My breath came out in a gasp every time he shoved inside. I braced my legs against his chest, then he lifted them to his shoulders, spreading me wide open. His groin slapped against my ass like a blacksmith's hammer on an anvil. My whole body shook with his pounding. And all I could feel was that hard shaft splitting me open.

All too soon, he gave a grunt, and I felt hot cream shooting into the condom deep inside my ass. Ben shoved hard against me, driving himself deep into my hole, then slowly relaxed. I was disappointed that it was over so soon. Then, I felt his hand close over my cock again. "Can't let the bronco go without his reward," he muttered, breathing hard. His hand was slippery with sweat and KY. My cock, which had wilted while he was fucking me, quickly revived. Within seconds, I was shoving forward again, gasping as he pumped my cock. I barely noticed when he pulled his wilting cock from my ass.

I groaned, feeling the hot juice surge up within my balls. Ben's hand moved faster, slapping against my belly. My hips shoved against him, my back arching away from the floor as my balls erupted. I'd never had such an intense climax. It felt like my cock was a firehose, gushing cream all over my chest and belly. I whimpered as Ben pumped me dry, wanting him to stop—but wanting him to go on forever.

When I could think clearly again, Ben had stretched out beside me on the hay. His hand roamed over my chest—not to excite me, but soothingly. I rolled towards him, and our lips met. Our sticky cocks, trapped between us, rubbed together. I could tell from the throb already starting in my balls that I was going to want seconds.

"About that brand—" I muttered, feeling a sudden stab of remorse.

"Forget it," Ben replied. "I reckon we both learned a lesson today—and you're going to be wearing my brand the rest of this summer."

I pulled my face away to look into those twinkling blue eyes. "We'll just see who's wearing the brand, mister," I said. With a twist, I rolled on top of him, then pinned his arms to the hay while I reached for another condom.

He grinned up at me. "Get your iron hot then, 'cause I'm ready for it."

CONFESSIONS OF A CAMP COUNSELOR

J . D . R y a n

"THIS IS WHERE WE'LL BE LIVING FOR THE NEXT FEW MONTHS, GOLDIE."
The head ranger studied me for a moment. "You don't mind if we call
you Goldie, do you?"

I shrugged. With a last name like Goldfarb, I was grateful I wasn't
ending with an even worse nickname. Besides, I was blond. It fit.

I'd signed on for a tour of duty with the State Park Service for the
summer before going to college. For the next few months, I was
going to be the Recreation Specialist at Hamilton State Park, a coastal
park set on an island of a hundred acres of woodland. My main job
was to organize games for the kiddies while Mom and Dad hiked or
swam or went shopping in the nearby town. My partner at the
visitors' center would run the science end of things, educating the
tourists about nature.

Jim, the head ranger, was giving me a quick tour around the cabin
where we would sleep and spend our free time. We had a tiny kitchen,
a communal shower, a living room with a dilapadated sofa and chairs,
and a washer/dryer in a shed outside. Jim and Matthew, the two full
time rangers, had bought niceties like a small color TV set and a
microwave, but I was firmly warned about "playing with them."

As we wound up in the bedroom I'd be sharing with the park
naturalist, Jim gave me a stern glare. "Park staff," he told me, "don't
mingle with visitors."

I nodded. I took his warning to mean I was not supposed to screw
any tourists. That wasn't bad. I'd hardly been the Studmuffin of
Greenbriar High. Of course, coming out of a graduating class of only
thirty, I hadn't had too much choice.

I dropped my duffel bag on the bed and followed Jim back down the sandy pathway to the campsites. The visitors' center was about half a mile from our bunkhouse. Not wanting Jim to think I was some kind of nerd, I did my best to keep up with him along the path. Mostly I ended up trotting behind his tall, lean figure as he strode along.

Jim looked like every picture I'd ever seen of a park ranger: whip-cord strong, dark and rugged from a life spent outdoors. He was clean-shaven, and kept his dark brown hair in a buzz cut. I liked the way his shirt fell open to show a dark V of hair. I wished I looked like that, instead of scrawny and pale.

I stared at the centuries-old pines and oaks shading the path and campsite as we passed through them. We didn't have trees like them on the other side of the state. I promised myself that I'd spend my first day off wandering under their low-hanging limbs. The thick carpet of old leaves and pine needles cushioned the sound as we walked so that I could hear bird's chirping in the trees.

We rounded a curve, and I saw the visitor's center beyond the tents of our early season tourists. Jim informed me that the only visitors I was likely to see today would be hiking, bird-watching, or fishing from the shore, so I could work on the center in peace.

I spent the day cleaning the recreation end of the building. Ted, the naturalist, had worked here the previous summer. While he put his end of the building together, he passed along a lot of information. According to him, we had about a week to get the place ship-shape, before the weather enticed the average family into spending a week together in a tent or camper.

Ted was a short, wiry redhead with enough freckles to play "Connect the Dots" for hours. His shirt was open and I could see that his chest was muscular and covered in a thick mat of carrot-colored hair.

Ted had an odd sense of humor as well, or so I thought at the time. He told me that the two rangers would expect us to help clear trails and repair the signs along them once we'd finished with the visitor's center. Then he winked.

"We'll be all alone in the woods, just the four of us."

I tried to figure that one out, but the meaning eluded me. Finally, I shrugged and went back to tacking brightly colored posters onto the wall. By the end of the day, we had the place looking like a cross between an elementary school classroom and an eccentric scientist's back porch.

We admired each other's displays, then Ted and I posted dozens of neatly-lettered signs on the outside walls, explaining everything from the importance of staying on the park trails to the best way to spot a redheaded woodpecker. Ted explained that, on rainy days, the visitors could congregate under the center's overhang and fight boredom while waiting for the sun to come out.

Throughout the day, we sometimes heard the deep voices of the rangers in the woods—mostly stuff like "look out for that rotten log," or "poison ivy over here." Occasionally, we'd hear a quickly-stifled curse. For some reason, whenever the voices were especially loud, I'd look over to find Ted watching me with a funny smirk on his face.

"They must be pretty hot and sweaty by now," he said at one point, waggling his eyebrows at me. I had no idea what he might be trying to tell me, but I was starting to feel distinctly uncomfortable.

We finally reached the point when Ted suggested we call it a day. On the way back to the bunkhouse, Ted kept looking around, peering through the undergrowth along the sides of the trail. I was about to ask what he'd lost, when he threw out an arm and grabbed my shirt collar.

"There they are!" he whispered, jerking me behind a huge pine tree. The rough bark crumbled beneath my hands as I stumbled against the trunk. Ted waved me into silence, pointing towards the woods.

A curve of the main trail wound through the area, close to the private trail to our bunkhouse. I could see the burly figures of the two rangers across a small clearing. They'd taken off their shirts, and their tanned skin glistened in the fading sunlight, dripping with sweat.

Jim, the head ranger, towered over his assistant. He must have been at least 6 foot four. I watched his muscles ripple as he swung a machete at a recalcitrant vine. The other ranger, Matthew, may have been shorter, but I'd hate to bet on which one of the two would've won in a no-holds-barred fight. Matthew's burly chest was covered with thick, dark hair. I never even wondered if his thick build had an ounce of fat—he was obviously as solid as the ancient oak tree beneath which they worked.

I watched for a moment, spellbound by the sight. The two men, sweating beneath the trees, fascinated me. Then, I came to my senses and turned around.

Ted stood there with his mouth open, his eyes glazed. I was afraid the men would spot us and nudged him sharply. We crept back to the trail and jogged to the bunkhouse. Once inside, I was too embarrassed to ask Ted what exactly we'd been doing. The thought that maybe Ted—maybe me, too—had enjoyed the sight of those muscular men working in the hot afternoon sun never occurred to me. Not then, anyway.

When Matthew and Jim arrived, they'd already showered at the main building. I wondered at the little pang of disappointment when they walked into the bunkhouse fully clothed, but shrugged it off. Jim gathered the four of us around the table to make out a cooking and cleaning schedule.

"Matthew and I will take cooking duty tonight," he said in his rumbling bass voice. Ted shoved his foot against mine under the table, but I ignored him. "Hamburgers all right with you two?"

I nodded, trying not to make eye contact with Ted. Jim and Matthew busied themselves putting together a meal, while Ted and I located plates and silverware and set the table. Soon the smell of hamburgers filled the bunkhouse. Matthew pulled vegetables from the refrigerator and began making a salad.

I was acutely aware of the two big men in such close proximity to me. I got a whiff of shampoo and the aftershave they'd used. I found myself watching from the corner of my eyes as they worked together. They were a well-oiled team, each one knowing what the other was going to do next.

Matthew's big hands moved gracefully, chopping vegetables and tossing the salad. I kept finding my gaze wandering to the sight. His burly body fascinated me, especially watching his strong fingers manipulate the carrots and tomatoes. I caught myself after the third time, and turned away with a blush—only to find myself looking directly into Ted's twinkling brown eyes. My face flamed.

After dinner, Jim and Matthew excused themselves, leaving us to wash up.

"This is great," Ted said as the door swung shut. I was a little surprised that he'd say something serious instead of making another weird joke, but agreed happily.

"I think I'm really going to like this job," I said, stacking the final plate in the cabinet.

Ted chuckled. Something about the sound made me nervous again. I glanced at him.

"You too, huh?" he said with a smirk.

I crossed the kitchen to flop down onto the sofa. I wondered if it would be better to ignore his oddball quips, or just to come out and tell him I didn't get the joke. Ted finished the pan he was drying and collapsed into one of the overstuffed chairs.

I decided it was best to be truthful. "I don't have any idea what you've been hinting at, you know."

He leaned forward, studying me. "You were watching them just as much as I was," he said. "I hope you're not one of those hypocrites who try to pretend they don't enjoy a good-looking man."

My mouth fell open. Was that what we'd been doing? Then the light bulb flickered on.

"You're—" I had a hard time getting the words out. "You're gay?"

I'd never actually known a gay man personally before. Ted gave me a pitying look, then rolled his eyes.

"Oh, please," he said. "Don't give me that 'fresh off the farm' routine. I've got eyes. You'd have been perfectly happy if Jim and Matthew had stripped naked and started posing."

I felt my face flaming again. "I—it wasn't like that," I muttered lamely. "I was just—You started it!" I shouted in desperation. "You dragged me out there to watch them. I've never done anything like that in my life!"

"Really?" Ted sat up and faced me, leaning forward so suddenly that I flinched.

I edged as far away as the sofa allowed. Ted eyed me, disbelief evident in his face. "You mean you never even looked at another man before?" he asked.

"NO!" I growled. "And I'm not interested in starting. Could we talk about something else?" Something that would keep my mind off a sudden mental image of Matthew's sweaty chest, heaving with exertion, his strong hands working to clear the trail.

An evil grin spread across Ted's face. "Don't you wonder what they're doing out there?" he whispered.

"Fishing!" My heart was pounding so hard I thought I might be on the verge of an attack.

"Yeah?"

"They took their fishing rods, Ted."

He pointed across the floor. Against my better judgement, I looked in that direction. "If they're fishing," he said, "then why'd they leave the tackle box behind?"

Somehow—I'm still not quite sure how—I ended up following Ted down the darkened trail to the water. We'd left the flashlight behind so they wouldn't see us coming and I had to concentrate so hard on keeping on the trail that I almost forgot what we were doing.

Jim and Matthew sat in plain sight on the fishing dock. Ted jerked me behind a bush, clapping a hand over my mouth. I shoved him away.

My heart leaped into my throat as I peered out between the leaves, watching the two men. They weren't fishing. They'd removed their shirts, but this time their arms were around each other. Their lips were pressed together in a long, passionate kiss.

I felt a familiar throbbing between my legs. I wanted to run back to the bunkhouse, but my eyes wouldn't leave the figures on the beach. Jim and Matthew certainly didn't look like any idea I'd ever had of gay men. Neither did Ted, for that matter.

I thought about it. What did I actually know about gay men, anyhow? That they were more feminine than 'normal' men? None of these guys seemed to be anything but a real man. They didn't walk or talk funny. They even had body hair that I wished I had. I didn't know shit about being gay except that you did it with other guys. I'd just never imagined myself getting off on watching a couple of men making out.

But I was getting off on it. My cock was thickened into a full-blown woody, straining the fabric of my shorts. Jim and Matthew had no idea we were watching. Their hands roamed over hairy chests and slipped beneath khaki trousers. I was having trouble breathing.

Something moved beneath the bushes and leaped out at us. Ted and I screeched as we scrambled backwards. I was still trying to quiet my pounding heart when something clamped down on my shoulder. I screamed again.

"What the hell is going on here?" a deep voice demanded, just over my head.

Matthew had a firm hold on my T-shirt. Jim had a similar hold on Ted.

"You two know better than to go crawling around in a nesting site," Jim said sternly. "What if that quail had already laid her eggs?"

"Quail—?" Ted gasped. "It was just an quail."

We giggled nervously. I was acutely aware of the man beside me. My head was level with Matthew's trousers. I tried to edge discretely away from him, but his fist tightened on my shirt.

"Now suppose you two explain what you're doing out here," Jim said.

Neither Ted nor I replied. I was trying very hard to sink into the sand and disappear.

Matthew cleared his throat. "Maybe they wanted some fishing lessons," he suggested.

"Hmmm. You'd think they'd bring a fishing rod for that. Maybe they just want to show their appreciation for that fine meal we cooked."

Both men chuckled. "Right," Matthew said, giving my shirt a little tug. "They're probably dying to get on their knees and show us how much they enjoyed those hamburgers."

"What about it, guys?" Jim asked, leaning over us. "Did you come down here to show us how much you liked the food?"

Ted glanced at me. His teeth flashed in the moonlight as he

grinned. "Are you serious?" he asked.

Jim and Matthew were silent. I couldn't have made a sound if my life depended on it. Ted squirmed around until he was facing Jim's crotch.

"I really did like your cooking, Ranger Jim," Ted said with a chuckle. "Man, I wanted this thing since my first day on the job," he continued. I watched in amazement as Ted unzipped Jim's trousers, pulling out the longest cock I'd ever seen. It must have been eight or nine inches long, and as thick around as my wrist. My cock sprang back to attention.

Ted wrapped his lips around Jim's cock like it was a giant hot dog. I could feel my mouth dropping open as he dove onto that hunk of meat. Jim's fist clenched tightly. His other hand moved slowly to rest on Ted's dark hair, tousling the thick curls. I glanced at his face. His head was thrown back in pleasure. I could see the cords on the side of his thick neck.

I felt a hand on my back, and stiffened. Matthew let go of my shirt and started rubbing my shoulders. He knew exactly what to do and his big, meaty hands felt good. I started to relax as he knelt beside me.

"C'mon, Goldie," Ted said as he pulled off his mouthful of man-meat for a moment. "What are you waiting for?"

"I don't know what to do," I admitted. I looked up at Matthew. He moved in front of me and leaned over. Before I figured out what was happening, our lips met.

I'd never even dreamed of kissing a man, but Matthew made my knees weak. My mouth opened by itself, and I leaned forward. I loved the taste of him and the smell of his body. I wanted to see what it was like to run my hands through that thick chest hair, to see if the rest of him was covered just as thickly.

My fingers wandered through Matthew's forest of dark hair. Jim gasped and I knew I wanted to be able to make my ranger whimper like that.

Matthew's hands found my chest, sliding my T-shirt up. I started to get up, but he put one hand on my shoulder again and pressed me back down. His fingers closed over my nipples, and I let out a gasp that made Jim's sound feeble. Electricity shot straight down to my balls as Matthew rubbed and twisted my nubs.

I realized that he was teaching me what I ought to be doing. I managed to concentrate, and tried his technique on his own nipples. I was rewarded by a satisfied groan. Emboldened, I slipped my hands downwards and found his zipper.

A little voice in my head kept asking me what I thought I was doing out here. I ignored it. Matthew didn't have on any underwear, and his hard cock flopped out as soon as I had the zipper down.

I stared. Matthew's wasn't as big as Jim's but I liked it better—the straight hardness of the cock, the way it stood almost upright. It looked like it was ready to blast off from the hairy forest between his legs.

His balls hung low and heavy beneath the cock. I eased his trousers down around his ankles to see better. Matthew rested his hand on my head, stroking my hair. I put out a tentative hand to the furry balls. Matthew's cock jerked. He spread his legs a little, and I moved closer.

I took a deep breath of the heady man-smell rising from Matthew's crotch. I buried my nose in his balls, wrapping my hands around to cup his muscular ass. Matthew groaned again, and his cock pushed against my face.

I glanced over to see what Ted was doing. My jaw dropped.

Ted was lying on his back with his legs thrown over Jim's shoulders. Jim's cock slid in and out of Ted's ass. From the expression on Ted's face and the way he was panting, I could tell it felt good. Jim supported his weight on one bulging arm and had his other hand closed tightly over Ted's cock.

"Oh, God," I mumbled.

"Do you want to go back to the bunkhouse?" Matthew whispered. "It's OK if you do."

"I want you to teach me everything they're doing," I whispered back. I opened my mouth wide and closed it over the end of his cock. It tasted salty and spicy at the same time, and I could smell the tang of his pre-cum.

As I sucked Matthew's cock I watched Jim out of the corner of my eye. When Jim shoved forward, into Ted, I pulled my mouth back. When Jim pulled back, I dove forward onto Matthew's hard meat.

I wanted to be on my back, with a hairy, muscular man between my legs, just like Ted was. I nearly came from excitement as I accepted the fact. I tugged at Matthew's thick waist, leaning backwards to show him what I wanted.

"Wait a second," he whispered, reaching into his pocket. I stretched out on the cool sand and waited. I heard a rustling noise and smelled a freshly-opened condom. Then Matthew pulled my shorts off.

A chill ran over my body. This was it. What the hell was I doing? I felt like I was dreaming as I raised my legs to his shoulders. I felt cool air on my asshole and shivered.

Matthew lowered his head and closed his mouth over my cock. I gasped. I had no idea it felt this good. None of the girls I'd dated had ever wanted to try this. My balls churned. I stiffened, fighting it. I didn't want it to be over this quickly. Matthew seemed to understand and sat back on his haunches. I watched as he quickly rolled the rubber down his dick.

He moved his mouth to my chest, sucking and nibbling on my hard nubs. My body writhed beneath him. My hands clenched in his hair. I heard myself making little whimpering noises.

I felt fingers at my asshole then. I tried to relax, but my body tensed at the unknown sensation.

"It's okay," Matthew whispered, "I'll go really slow. It won't hurt."

He slid one finger past my puckered opening. I shivered. Matthew's tongue lapped at my nipples, sending little ripples of electricity through my body. He closed his fist over my cock, moving slowly and gently up and down. His finger slid in and out of my ass, in time with his pumping movements. I relaxed. Soon my hips started bouncing off the sand, shoving up as his big hand stroked my cock.

Somewhere along the way he'd gotten another finger into my ass, and I realized that two felt even better than one did. But I wasn't sure I was ready when I felt him slide his fingers out and position himself between my legs.

"I'll go slow," he promised again.

His hard cock pressed against my hole. My heart thudded in my chest. Beside me, I could hear Ted's gasping breath and Jim's grunts as he shot his load into Ted's eager ass. I raised my hips and pressed up against Matthew's cock.

My ass stretched wide around the thick manmeat. Slowly—so slowly that I almost didn't realize it was happening—he eased into my ass. The feel of his thick pubes brushing against my ass startled me. I had a man's cock inside me. I looked at him in shock.

Matthew grinned down at me. He leaned over and gave me a rough kiss, then propped himself up on both elbows. My ass was stretched wider than I'd ever thought possible. He pulled his cock slowly backwards.

Before I could complain, he pushed back inside. His hard rod massaged my prostate. I leaned my head back into the sand with a groan. Matthew thrust deep inside me, then pulled out again. Soon, his rhythm speeded up, and my hips started bouncing along. Within a minute or so, I was shoving off the sand as hard as I could, grunting with every thrust.

Matthew shoved hard against me with a groan, and his hot cream filled the condom, deep within my ass. It was over too soon, and I whimpered as he pulled out. He closed his fist over my cock, pumping it hard.

I squirmed beneath him as he milked my cock. I oozed pre-cum as his big fingers slid over my shaft. My balls tingled, then jerked. My load boiled up and I shoved my hips forward. I groaned, spewing cream everywhere. A wad hit my chest. I thought my cock was never going to stop shooting.

At last, I gave a quivering gasp and collapsed into a limp heap. Matthew stretched out beside me, one hand toying with my chest. I raised a hand to his furry body.

"So—?" Ted's voice wafted over from the other side of Matthew's body. "Now are you going to admit you're gay?"

"All right!" I snapped. "I'm gay. Are you happy now?"

"I am," Matthew said with a grin. He leaned over for another kiss. "I'd hate to think I'd busted your cherry for nothing."

I stared up at him for a minute. Then, I pulled him close. "Not for nothing," I told him. "But I'm going to need a lot of practice before I'm any good at it."

"Practice makes perfect," Ted retorted from the other side. He and

Jim had gotten to their feet. Neither was dressed, but their hands were entwined.

"We're going swimming," Jim said. "You guys come on in when you're done."

I looked at Matthew as they left. "When are we going to be done?" I asked.

He leaned over, his face only inches from mine. "When I think you're good enough to be called Recreation Specialist."

His hand slid between my ass-cheeks, tickling my pucker. I felt a tingle deep within my balls.

"I'm ready for my entrance exam, Ranger," I gasped.

MY SEX EDUCATION

Simon Sheppard

"SO WHY THE FUCK SHOULD I CARE ABOUT *WAR AND PEACE*, ANYWAY?"
Dirk asked me.

"Because—" I said, popping open another beer, "because it's a classic of world literature, that's why, and it's about man and his fate." I swigged down some Heineken. "Or something."

"Not convincing," Dirk said, and threw the thick book across the room at me. "If it's so classic, you read it."

"I have. In high school."

"I fucking hate you, genius," Dirk joked.

It was spring of my sophomore year at Berkeley. Dirk and I had been squeezed into a little apartment on Durant Street all semester, and I'd come to enjoy his teasing. I was sorry that next year he'd be going back to Holland. I'd never known a Dutch guy before. Where I grew up, a little town in the Central Valley, there were white guys, Latinos like me, and that was about it. Berkeley was different, with students from all over the world. The previous semester, I'd been living with my girlfriend, Sarah, a neo-hippie type I'd met in PolySci. But we broke up, me being insufficiently groovy as it turned out, and I'd needed a place to live. In a university town in the middle of America's toughest housing market, I needed a place to live bad. So I'd answered an ad tacked to the Union bulletin board and ended up moving in with Dirk. It was just a crummy studio apartment, but Dirk was running out of money, I needed a place, and so we figured we could stand each other for a few months.

Dirk was blond, handsome, smart, and funny. And tall, 6-foot-5, although he assured me that back in Holland, he was just of average height. We were jammed into close quarters, but I wasn't looking to find another girlfriend—not until I got over Sarah—so I figured that I could probably do without privacy. I also figured that, if any girlfriend of mine met Dirk, I'd be in trouble; the guy had all the makings of a pussy magnet.

And that, apparently, was how things were. Shortly after I moved in, Dirk started spending nights out. A lot of nights out. I'd wake up, look over at his bed, still not slept in, and know that the Dutchboy got laid again, the lucky bastard. But whoever she was, Dirk was pretty cagey about it. I never met his girlfriend, or even saw him around campus with a woman in a couple-type pose.

It wasn't till early May, when we'd come back from a Green Day concert at the Greek Theater—we were still pretty stoned—that I found out why.

"So who is she?" I asked, over a slice of pizza that had just come out of the microwave.

"She who?" asked Dirk.

"Your girlfriend," I said. "The one you've been seeing."

Dirk took a gulp of beer. "It's a he," he said.

"What? Who is?"

"I've been seeing a he, not a she. His name is Scott. My boyfriend Scott."

I didn't know what to say. I finished my pizza and left the apartment.

Walking down Telegraph Avenue, I told myself I wasn't pissed off because Dirk was gay, I was pissed off because he hadn't told me the truth. Or so I told myself.

The next few weeks around the apartment were tense. I stopped lounging around in my underwear. Whenever I took a shower, I made sure I was dressed before I walked out of the bathroom. I started wearing sweat pants to bed. If it had been possible to find another place to live, I would have. I spent less time at home. Dirk spent most nights out. And we never talked about his love life.

Not until the night he threw *War and Peace* at me.

"I fucking hate you, genius," Dirk said, jokingly.

I picked Tolstoy up off the floor.

"Hey," Dirk continued, "are you mad at me?"

"No."

"You are, aren't you?" He unfolded his tall, lean frame from the chair.

"Why didn't you tell me you were gay?"

"I'm not gay," he said, looking down at me slouched on the futon. "I'm bisexual. Most people are bisexual, you know, if they'd just relax and admit it to themselves."

"Uh-huh."

"Listen," Dirk said in that deep, Dutch-accented voice of his, "are you afraid I'm attracted to you? Or are you afraid that I'm not?"

"Jesus, my roommate sucks cock," I said. "What do you want me to say?"

Dirk smiled. "I do it rather well, too."

"I don't want to know," I said. "I'm going out for a walk." But as I walked through the warm California night, I found myself thinking about Dirk—blond, handsome Dirk—kneeling, with his mouth open. Sucking some guy's dick. And I found myself wondering how that mouth would feel on me.

It was two weeks later. I was lying on my futon, drifting off to sleep, when I heard Dirk's key in the lock. He walked in without turning on the lights and threw himself onto his bed. I heard him sobbing in the darkness.

"Dirk," I asked softly, "what's wrong?"

"Scott left me," he said in a tortured voice. "Or I left him. He's been seeing this other guy, a basketball player. The bastard."

"Which one's the bastard," I asked, "Scott or the basketball player?"

"Both, I guess," he said with a little laugh. I thought maybe he'd calmed down, but then he started crying again. Ever since my mother left my dad, I've been uncomfortable around crying men. But I got up from the futon, walked over to his bed, and laid a hand on his shaking shoulder. He reached around and laid his hand on mine. I just wanted to act emotionally supportive in a brotherly sort of way, but unfortunately my dick was getting hard. I was surprised. And confused. And hard. He said something.

"What?" I said, not sure if I heard right.

"Hold me," he repeated.

I got into bed with him and awkwardly laid my arm around his shoulder.

"Closer," he said. "Please."

I took him in my arms and pressed my chest against his back. My throbbing dick was just inches away from his butt. He snuggled back up against me. I figured he had to have noticed the state of my cock. Then he reached his long arm back around and pressed my body against his. The fleecy fabric of my sweatpants felt great against my hard shaft. I started gently dry humping against him.

"Uh, Dirk, I'm not taking advantage of you in your hour of need?"

"Not at all. In Holland, we have a saying—"

But I never did find out what that saying was, because Dirk gasped as I slipped my hand inside his shirt. I knew from what Sarah had done to me that it feels great to have your nipples played with. I slid my hand along his chest hair, found his left nipple, and gently squeezed.

Wait," Dirk said. He pried himself loose from my arms, stood, and lit a candle on the bedside table. I could see that his eyes were a bleary red. The were tear tracks on his cheeks. It turned me on.

I lay there, hardly daring to breathe, as he kicked off his boots and began to unbutton his shirt. I'd seen plenty of guys' chests before, of course—at the beach, at the gym, just hanging around. But no one's chest had ever looked like Dirk's did in that candlelight. It was beautiful.

He unbuckled his belt and unzipped the fly of his khakis, letting them slip to mid-thigh. He was wearing white boxer shorts. I'd seen his cock before, but never hard. It was big, much bigger than mine. Its glossy, swollen head was poking out of one of the legs of the boxers. I knew it would be a bad idea to touch it, but I wanted to touch it, bad.

"You gonna keep those sweatpants on?" Dirk asked. I nodded stupidly. "Then I'll keep my underwear on." He looked down and smiled. "Not that it'll do a lot of good." He took a step toward the bed, and stood there, towering above me, nearly naked in the candle-light. "You ever touched another guy before?"

I shook my head. "Not since sixth grade," I said.

"Why do I find that so easy to believe?" he said, reaching down for my hand and guiding it to his cock. At first I just grabbed the base of his hard-on through his shorts, the flesh hot through the thin white cotton. Then I moved my fingers down to his naked skin, his hand still holding my wrist. I squeezed the swollen head of his prick, rubbing my thumb over his moist slit.

"You like the way it feels?" he asked.

I nodded.

"Good. So do I," Dirk said. "Now just lie back."

I did as I was told. He tugged his boxers down, let his pants fall to his ankles and stepped out of them. His swollen cock stood straight out, pointing in front of him, pointing in my direction. I knew that gay men liked to suck cock, more than women did. I wondered what that big thing would feel like in my mouth. And I wondered what Dirk's mouth would feel like on me. That, I was about to find out.

Dirk sank to his knees and pulled the waistband of my sweatpants down, down just enough for my cock and my swollen balls to spring free. He licked the underside of my shaft hungrily, then slid his wet mouth down the length of my dick, till I could feel the back of his throat working my dickhead. He did it a lot better than Sarah ever had and, unlike her, he didn't smell of patchouli.

I grabbed the back of his blond head and gently guided it as he moved up and down on my dick. Nobody had ever seemed to want my cock so much. I felt like I was going to explode. I could see now why guys wanted to be gay.

I hated it when he let my hard-on slide out of his mouth, but it turned out he had something else in mind. He went into the drawer of his bedside table and pulled out a condom and a little bottle of lube. He tore open the foil package with his teeth and expertly rolled the rubber down over my shaft, then lubed it up and jacked it off till it was once again rock-hard and ready to shoot. Then he rose to his feet and clambered over me, till he was squatting on the bed, straddling me, my dick rubbing right against the crack of his ass. Even through the rubber, the friction of his butt against me felt intense.

I'd always figured that getting fucked up the ass would hurt, but when Dirk raised himself up on his knees, reached back and guided my dick to his hole, and then sat back, my cock slipped right into him and he looked like it didn't hurt at all. Being inside him felt incredible, like a cunt but tighter. He rocked himself on my dick, sliding up and down on my hard-on while I thrust up into him. I looked at him, at his shining blond hair, his handsome face, his lean body shiny with sweat. And at his cock, hard and throbbing, pre-cum drooling from his slit.

I reached down and grabbed his hot dick and started jacking him off, lubed by his own juice. It was incredible, knowing that his cock was feeling what mine was feeling too, a cycle of energy unlike anything I'd ever felt during sex. And then suddenly he was coming, spraying hot gobs all over my chest, and his ass muscles clenched, and I couldn't hold back and I shot off in his ass. It was amazing. Just fucking amazing.

In a few minutes, after we'd stopped shaking and caught our breath, he raised himself up from me, peeled the rubber off my half-hard cock, and lay down beside me. He reached for me, then hesitated. I reached for his hand and guided it to my chest.

"Feeling better?" I asked.

"Yep," said Dirk. "I guess Scott's not the only fish in the ocean."

"In the sea," I corrected him. "And neither is Sarah."

He put his mouth to mine and hesitated. I parted my lips. Our tongues met. I wrapped my arms around him.

I was already drifting off to sleep when I heard him ask the question. "OK, genius," Dirk said, "now are you going to explain goddamn *War And Peace*?"

CAMP OUT ORGY— THE INITIATION

Jay Starre

I WAS DOING IT. FINALLY. AFTER EIGHTEEN YEARS. EIGHTEEN LONG, boring—dutiful—years.

I was letting my hair down. Doing exactly what I wanted to do. I hadn't asked my parents if I could go camping with my roommates and their friends. I'd just done it. I'd drunk enough beer to get a buzz going, too.

I almost laughed there under the night desert sky. Daddy dearest would cut me off without a thought if he knew about the beer. No, he'd think it out first. He'd have me back home in our small town on the Mexican border and every man in the church watching me like a hawk. They'd feel that they had to watch the preacher's boy for more signs of Satan taking him down the well-worn path to hell. Daddy would make them think it was their duty to watch me.

Well, I was free now. The folks and the church were way out from Tempe and I was in Phoenix. I could finally be me. Whoever me was. I was hoping my roommates would help me out there. Chad and Grant were just so cool. I couldn't have been any luckier when roommates were being assigned. And their buddies, Tim and Derek ... They were the greatest four guys I could imagine. All four of them were from Phoenix and so different from the boys I'd known growing up. I just hoped they liked me, but I was guessing they did—otherwise, they wouldn't have invited me along on this camp out. Would they?

I wanted so bad to be a brand new Caleb Hansen.

We were fifty miles out in the desert—five of us guys on a camp out. We had drunk beer and just been grown up men being men. The fire had burned down to coals. Far off coyotes bayed at the sliver of moon that sat on the horizon. The night was otherwise pitch dark around me.

I lay on my sleeping bag between Chad and Grant in just my T-shirt and briefs and gazed up at the stars above. I was pleasantly woozy and basking in the joy of having newfound friends. I was floating towards sleep when a hand grazed my stomach.

I froze. The hand rested right on my navel, exactly where my T-shirt had slid up as I crossed my arms behind my head and stared up at the night sky. It didn't move, it just rested there as I breathed slowly, rising and falling with the movement of my stomach. Chad's hand was on my belly, resting with the palm down and the fingers outstretched.

I didn't know what to do and I sure didn't want to mess up the friendship I had started with my roommates. I wondered if this was some kind of initiation that big city boys put guys through before accepting them as friends.

I began to breathe faster, I couldn't help it. If Chad had his hand on my stomach, I was not going to object. He was a tall city dude from Phoenix who, to me, was the ultimate in cool, with a buzz-cut and an earring and a chain tattoo snaking around one of his muscled biceps. It was his jeep we had taken out on our desert ride. He had managed to procure the beer, and he had come up with the idea for this trip. Blond and laughing, he had impressed me as secure and sure of himself in the short time I'd known him.

A coyote howled again and his hand moved. It slid down my belly and its fingers were at the band of my underwear. I realized I was trembling and tried to stop. I was afraid of showing my fear. If something queer happened—say that hand actually moved lower and touched my dick—I didn't know what in the hell to do. What would my new friends think of me? What if I squealed and slapped Chad's hand away? Would he consider me some kind of uptight freak?

While I was figuring out how I was going to react, the hand moved again, all at once sliding under the waistband into my shorts. Its fingers cupped around my dick and pulled the skin off my knob. It took about two seconds of that and I was as hard as a board. I stared up at the stars and didn't know what to do.

I moaned. As soon as the sound came out of my mouth, I writhed in embarrassment, which made my dick thrust upwards into the fingers that were clasped around it. Chad seemed to take that as encouragement. He began to pump my cock slowly.

I gritted my teeth. The feeling in my dick was overpowering. Chad's hand was tight around my rod, squeezing while it pumped. I humped upward, unable to prevent myself from doing so.

I froze when I felt another hand touch my hip. My eyes bulged as it began to pull down my undershorts, exposing my crotch to the night air. That hand dragged my shorts down while Chad scooted his free hand under my butt and lifted my ass. Soft cotton slid over my ass-cheeks down to my thighs, to my ankles and disappeared. My butt was bare on the sleeping bag, and my dick and balls were right out in the open.

I figured right then that I had to be queer. I loved what was happening to me! I wanted Chad touching me! Grant, too. Only, what were they going to think now that they knew?

Sensations bombarded my body. One hand was stroking my balls, rolling them and tickling my hairy sack. The other hand was moving all over my dick, pinching, pulling and squeezing.

I was once again shocked when a third hand slid right under my butt and cupped it. I knew that hand was Grant's. It groped at my butt, rubbing all over it, with much more aggressiveness than the hands on my dick and balls.

Grant was my other new roommate. He was the opposite of Chad. Tall, lean and dark haired, he was friendly in a quiet way. He laughed at Chad's jokes but was not the one to offer up much in the way of conversation. He was an athlete, attending Arizona on a basketball scholarship. I was in awe of him, as well.

Now his large hand was probing my butt-crack, and I was clamping my butt cheeks and opening them up alternately. When his hand got right into the crack and poked at my hole, I let out a low yelp that sounded like a gunshot in the silence of the night.

Immediately after I had uttered that cry, a face covered mine and lips pressed over my mouth. A tongue slid between my lips, muffling another groan. It was Grant kissing me, his hand was still down under my ass with his finger grinding against my pucker. His body was leaned into mine as his mouth smothered me.

The heat of his lean body pressing into my side added to the fires already raging up and down the length of me. I could tell he was naked from his burning flesh mashed into me. His hard cock ground against the right side of my stomach.

I suddenly felt something warm and wet sliding over the head of my aching rod. Lips were caressing my dick, then a tongue swiped it wetly. The hand pumping my dick fed it into the mouth covering it. A deep groan bubbled up from the depths of my heaving chest, muffled by the tongue probing the insides of my mouth. The mouth over my dick began to suck as the hand pumped it in and out of the wet cavern.

Nothing had ever happened to me like this before. I stared upwards at the swirling stars and the shadowed face above me. The desert silence around us was only broken by some heavy breathing and the suckling sounds of that mouth over my cock.

Someone pulled my legs wide apart. There was no way of knowing, but I imagined it was Tim and Derek who had hold of my feet. No one was saying a word, and I could only see the stars above me and the dark head that was feeding me tongue.

Tim and Derek were Chad's friends who'd come camping with us. They were both short and well-built, they were also from Phoenix and had the big city type of cool I was desperately searching for. I tried to tell myself that, if it was their hands pulling my feet apart, I didn't mind. Only, there was still that suspicion in my head that this was all some sort of test.

I realized at that point that these four guys, all of whom were the coolest I had ever met, were the ones acting queer. It didn't matter if I liked what they were doing, they were the ones doing it—they were as queer as me. That kicked me into another—and profound— realization. If they could do that, and not be freaks, then why couldn't I? Why couldn't I love these sensations and be queer and not be a freak? Something just gave way then, and I surrendered to the flow of it all. I felt like both laughing and screaming at the same time. If there hadn't been a mouth over mine with its tongue possessing mine, I'm certain I would have.

Meanwhile, a finger had zeroed in on my butthole, which was wide open now that my legs were pulled apart. I thought it was Grant's finger probing me, his hard body still pressed against me and his equally hard cock rubbing into my side lustily. While Chad mouthed and sucked my throbbing dick, Grant probed into my asshole. He worked at it as he banged my side with his dick, jabbing that hard finger right into the center of my virgin anus and pushing past the puckered rim. He was inside me almost at once. It ached pleasurably as that finger sank deeper, the entire thing inside me in no time at all.

Hands stroked my thighs and butt. My ass cheeks were pulled apart, allowing the finger up my hole to go deeper as it was frigged in and out in a maddening rhythm. In the fog of my own lust I heard whispers, but could not quite make out their muffled meaning. I did hear the word "rubber" mentioned twice, and some movement around me as if perhaps they were fumbling for something.

I heard hawking and felt spit splatter my asshole. More of the same followed and the finger fucking me slid easier and deeper as its rhythm increased. They were spitting on my asshole and Grant was using that oral lube the better to finger my hole. The very thought of it nearly drove me over the edge.

My cock was on fire, and my balls were tight up against the base of my hard dick. I was wracked with spasms of heat and lust. But I did not cum, although I felt as if an explosion was imminent.

The finger inside my butt was yanked out and something larger and blunt was pressed against my hole. I knew it was a dick. The pit of my stomach clenched; the realization that I was getting fucked overwhelmed all the other sensations wracking my tortured body. I moaned, loud in the night, and sucked the tongue inside my mouth deep.

I relaxed my asshole. Something gave way, in my soul as much as in my body. My thighs were pulled wide apart and my spit-wet butthole was gaping open to the night air. The dick pressing into it just slid inside me with practically no resistance.

The feeling of fullness was incredible. A real live cock was in my cherry butthole, and I was loving it. Someone else moaned, I think it was Tim or Derek, whoever was putting his cock up my hole. My entire lower body was floating, riding the cock that began to fuck in and out of me. I writhed around on that prick, and the mouth that was sucking on my dick. I twisted my hips and torso so that more of both were given to me. My dick began to spasm, and a load of cream lurched upwards from my tight balls through the pulsing shaft and into the sucking mouth engulfing it.

My orgasm was entirely different than the few I had previously experienced. It merely pulsed through me, like a wave on the ocean. There was no gut-wrenching explosion, and neither did it end at once. It went on and on, the dick now being plowed in and out of my willing asshole a part of each spurt of cum that oozed from my dickhead. I gave in to it totally, riding the wave and staring up at the blazing stars. A pair of shooting stars briefly warmed the sky, a vision that somehow exemplified the incredible experience I was having.

The dick inside me pulled out, and I felt warm cream splatter my belly. I was shaking all over by then, my orgasm subsided, but my desire was not in the least satiated. There were more whispers.

When another dick entered me, I actually reached down and felt for it, my hands wending their way through a tangle of hands and bodies that surrounded me. I found my own butthole and felt the fat latex-covered dick that was sliding into me. The emotional thrill of feeling a dick going up me overrode all else. I had my hand on the slippery shaft that was fucking me.

The center of my lust was in my pulsing anal slot and the dick filling it. When that fat cock was pulled out and another load of cum was deposited on my ass cheeks, I was prepared for anything the four of them had to offer. I was a willing hole, there was no question of it.

They moved me, flipping me over and lifting me up on my hands and knees. One of them crawled under me and his mouth soon engulfed my still hard dick. I gasped out loud, but then grunted with the sudden intrusion of another dick into my stretched and slick butt tunnel. This dick was definitely fatter and longer than the others, and I imagined it was Grant's, his lanky height matched by the long spear between his legs. And I did feel speared—this was by far the deepest penetration I had yet to experience. That dick went far up into my guts, and it rode me with gusto. I was sure it was Grant by then; he had been thrusting that same hard bone into my side for the past half hour.

I wanted to be sucked and fucked and fondled. The four pairs of hands stroked every part of my body, from my nipples to the backs of my thighs. I grunted and mewled like a dog as I was fucked, our mutual moans of lust the only sounds in the night.

Grant wrapped his long arms around my chest and plowed my ass, his mouth on my neck, lapping at it with hungry swipes. I felt a deep sense of being wanted, of being desired. They wanted to fuck me, they were enjoying my body. I was not on the outside looking in, I was the focus of these four hot guys' entire attention.

That thought was enough to push me into my second orgasm. This one was violent, matching the pounding of some inner spot that the big dork inside me was steadily massaging. My butthole and my dick both came. This time I almost wept with the intensity of it. The mouth on my spewing cock swallowed eagerly, sucking me dry.

Grant came up my butt, filling the condom as I was filling someone's mouth with spunk. When he pulled out, another dick replaced his. This one slithered up my sloppy, open asshole easily.

I lay my head down on my arms and stared at the horizon. Another shooting star appeared and then was gone, ephemeral and ghostly. My body rocked in the rhythm of the cock pounding me from behind. I was content to kneel there and be used, my own dick now limp and drained. The hands on me continued their lazy fondling, all of us having cum except the owner of the cock now inside me.

I knew it was Chad—he was the leader. I knew that as well. He had orchestrated all this, I was certain of it. This was my initiation into his circle. Now he was fucking me, driving into my well-used and slick ass channel. He had what he wanted. I gave it up to him, spreading my thighs wider, wiggling my butt around his dick, actually milking it with my anal muscles.

When he came, he pulled out, rolled me on my back and lay over me, spraying his cum on my stomach and chest. He kissed me, driving his tongue deep and moaning, his body shaking in the last throes of his orgasm. The others were all around us, lying on either side, their bodies entwined with ours.

My eyes were wide open, the great wheel of the milky way a bright blaze above us. The universe seemed so vast, a billion suns and more merely small twinkling lights in a night sky. The warmth of the bodies surrounding me was reassuring, the steady breathing of my new friends comforting.

HIGH SCHOOL REUNION

Chad Stevens

I WAS FLYING TO LOS ANGELES, SITTING BETWEEN TWO HOT GUYS. MY idol from high school, Luke St. James, sat in the aisle seat. He had dark hair, classic facial features, brown eyes. The guy sitting by the window had very blonde hair, fair skin and vivid blue eyes. I couldn't believe they were both flirting with me.

"You're going to love it in Los Angeles," the blond said. The cabin was dark. I glanced down at his crotch. He had an impressive woody in his jeans. He took my hand and placed it on his basket.

"I want to show you around," Luke said. I turned to stare into his gorgeous brown eyes. My eyes dropped to his crotch and I saw he too sported an enormous erection. He took my right hand and forced it into his pocket. Except there was no pocket. Just skin and pubes. And I was touching his throbbing hard-on.

"You like it?" he smiled at me.

"Yeah."

The blonde tapped me on the shoulder. I turned toward him and saw his cock fully exposed and throbbing.

"What do you think of this?" he asked. He pressed my left hand onto his man-meat. I squeezed out a dollop of pre-cum.

"Go ahead and suck it," he coaxed. I couldn't resist.

"Get back here, cutie pie," Luke whispered, his voice smooth and sexy. He too had his cock out. It was firm and thick. I turned toward him and engulfed his cock. Pressure on my shoulder brought me back to the blond. A tug on my leg brought me back to Luke.

"What's going on here?" I broke away from my work to see the very sexy redheaded flight attendant. He was wearing his name badge around his neck and nothing else. He too was sporting quite a hefty hard-on, which I quickly took into my anxious mouth.

We hit an air pocket and I left my stomach five thousand feet higher up than where I was sitting. My eyes popped open.

"Are you all right?"

I realized my mouth was open and quickly shut it. I was sitting between a very large woman in the aisle seat and a scary-looking big-ass football-player-type guy in the window seat.

"That must have been some dream you were having," the woman said. "You were squirming around like nobody's business."

To my horror I noticed my erection was quite apparent. My dick had always been larger than those of most of the guys in gym class. Being 5'7" and weighing in at only 130 pounds, the size of my dick was quite pronounced. I went to grab a magazine from the seat pocket in front of me but only found a barf bag. It would have to do. I snatched the bag and placed it in my lap.

Both seatmates turned away from me. The rest of the flight from Pittsburgh to Los Angeles was uneventful.

Luke St. James was meeting me at the airport. He had been two years ahead of me in high school and, when he went off to college, I figured I'd never see him again. We ran into each other the summer between my junior and senior years, however; and he suggested I consider UCLA. He gave me his phone number.

I couldn't get him out of my mind after that. With the help of scholarships and student loans I was all set to do UCLA, at least for the first year. I called Luke and told him of my plans to come West. He actually offered to pick me up at the airport and show me around campus.

35,000 feet over Kansas, I began to regret my decision to follow him. What would Luke do if he knew I was gay and attracted to him? Barely 18, I was filled with tons of doubts and fears.

"Hey, Jeremy Johnson," Luke yelled, waving wildly, as I entered the terminal. I was suddenly conscious of the crowds around us. I felt like such a dork. He smiled and the dimples I'd imagined touching reintroduced themselves to me. My heart did flip-flops.

"Over here, J.J.," Luke continued, making a scene. I quickly shot my hand up and hoped he'd act normal now that he knew I'd seen him.

When I got to him, he wrapped his arms around me in a tight bear hug and I wanted to die right there. He felt so wonderful. Then I felt his warm, moist lips briefly on my neck. I was sure I was imagining that. This was Luke St. James, the most popular guy back in high school.

"It's great to see you again, kid," he said. Was he blushing? Nah, couldn't be.

He took my bag and put his arm around my waist. My erection took charge, tenting my khakis. Damn, why didn't I wear briefs instead of boxers? I nervously glanced around, imagining everyone staring at us. Nobody even noticed.

"I appreciate you coming to pick me up and all," I said. "You really didn't have to do this."

"No problem, J.J.. It's great seeing you again. You've grown into quite a looker."

I knew I was considered pretty good looking back at school. But Luke noticing?

"You're pretty hot yourself," I said before I could stop myself. What a stupid thing to say. Why would one guy call another guy hot? How gay was that?

We stepped out into warm sunlight. Everyone was tan. Palm trees were everywhere where there wasn't asphalt or concrete. Luke packed me into his bright red Miata and pulled off his shirt.

"Nice car," I said, nervously trying not to eye his chest.

"A graduation present from the folks. They like to buy my love. Go figure. I hope you don't mind if I leave the top down."

"Nope."

Despite my best effort, my gaze locked on his chest. It was finely chiseled with just a smattering of black hair. His brown nipples were hard; each surrounded by a small circle of hair.

Luke reached over and toussled my head. "I can't tell you how glad I am so see you again."

"Really?" I asked.

"Yes, really."

I was getting lost in Luke St. Clair. It'd be so awesome if he was gay too and liked me.

Luke was weaving in and out of the traffic on Century Blvd. At a stop light, he placed his hand on my knee. I froze. Then it was gone and he was taking my hand and pulling it towards himself. He held my open palm on his thigh as he maneuvered his way through a few yellow lights. I glanced over at Luke. His eyes were on the road.

We buzzed onto the San Diego freeway. I gripped my seat. Somehow he managed to speed around slow moving cars, in and out of lanes, all with one hand. He never let go of my hand on his thigh. Several times I thought Luke was about to hit a car in front of us. I was terrified. I pressed my foot into a non-existent brake.

I glanced over at his crotch and noticed his beautiful, muscular legs. His large package was bulging noticeably. I wanted to touch his crotch. But this was Luke. I was so confused I didn't know what to do.

"See something you like, J.J.?" Luke asked.

I was horrified. What did he think of me? "Sorry," I whispered.

"I was just teasing you. Relax. We're going to have a great time. I promise."

Luke took my hand and placed it directly on his crotch. I felt his hard cock under my sweaty fingers. I shuddered with excitement.

All I could do was hold on, both to my seat and Luke's crotch, until we exited at Wilshire Blvd.

In minutes we were stuck in traffic on Westwood Blvd. Stores, offices and movie theaters lined the street. Lots of people were out and about.

At a red light, Luke removed his hand from mine. Reluctantly I pulled it away. Luke looked over at me and smiled. Then I noticed he was unzipping his shorts. He pulled out his hard-on. My mouth dropped open as Luke took my shaking hand and placed it on his pole. His tool pumped out a glob of glistening pre-cum.

I wanted to take it into my mouth. But how could I? There were all these people around. Luke was driving and—well… he was Luke.

"Go ahead," he invited.

"Huh?"

"Go ahead and suck it. You know you want to."

I stared at his cock and lost every thought I'd ever had. "Yeah. I guess I do."

Luke gently guided my head down onto his throbbing member. It was broad daylight and we were in traffic and I was putting my mouth on my fantasy man's pole. The skin was smooth and silky. The pre-cum tasted a bit salty, slightly sticky, and wonderful.

I licked gently at the tip of Luke's cock, while gripping the monster meat in my hand. Then my mind stopped thinking and my body took over. I engulfed the hard, pulsing member in my mouth and held on. All the way down my throat I took Luke's firm, thick dick. It had to be at least as long as mine and just a bit wider.

I loved it. The taste, the texture. I could smell Luke's musky odor and was in love. Like a madman I sucked and sucked, occasionally licking Luke's large, tight ball-sack.

"Whoa! Slow down, J.J.," Luke said, pulling my mouth off his bright red cock. The veins were large and pumped. "Let's take a break and wait until we get home." With excruciating effort Luke tucked away his manhood and zipped up. We drove in silence for a while. I was still breathing quite heavily.

"Are you okay?" Luke asked.

"Uh, yeah—sorry." I shook my head, feeling the dry heated air of LA wash over me. Damn. That had been just another one of my fantasies.

"Well, you're gonna have to start paying some more attention to me, guy. It's like I was talking to myself here." Luke smiled. I didn't dare look at his crotch.

"Look up ahead," Luke said.

I followed his gaze and saw the entrance to UCLA. I was overwhelmed by the enormity of the place. So many buildings. I just knew I would never find my way around.

"Wow," I managed. "It's awesome."

"I'll take you around later. But first we need to get you moved in and catch up with each other."

"Y—yeah, Luke," I stammered. "That would be great."

Luke drove into a pleasant neighborhood of apartments and houses on the edge of the campus. He pulled up to a duplex and parked the car in the driveway. It was a quaint, one-storey Spanish-style house with a little concrete porch in front of each of the two doors.

"This is it," he said, opening his car door and getting out. I undid my seatbelt and followed him.

"It's nice," I said, again feeling nervous. God! I was going to be living with my fantasy man next semester. I just stared into Luke's beautiful brown eyes. I wanted to cry I wanted him so bad. I'd never be able to keep my hands off of him if I lived with him.

"Well don't look so upset," he said. "If you really don't like it, it's no big deal. But at least look at the place. It's rather small and only has one bathroom—and one bedroom."

"No, no. It's not that. I'm just so surprised that you want me for a roommate. I was so afraid of being all alone here." One bedroom? I knew I'd be in hell.

"So this is the bedroom," I said. There was one queen-sized bed.

"What do you think?" Luke asked. He placed his hand on my shoulder.

"It's a nice place," I mumbled hesitantly. "But—well, where am I going to sleep?"

"We need to talk," he sat on the edge of the bed and patted the space next to him. I tentatively joined him.

Luke turned towards me. His bare leg rested against mine. His touch was electrifying. I was again having a hard time breathing. I pinched my leg to see if I was awake this time.

"What are you doing?" Luke asked, staring at my hand.

"Nothing, just nervous."

"So am I," Luke said.

"Why should you be nervous? You've got everything going for you. Looks. Money. A girl or two, I'll bet."

"That's what we need to talk about," Luke said.

"It's okay that you have a girlfriend. I mean… Maybe I should say that it's none of my business. It has nothing to do with me. You know … I'm sorry, I guess I'm babbling."

"There's no girlfriend, J.J.. Please look at me."

I looked into Luke's eyes.

"There is someone special, though. I knew it from the moment we met. I watched this person grow up, in fact. Mature into quite a fine young adult."

"Uh huh," I said, swimming through waves of jealousy.

"I have strong feelings for this person, but I'm having a very difficult time telling him."

"Him?"

"Yes, J.J.. You."

"You're kidding, right?" This had to be another dream. Luke couldn't possibly be talking about me.

"J.J., I'm gay. I suspect you are too. And I'm hoping you feel just a little bit for me."

I hesitated. Should I tell him the truth? What the heck, it was now or never. "I feel more than a little bit for you, Luke. I always have."

He smiled and took me in his arms. He leaned back and kissed my cheek. Then he kissed my chin. His lips met mine and he kissed them, gently at first. Then harder. He forced my mouth open and invaded it with his slippery tongue. It was both cool and hot.

My resistance melted away. Passion took over and I lunged my tongue into Luke's hot mouth. We dueled like this back and forth for quite some time.

He removed his shoes, socks and shorts and sat naked beside me. His body was magnificent. His cock was a work of art.

"Are you nervous?" Luke asked, almost shyly.

I shuddered. "Yeah."

"Me too. But don't worry. God, you have beautiful green eyes." I blushed. "Stand up, J.J.. I want you naked."

Luke unbuttoned my shirt and slipped it over my shoulders, letting it fall to the floor. He unbuttoned my belt, unsnapped my trousers and unzipped my fly. I stepped out of my loafers and out of my pants. Standing there in front of him, I hesitated only a moment before I shucked my boxer shorts. I peeled off my socks and stood back up, letting my fantasy lover finally see me.

He wrapped his arms around me as he stood up. His bare skin against mine was totally awesome. My heart was beating so wildly I though I would have a heart attack. Our cocks were pressed hard against each other, super hot.

He guided me onto the bed and we both tumbled on top of the slightly messy comforter. We clung to each other like we were afraid to let go. In fact I was.

Luke again pressed his lips against mine. The taste of his mouth was so amazing. He kissed my neck and ran his tongue down my hairless chest, stopping to gently nibble on each of my hard nipples. I shuddered when his tongue continued down my chest. He stopped at my belly button and sucked ever so softly.

When his lips reached my bush I sucked in my breath. He took my hard, throbbing member into his mouth and I almost lost it right there.

It felt like a volt of electricity shot up my spine with every movement of Luke's tongue on my sensitive cockhead. My dick pulsed.

I couldn't move, but just laid back and let Luke take control. I stared down at him, admiring his smooth firm ass, his strong back, and those hairy legs. He looked up at me and smiled. His chin was wet with saliva and pre-cum.

I was scared of what I felt for him. What if he really didn't feel the same way? What if it was all a lie? What if he just wanted a quick fuck and then out the door with me? How could I face him again?

His mouth engulfed my entire ball-sac.

"Whoa," I said, without thinking. My groin was so sensitive I could hardly stand it. I felt like I was on fire.

"Are you okay?" he asked. "Are you sure you're all right with this?"

"Oh yeah. I just don't want to spoil anything."

"Don't worry about that." He smiled. "You're doing just fine. We've got a real chemistry thing happening here, in case you haven't noticed. I've never had that with anyone else. I just thought you'd like to know."

"Then you are serious?"

"Yes, J.J.. Very. And I'm not just saying that."

I looked into his eyes and believed him.

"Would you let me fuck you?" Luke asked hesitantly. "I know it's your first time, but I hope you'll like it."

I looked down his body again. I remembered that tool of his. I couldn't imagine it going into my ass comfortably. But, sooner or later, it was going to come to this. If I was going to live with him, getting fucked was going to happen. We might as well go ahead and get the preliminaries out of the way, no matter how it hurt this time. "Yeah."

Luke opened his nightstand drawer, pulling out a plastic bottle of lube and a condom. I lay back on the bed. Not knowing what else to do I bent my legs at the knees and spread them apart. I realized I was looking forward to having Luke St. Clair in me.

"Are you sure you haven't done this before?"

"No," I said. "Am I doing it wrong?"

"It's okay, J.J.. I'm just kidding."

Luke poured a gob of lube on his fingers and massaged my asshole. He probed with one finger, then two. My pucker spasmed with pleasure. At the same time, I feared what was coming next— almost as much as I wanted it. Luke slowly pushed his fingers inside me. At the same time he stroked my bouncing cock. His touch was hot, yet gentle.

Feeling Luke's fingers inside me felt so right. I could feel my balls churning with pent up cum juice.

"Ready?" I nodded and, one-handed, he rolled a condom over his dick. He removed his fingers and pointed his latex-covered cock at my hole without waiting for an answer. I watched him crawl into place, my brain telling me over and over that he was too big for me. Screaming it at me. I was scared to death. His dick was so big. I didn't see how it would ever fit. Luke lifted my legs up onto his chest.

I felt the blunt head of his cock begin to press against my hole. I stared at the inches of shaft I could see below my balls. "Look up here, J.J.. Look me right in the eye. Come on, baby, do it."

I looked up. Our eyes locked. In that eternity, it was as if Luke was controlling me with his eyes. Like I could feel nothing except that which he permitted me. I knew his cock was entering me, that it knob was stretching my sphincter. I knew that my anal muscles were relaxing to let him inside me. He willed me to open for him as he continued to slip gently into me. There was no pain, just a growing sense of union with Luke St. Clair.

I felt his pubes scratch at the insides of my thighs and nuzzle my balls. He gripped my dick and I realized it had lost some of its hardness. He began to stroke me and I sprang back hard and drooling for him. The pressure of Luke's cockhead against my prostate was the most exciting feeling I ever had in my life.

Luke backed up a bit, then entered again. Fully. He pumped away at my pole. Slowly at first, then faster and faster. In synch with his thrusts into my ass. I ground against him as he pushed into me, humping his hand. An unknown need possessing me and driving my body.

I lost it. I could stand it no longer and exploded. Wave after wave of hot jism flew everywhere.

"What a gusher you are." Luke smiled down at me. His smile took on a serious expression. His breathing became ragged. He started to moan, his head snapped back. His thrusts became shorter and harder. He pushed all the way in. His cock seemed to grow larger inside me.

"Oh God," he cried out. Sweat broke out on his forehead. His hot cum seemed to fill my soul.

Luke carefully pulled out of me.

We embraced and kissed for quite a while, then finally broke apart.

"That was great!" I gushed.

"You ain't seen nothing yet, kid," Luke said. "I'm gonna show you a whole new world out here. Consider it a part of your education."

Luke held me in his arms and I felt loved. I knew I would be very happy here.

ABOUT THE AUTHORS

BARRY ALEXANDER (Student Union)—Barry is the author of *All The Right Places* (Badboy Press, 1998). He has also been published in *Skinflicks 1 & 2* (Companion), *Casting Couch Confessions* (Companion), and *Friction* (Alyson). Barry lives in Iowa.

SAM ARCHER (Teacher's Pet)—Sam's work has appeared in *In Touch* and *Freshmen* magazines. A Louisiana native who now lives in Arkansas, Sam has spent most of his 35 years as a writer, hitchhiker, and house guest.

JORDAN BAKER (Straight—As a Board)—Jordan has had stories published in *Indulge, In Touch,* and *Hustler*, as well as in *Rentboys* (Companion) and numerous literary magazines. He lives in Arkansas.

RICHARD BELLINGHAM (Randy Roommates)—Richard's stories have appeared in *In Touch* as well as in two of Dave MacMillan's other anthologies, *Sons of the Moon* (Nocturnis) and *Loveseats* (Nocturnis). He lives in England, and he recently graduated from the University of London.

ROBBIE CRAMER (Rally 'Round the Flagpole)—Robbie is a film student who lives in Seattle, Washington. This is his first published story.

BILL CRIMMIN (Dirty Laundry Boys)—Bill was first published in *Casting Couch Confessions* (Companion). His stories have also appeared in *Loveseats* (Nocturnis) and *Sons Of The Moon* (Nocturnis). He lives in London.

GRANT FOSTER (Jock Itch) has contributed short stories to a number of magazines and anthologies. In addition to his fiction, he also writes articles about travel and gay history. Grant lives in rural Washington state.

J.L. GORDEN (Farm Boys) has been writing and selling stories to gay magazines for more than ten years. He has appeared in *In Touch, Men,* and *Hot/Shots!*

DAK HUNTER (Phi Beta Sucka) has been a theatre critic and feature writer for various magazines and newspapers in Orange County, California. His first short story was published in *Skinflicks* (Companion). Dak lives in Long Beach.

DAVE MACMILLAN (The Boys Club)—Dave edited *Casting Couch Confessions* (Companion), and the forthcoming anthologies, *Loveseats* (Nocturnis) and *Sons Of The Moon* (Nocturnis). He lives in Atlanta ,Georgia.

HOWIE MARSHALL (Frisky Frat Boys)—Howie has been jotting down his exploits in the bayou country of Louisiana, where he lives, for years. This is his first published story.

RODDY MARTIN (Cherry Boy in the Big Apple)—Roddy's work has appeared in *Friction* (Alyson), *Best Gay Erotica 1998, In Touch*, and *Blackmale*. He lives in Pennsylvania.

ALAN W. MILLS (The Coming Out Party)—Alan is a California-born writer and poet living in West Hollywood. He's also the editor of *In Touch, Indulge*, and *Blackmale* magazines. His stories have appeared in *Friction 2* (Alyson), *Skinflicks 1 & 2* (Companion).

BRYAN NAKAI (Summer Blow Job)—Bryan's stories have appeared in *Casting Couch Confessions* (Companion) and *Skinflicks 2* (Companion). He is a Native American living in Albuquerque.

J.D. RYAN (Confessions of a Camp Counselor)—J.D.'s work has appeared in *Casting Couch Confessions* (Companion) and in *In Touch, Bunkhouse,* and *Honcho* magazines. He lives in South Carolina.

SIMON SHEPPARD (My Sex Education)—Simon is the co-editor, with M. Christian, of the anthology *Rough Stuff: Tales of Gay Men, Sex and Power*. His work has appeared in *Skinflicks 1 & 2* (Companion), *Casting Couch Confessions* (Companion), and many other anthologies. He lives in San Francisco.

JAY STARRE (Camp Out Orgy)—Jay's work has appeared in *In Touch, Mandate*, and *Bunkhouse* magazines. Born in Los Angeles, Jay immigrated to Canada at nineteen. He presently lives in Vancouver. He is now a personal trainer and full-time writer.

CHAD STEVENS (High School Reunion)—Chad's work has appeared in *In Touch* and *Hot/Shots!* under the psuedonym Charlie Stevens and in *Skinflicks 2* (Companion). He has also sold a video script. He resides in Redondo Beach, California.

companion press sex book catalog

BAD BOYS Of Video #1
Porn Star Interviews
By Mickey Skee
224 pages, 5-1/2 x 8-1/2
ISBN# 1-889138-12-6
$12.95 Softcover (Photos)

BAD BOYS Of Video #2
Porn Star Interviews
By Mickey Skee
224 pages, 5-1/2 x 8-1/2
ISBN# 1-889138-19-3
$14.95 Softcover (Photos)

The "BEST OF"
Gay Adult Video 1998
By Mickey Skee
208 pages, 5-1/2 x 8-1/2
ISBN# 1-889138-10-X
$12.95 Softcover (Photos)

The "BEST OF"
Gay Adult Video 1999
By Mickey Skee
208 pages, 5-1/2 x 8-1/2
ISBN# 1-889138-14-2
$12.95 Softcover (Photos)

The "BEST OF"
Gay Adult Video 2000
By Mickey Skee
224 pages, 5-1/2 x 8-1/2
ISBN# 1-889138-21-5
$14.95 Softcover (Photos)

CAMPY, VAMPY, TRAMPY
Movie Quotes
By Steve Stewart
212 pages, 4-1/4 x 6-3/4
ISBN# 0-9625277-6-9
$9.95 Softcover

CASTING COUCH CONFESSIONS
17 Gay Erotic Tales (fiction)
Edited by David MacMillan
192 pages, 5-1/2 x 8-1/2
ISBN# 1-889138-17-7
$14.95 Softcover

COMING OF AGE Movie & Video
Guide, By Don Lort
216 pages, 8-1/2 x 11
ISBN# 1-889138-02-9
$18.95 Softcover

The Films of KEN RYKER
By Mickey Skee
152 pages, 8-1/2 x 11
ISBN# 1-889138-08-8
$18.95 Softcover (Photos)

The Films of KRISTEN BJORN
By Jamoo
152 pages, 8-1/2 x 11
ISBN# 1-889138-00-2
$18.95 Softcover (Photos)

THE FRESHMAN CLUB
18 Gay Erotic Virgin Tales
Edited by David MacMillan
192 pages, 5-1/2 x 8-1/2
ISBN# 1-889138-27-4
$14.95 Softcover (fiction)

FULL FRONTAL, 2nd Edition
Male Nudity Video Guide
Edited by Steve Stewart
144 pages, 5-1/2 x 8-1/2
ISBN# 1-889138-11-8
$12.95 Softcover

GAY HOLLYWOOD, 2nd Edition
Film & Video Guide (non-hardcore)
Edited by Steve Stewart
352 pages, 7 x 8-1/2
ISBN# 0-9625277-5-0
$15.95 Softcover (Photos)

HOLLYWOOD HARDCORE
DIARIES
14 Erotic Tales (fiction)
By Mickey Skee
192 pages, 5-1/2 x 8-1/2
ISBN# 1-889138-15-0
$12.95 Softcover

LITTLE JOE SUPERSTAR
The Films of Joe Dallesandro
By Michael Ferguson
216 pages, 8-1/2 x 11
ISBN# 1-889138-09-6
$18.95 Softcover (Photos)

PENIS PUNS
Movie Quotes
By Steve Stewart
118 pages, 6 x 4-1/4
ISBN# 1-889138-07-X
$5.95 Softcover

RENT BOYS
18 Erotic Hustler & Escort Tales
Edited by David MacMillan
192 pages, 5-1/2 x 8-1/2
ISBN# 1-889138-25-8
$14.95 Softcover (fiction)

SKIN FLICKS #1
15 Gay Erotic Tales (fiction)
Edited by Bruce Wayne
192 pages, 5-1/2 x 8-1/2
ISBN# 1-889138-16-9
$12.95 Softcover

SKIN FLICKS #2
18 Gay Erotic Tales (fiction)
Edited by David MacMillan
192 pages, 5-1/2 x 8-1/2
ISBN# 1-889138-26-6
$14.95 Softcover

STAR DIRECTORY
Over 2,000 Porn Star Videographies
Edited by Bruce Wayne
384 pages, 5-1/2 x 8-1/2
ISBN# 0-9625277-22-3
$18.95 Softcover

SUPERSTARS #1
Porn Star Profiles
By Jamoo
204 pages, 5-1/2 x 8-1/8
ISBN# 0-9625277-9-3
$12.95 Softcover (Photos)

SUPERSTARS #2
Porn Star Profiles
By Jamoo
224 pages, 5-1/2 x 8-1/2
ISBN# 1-889138-20-7
$14.95 Softcover (Photos)

THE VOYEUR VIDEO GUIDE
To Gay Softcore Videos
Edited by Steve Stewart
144 pages, 5-1/2 x 8-1/8
ISBN# 1-889138-05-3
$12.95 Softcover (Photos)

X-RATED Gay Video Guide
Edited by Sabin
448 pages, 5-1/2 x 8-1/8
ISBN# 1-889138-03-7
$12.95 Softcover

companion press order form

PO Box 2575, Laguna Hills, CA 92654 USA

Phone: (949) 362-9726 Fax: (949) 362-4489

Please include your phone number or E-MAIL ADDRESS (for questions about your order):

_____

PRINT Name _____

Address _____

City _____ State _____ Zip _____

PLEASE PRINT CLEARLY. USE EXTRA SHEET OF PAPER IF NECESSARY

Qty	Order or ISBN # last 3 digits only	Title	Price (each)	Price

SHIPPING & HANDLING CHARGES—BOOKS ONLY
U.S. Shipping & Handling Charges (U.S. ONLY)
First book $4.00. $1.00 for each additional book.
Canada Shipping & Handling Charges (Canada)
First book $5.00. $1.00 for each additional book.
Outside U.S. Shipping & Handling Charges (Outside U.S.)
First book $20.00. $1.00 for each additional book.
RUSH FedEx Delivery Charges (U.S. ONLY)
Check one and ADD to above charges ❑ Overnight, **Add** $35.00
❑ 2nd Day, **Add** $25.00 ❑ Saturday Delivery, **Add** $45.00.
CREDIT CARD or MONEY ORDERS ONLY for rush delivery.

Subtotal	$
Discount or Credit (if any)	-
California Residents add **7.75% Sales Tax**	$
Shipping & Handling **See left for rates**	$
ADD RUSH FedEx Delivery Charge	$
TOTAL	$

Check Payment Method
❑ Visa ❑ MasterCard ❑ American Express ❑ Money Order
❑ Check (U.S. only) (**Allow 6-8 weeks.**) Make check payable to COMPANION PRESS.

VISA   MasterCard   AMERICAN EXPRESS

Credit card # _____ | Exp. date | _____

X Signature required for all orders

I certify by my signature that I am over 21 years old and desire to receive sexually-oriented material. My signature here also authorizes my credit card charge if I am paying for my order by Visa, MasterCard or American Express. We cannot ship your order without your signature.

❑ **Here is my $5. Please send me your complete book flyers. I do not wish to order at this time. (I understand that my $5 will be refunded with my first purchase).**

01/2000